What was wrong with the old Roxie?

His words had stuck with her. And his kiss.

It was difficult to forget a kiss like that, especially coming from someone...well, someone like Byron. She'd spent more time than she'd like to admit trying not to think about the kiss—about how sweet it was. She'd forgotten kisses could be so sweet. She'd tried extra hard to forget how his lips had lingered. And how in lingering he'd awakened starbursts inside of her. Small starbursts of eternity.

Roxie frowned deeply now. Being touched... It had been so long since she had *really* been touched. The hollowness in her had turned into a resounding ache, and for a few moments, she'd thought about bringing Byron's mouth back down to hers. For a few moments, she'd craved more than his companionship. She'd craved the contact. The promise of heat that came with it.

But had she wanted it—had she wanted *him*— for the single reason that heat could erode loneliness? There was trust there. There was affection. For those small starbursts of eternity, there had been longing and the promise of flame. It had been too long since she'd felt the sheer, electrical pulse of new chemistry.

Why did it seem like so long since she'd felt the flame? The passion?

Dear Reader,

Welcome to Roxie's story! Or is it Byron's story? In the grand scheme of things, it's really both. This in fact was my plan, or scheme, all along, you see—to get these two kids together. They both may hate me for how it all came about—the deep-rutted forays they had to scale to get to the first page of *Wooing the Wedding Planner*. Can you lose sleep over the fate of people who live solely in your imagination? Why, yes. I'm convinced that all my characters hate me at some point, which is why I push, cajole...sometimes drag them to that place they reach at the end of their journey, as we see it—the completion of their story and the happy ending they deserve.

We all have people in our lives who have been through their fair share of tribulations and deserve nothing less than a happy-ever-after. Or perhaps just peace. For me and everyone who knows and loves them, in fiction and reality, Roxie and Byron are two such people. And it's my profound pleasure to say that they do find happiness and peace in the end...after, of course, plenty of pushing and cajoling from their sadistic plotter—that's me!

Wherever it does find you—on a subway bench, riffling through pages in a bookshop, on your lunch break or simply tucked up in bed after a long day—I hope you enjoy Roxie and Byron's journey. Look for more books in my series with Superromance coming soon!

Love,

Amber Leigh

AMBER LEIGH WILLIAMS

Wooing the Wedding Planner

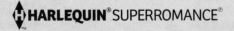

Recycling programs
for this product may
not exist in your area.

ISBN-13: 978-0-373-64012-6

Wooing the Wedding Planner

Copyright © 2017 by Amber Leigh Williams

Printed in U.S.A.

Amber Leigh Williams lives on the US Gulf Coast. A Southern girl at heart, she lives for beach days, the smell of real books and spending time with her husband, Jacob, and their two young children. When she's not keeping up with rambunctious little ones—and two large dogs—she can usually be found reading a good romance or cooking up something new in her kitchen. Amber is represented by the D4EO Literary Agency. Learn more at www.amberleighwilliams.com.

Books by Amber Leigh Williams

HARLEQUIN SUPERROMANCE

A Place with Briar
Married One Night
His Rebel Heart

Visit the Author Profile page at Harlequin.com for more titles.

To my tribe—those who fall asleep reading and those who dream in pages. Wishing you a sea of endless books to sail and soothe you through this life.

And to those who waited for Byron's story. Cheers!

CHAPTER ONE

MONDAYS SUCKED ENOUGH without the grim implications of Valentine's Day.

Byron Strong thought seriously about calling in sick. Then he remembered what had happened the last time he'd done just that. Not a half hour after he'd vetoed the workday, he found his father, mother and two sisters on the threshold offering him a bevy of pity food and head patting.

Byron cringed. *No. Not the head patting.* The idea chased him from the seductive warmth of flannel sheets and into the shower, where he confronted the scalding spray, head up and shoulders back.

His ritual morning routine helped dull his unmotivated subconscious. He made himself a double espresso with the top-rated espresso machine he'd splurged on—money very well spent. Meticulously, he did all the things any other sane man in his shoes would've liked to skip today of all days—shaved, brushed, flossed… He checked the weather before choosing khaki slacks, a black tie and a black sports coat. He stuffed his dress shoes in his briefcase before donning his favorite Nike running shoes and an overcoat and hoofing it to work.

If the hot shower hadn't shocked him awake, the chill whistling through the streets of Fairhope, Alabama, did. It was a brisk five-block walk to the office, mostly uphill. In the spring, it seemed everyone who lived close to downtown strolled to work in the mornings. In winter, usually only those who needed the exercise or a swift wake-up call ventured out without transport. Byron had memorized the cheery bright storefronts, quaint shops, charming courtyards, alleyways and French Creole architecture that were all trademark to Fairhope's appeal.

Fairhope was nothing short of spectacular in the spring—like something from a book or a dream. By June, the weather was hot enough to melt plastic. By August, only the brave walked the scalding pavement. The rest—the wise—remained behind cool glass and central air. Winter weather didn't show up until late November. Maybe. It rarely snowed, and when it did it came down more wet than fluffy, coating everything in ice.

The few months of cold made the residents of the bay-front village wish for their blistering summers that melted plastic and tarmac and made even the hummingbird mosquitoes fight for shade.

Ducking his head, Byron kept his face out of the wind and prayed the office coffeepot had already punched in.

Grimsby, Strong & Associates was on Fels Avenue. Byron entered through the back door of the small accounting firm, which was his baby. He lifted the cross-body strap of his briefcase over his head.

The scent of coffee hit him. He almost groaned in relief and made a beeline for it.

Tobias Grimsby, his brother-in-law, planted his six-feet-seven-inch frame in the kitchen doorway and brought Byron up short. "Dude. You know what day it is. Right?" Wariness coated every inch of his espresso-toned face.

"I'm a human popsicle," Byron muttered. Desperate to get to the coffee, he ducked under Grim's arm. "Out of my way."

Grim stayed on his bumper. "You want to go home?" he asked in his deep Kentucky baritone. "Go if you wanna."

Byron tried not to dive for the pot. It was a near thing. He poured a mug to the lip, drank it straight. Refilled. "I've got a meeting with Mr. Stepinsky at nine. Your appointment with the Levinsens isn't until eleven. You didn't have to come in early."

"But it's *Valentine's Day*," Grim proclaimed

with all the gravity of a general briefing his troops on a mortal campaign.

Byron offered Grim as deadpan a look as he could manage. "Damn. Sorry, man. I didn't get you anything."

Grim tilted his head slightly, measuring Byron's face. "So...you're okay?"

Byron jerked a shoulder and eyed the box of croissants their secretary, Kath, had picked up from the bakery. Yeah; he could do fifty extra sit-ups if it meant chowing down on one of those bad boys. "As far as I'm concerned, it's just another Monday." He sipped his coffee and clapped Grim on the arm. "Relax. You've got the Carltons today at two?"

"Two thirty," Grim corrected.

"You'll be lucky to get out of here before your hot date tonight."

"Ah," Grim said, reaching up to scratch the underside of his chin. "About that. I was thinking we could do a guys' night. Just us."

The mug stopped halfway to Byron's mouth. He narrowed his eyes on Grim's innocent expression. "This is your first date night with 'Cilla in weeks and you want to spend it with me?" He frowned. "Is this some half-cocked scheme the two of you cooked up?"

"There's no scheme," Grim said with derision that didn't quite ring true. "Maybe 'Cilla's sick of me. Maybe I'm sick of her. The further along she gets, the crankier she is."

"It's a mother-effing pity party with 'Cilla's prints all over it," Byron said, pointing at Grim. "And denying it further will only insult my intelligence."

Grim's eyes rolled briefly before he sighed, his shoulders settling into a yielding line. "I told the woman it was a bad plan. You can spot a lie miles offshore. She doesn't listen."

The sound of the phone in his office drew his attention. Byron snatched a croissant. "Do me a favor. Let's not talk about this anymore."

"It's probably your mother," Grim warned.

Dear God, he hoped not. They couldn't be starting this early. *Not all of them.* Byron walked through the first door on the right. He set his briefcase behind the desk and settled into the rolling chair before reaching for the phone. Bringing it to his ear, he answered, "This is Byron Strong."

"Byron. It's your mother."

Byron closed his eyes. He reached for his temples, where a headache was already starting to gnaw. "Hi, Ma. Happy Valentine's."

"That's exactly why I'm calling—"

"So you got the flowers," Byron interrupted smoothly. "I told Adrian orchids."

"Yes," Vera stated. "They're beautiful. You did good."

"My *mitéra* deserves nothing less." He tapped his knuckles on his desk calendar. "Hey, listen, I'd love to chat, but I've got an early meeting. Can I call you back?"

"No, you may not," Vera said, undeterred. "I called to invite you to dinner this evening."

Byron rolled his head against the chair. "Ma…"

"No, no. It's all planned. We're doing chickens. Your father wants to try his hand at roasting them."

"That's…tempting." Byron fought a grimace as he recalled the last time his well-meaning yet culinarily deficient father had tried to roast something. His stomach roiled. "Yeah. I'm gonna pass."

"And why is that?" Vera asked, tone sharpening to cleave.

"Because I've already fielded one pity party this morning," he explained, frowning at the door to Grim's office across the hall. "Don't you think I know what you're doing?"

"I just want to make sure you're okay."

Byron's gaze fell on the framed black-and-white photo on his desk. It was the five of them—Byron; his father, Constantine; his mother, Vera; and his sisters, Priscilla and Vivienne—standing on the beach in Gulf Shores. On Christmas Day, they always drove to the coast to sit shoulder to shoulder in the sand, drink eggnog out of flasks, wrap themselves in woolen blankets and watch the waves charge and thunder into shore. He scanned one smiling face and then another before closing his eyes again and pinching the skin between them. *Nosy. But well-meaning. Every single one of them.* He lowered his voice as he spoke again. "It's been six years."

"Six years today," she reminded him.

"I'm aware," he told her.

"So you won't change your mind about dinner?"

Byron's mouth moved into something like a smile. "I want you and Pop to go out. Find a Greek place. Drink a bottle of ouzo. Make out in front of somebody other than me."

Vera gave a quiet laugh. "Well. I suppose we could do that. But only if you promise—"

"I won't spend the night at home in my bathrobe," Byron said quickly. "Gerald hosted a poker night at his place over the weekend and I lost, which means I'll be picking up his wife's shift at the tavern, since she's still on maternity leave."

"And after that?"

"I just got the new season of *Game of Thrones* on DVD," Byron assured her. "With that and a six-pack of Stella in the fridge, Valentine's Day couldn't end any better."

"Hmm."

Byron went another route, a sincere one. "Hey, Ma? I love ya."

Vera sighed. "I love you, too. You're my only son."

"I know," Byron replied. "And I mean it—happy Valentine's Day."

"Call me later."

"Will do. Bye." Byron hung up the phone. He eyed his coffee. Cold now. With a frown, he turned toward his computer monitor to switch it on. "Hey, Kath," he called. "Can you bring me another cup of coffee, please?"

No sooner had the computer hummed to life than the sunny voice of Constantine Strong filled the room. "No need, darlin'. I got what our boy needs right here."

"Jiminy Christmas," Byron muttered, exasperated.

"Christmas was a month and a half ago," Constantine stated as he folded his tall, skinny frame into one of the guest chairs on the other side of the desk. With his too-long legs spread wide in a comfortable slouch, the effect was very *praying mantis*. "Wake up, son. It's nearly Mardi Gras."

"What's that you've got there?" Byron asked suspiciously as his father set one of the go cups he carried onto the desk.

"Oh, just a little rocket fuel for my space pirate." Constantine grinned, a reminiscent gleam in his eye that took Byron back to his childhood obsession with the final frontier.

He eyed the cup. *Great.* Now they were going after his weakness for controlled substances. This put last year's cheese basket to shame. "I'm fine, damn it."

The mantis eyed Byron through rose-tinted lenses. There weren't too many lines in Constantine's face, although his long hair, pulled back into his typical man bun, had gone gray a decade before. He sported snug mustard-hued pants, a red shirt and a navy blue peacoat, and had a silver loop on his left lobe, where a black shark's tooth dangled. He looked absurd, off-the-wall and somehow together and completely at ease—one with the earth. An aging hippie who refused to be anything but himself. "Go on," he said finally, gesturing to the go cup. "You know you want it."

Byron reached for it. Hot. *Mm, yeah.* Just the way he liked it… "Only if we play a round of 'Guess Who's *Not* Coming to Dinner.'"

Constantine's face fell. "How did you know?"

"Your offerings are well-placed but transparent," Byron told him.

"Your mother called." Constantine checked his wristwatch. "Should've known. She starts earlier than Christ and she's always twelve steps ahead of me."

"You both should really start texting," Byron

suggested as he logged in to the office system. "It'll save time and confusion. Plus, you two would tear up some sexting. Not that you're hearing it from me." He took a sip from the go cup and his brows came together as he swallowed. He eyed the logo on the front. "What the—"

"Ah." Constantine quickly lifted the cup from his knee and switched it for Byron's. "I believe that's mine."

"Sprinkles and whipped cream?" Byron asked. "You're approaching sixty."

"What do I always say to you kids about aging?" Constantine asked, his eyes sage behind wire frames. "'We don't grow older, we grow riper.'"

"That was Picasso, not you, *pappou*. And if by *riper* you mean the charred remains of those chickens you were going to roast me and Ma tonight, for once I'll agree with you."

Constantine barked a laugh. He slapped his knee and leaned forward, his natural geniality flowing warmly into the room. It sieved its merry way through the defensive pall Byron had donned automatically that morning. A true smile spread across Byron's face. For a moment, the two men just looked at one another. Byron heard the silent message his father transmuted with a softened grin—*you're okay*. Gratitude filled Byron until he nearly swelled at the seams. He lifted the coffee and took a long sip. The dark roast slid down his throat, enlivening. "That's the stuff," he muttered appreciatively.

"Told you," Constantine said, crossing his ankle over his knee. Now he looked like a dandied-up cricket ready to break into a toe-tapping reel. "I've always got what my boy needs. And speaking of…" He pulled something from the breast pocket of his jacket and, with a flick of his wrist, tossed it Byron's way.

Byron swiped the key ring out of the air. "What's this?" he asked, studying the two silver keys dangling from the hoop. He frowned at the address written on both in permanent ink.

77 Serendipity.

His heart skipped a beat and hit the next hard. "Pop. What is this?"

"I ran by the retirement village yesterday morning to see our girl," Constantine informed him.

Byron beamed at the mention of his great-aunt, Athena. "How's she doing?"

"Yapped my ear off for three hours straight, so I'd say she's doing pretty fine," Constantine considered. "Had lots to say about *you*. And the house."

"The house," Byron breathed, tightening his grip on the keys.

"It's what you want, isn't it?" Constantine asked with a knowing smile. "At least it seems that's what you told her not too long ago. She's got it set in her head that the place is yours. She even says there's no use waiting for the will…what with the rest of your life ahead of you. Unless, of course, you've changed your mind…"

Changed his mind? Was his father crazy? Byron had been in love a few times in his life. But his first love had been and always would be his great-aunt Athena's old Victorian house. The secret cupboards. The creaky walnut floors. The odd pitch of the upper-floor ceilings. The gingerbread trim. The old-timey wood-burning stove that had been replaced by a newer model fifteen years ago, but still retained the original stone surround. One of Byron's first memories was of lying on the second-floor landing, watching the light wash through the stained-glass window his great-uncle Ari had bought in Greece to remind his wife of the homeland she'd left behind for him.

Byron and his sisters had chased ghosts and dreams in that house. He'd pushed Priscilla out of the Japanese magnolia in the backyard, resulting in a broken arm for her and a month at the mercy of Ari's hard-labor tutelage for him. He'd replaced the treads on the stairs, put up crown molding, and helped Ari build a detached two-car garage with a comfortable space above it where Athena could host her sewing circle.

When Ari passed, Byron had nixed plans for

summer courses in order to help Athena adjust, living in the garage apartment for a time. When he decided to live on the Eastern Shore for good, Athena—by that point in assisted living—offered him the use of the loft again, since the house was under long-term lease to an elderly couple, the Goodchilds. The Goodchilds seemed to like having a built-in handyman and yard boy. They let him keep his Camaro in the garage next to their El Camino and invited him to use the basement as a place for his exercise equipment.

Byron knew the Goodchilds hadn't renewed their lease on the Victorian. Mrs. Goodchild could no longer manage the stairs. However, he had assumed that interest in the house would be sky-high. It was a prize. Sure, it had its quirks. All old houses did. However, the Victorian had historic, architectural and—for Byron—extreme sentimental value. Who wouldn't bribe the Almighty Himself to live there?

He closed his fist around the keys. "When?" he asked.

Constantine lifted his shoulders. "Why not tomorrow?"

Byron's brows drew together. "Didn't Ma crack down on you for verbal contracts?"

"This is different," Constantine said. He was serious. Byron rarely saw his father so serious. He had to swallow a few times to digest it. "It's family. Athena. You. The house. It's all in the family. I'm sure Athena would gift it to you outright—"

"No, I'm buying it outright," Byron argued.

"Even if the loan goes toward your inheritance anyway?" Constantine asked.

"I want my name on it. I also want the appraisal estimate. Nothing lowball."

Constantine knew better than to argue the point. As the family real estate business was shared between him and Vera, he usually found houses to renovate and flip into lease homes, while Vera handled the actual leasing and brokerage part of the equation.

Constantine did have a point, however. With its claim to family heritage and Byron's long-held interest, the Victorian perhaps called for a more casual approach.

"Take some of your things over tonight and see how you adjust," Constantine was saying. "If you don't have any second thoughts over the next forty-eight hours, I'll bring the papers Wednesday." He lifted the go cup to punctuate the question.

Byron felt another smile, big and true, on his lips, and he liked it there. He raised his own cup. "I'll drink to that."

A knock on the door prevented him from raising the coffee to his mouth. Kath peered inside the office, her silver hair gathered on top of her head in a twist that pulled the corners of her eyes into a slant. "Good. You're already in." She spotted Constantine, stopped midspeech and smiled. "Oh. Sorry, Mr. Strong. I didn't see you arrive."

"I snuck in," Constantine said with a wink. "How're you, Kathleen?"

Byron sipped his coffee as his father worked the charm on the older woman, bringing a pretty blush to her cheeks. Both his parents were compulsive flirts. They were also two of the happiest compulsive flirts he'd ever seen.

Strongs are like Magellanic, gentoo and royal penguins all wrapped up in one very Greek, very reformed package, Constantine had told his three children all their lives. *We're crazy enough to mate once, for life, and the male and female are equals.*

You know way too much about penguins, Dad, a surly teenage Byron had once remarked. At the time he'd thought it was a strikingly conventional belief for a man who was in no way conventional.

Yet the belief held weight not even the staunchest cynic could deny. Byron's parents had been married for thirty-five years and were still madly in love—so much so that open affection refused to die off between them. Byron had seen enough parental PDA over the years to make a Friday-night dinner with his mother and father go from gag-worthy to blasé.

The belief had held for Priscilla, as well. She'd married Grim right out of college. The two had been married for a decade and were impatiently awaiting the birth of their first child. In addition, Vivienne's wedding to her boyfriend of four years, Sidney, was only a few short weeks away.

That "mate once for life" business was all too real. And that was the trouble.

Byron lifted his chin, catching Kath's gaze. "What can we do for you?"

The twinkle Constantine had brought to the woman's eyes faded out. "The Xerox machine is on the fritz."

Byron pushed up from his chair. *"Again?"*

She held up her hands. "I've tried the manual. I've tried customer service. I even channeled Pelé and gave the dang thing a few kicks like you did last week. Until the maintenance guy gets here later in the week, I'll have to run to the library to see if they'll let me use theirs."

Byron shook his head. "It's too cold out. You stay in. I'll go to the library."

"But you have a meeting," she reminded him.

"I'll have plenty of time to get back and prep." Pointing at the manila folder she'd folded against her chest, he asked, "Is this what we need copied?"

Kath relinquished the papers. "They're for

today and tomorrow's appointments. I usually make three copies of everything. One for records, one for the client and one spare."

"I'll take care of it," Byron said.

Kath eyed Constantine over Byron's shoulder. "You and the missus sure raised this one right."

"Ah, I'm a bad influence," Constantine said with a smirk. "This one's the work of his mother."

"Whatever the case, he's gentleman to the bone," Kath noted. "The world could use several more just like him."

Byron tossed a heated glance into Grim's office when he heard his business partner snigger. "Thank you, Kath."

"Thank you, sir," she said as she returned to the lobby.

As Byron stuffed the folder into his satchel and pulled on his coat and scarf, his father buttoned his peacoat. He peered into Grim's office and asked after Priscilla and the baby before joining Byron at the door while saying, "Vivi's flight was delayed again."

"She still hasn't flown out?" Byron asked, pushing the door open into the cold. Byron didn't particularly care for his sister being on another continent, not to mention a third-world country. The flying didn't soothe him either. She and her fiancé, Sidney, treasured their humanitarian calling. Their work was important, but Byron would feel a lot less edgy when his baby sister was back on home soil. "She's going to miss her own wedding."

"She'll be here. Don't you worry." Constantine clapped an arm around Byron's shoulders. "Remember, you need us, we're here."

"Yeah, I got that," Byron said, amused.

"Go see Athena."

"First chance I get," Byron promised. He wrapped an arm around his father. "Come here, you old geezer."

"Ah." Constantine squeezed him into a bear hug, rubbing circles over Byron's back just as he had when he was a child. He gave him a few thumps for good measure. "Fruit of my loins."

"Pop, word of advice," Byron quipped. "Don't talk about your loins when you're hugging people. Unless it's Ma. In which case please ensure the rest of us aren't anywhere within hearing distance."

A laugh rolled through Constantine's torso. He grabbed Byron's face and kissed him square on the mouth. "I love ya."

Byron rubbed his lips together. "Save some for her, huh?"

Constantine opened the driver's door of the Prius and folded his long frame behind the wheel, defying everything Byron knew about logic. He winked. "Valentine's Day, leap year, Lincoln's birthday…" He cranked the Prius to life. "Doesn't matter what day it is. My girl gets the lion's share."

Byron threw his father a casual salute. He waited for him to leave the parking lot before starting off for the library to the north. He bypassed the children's park, taking a shortcut between the buildings that walled off Fairhope's version of the French Quarter to cut the wind off his face.

As he came out onto De La Mare and turned east toward Section, he collided with the brunt of an icy gale. His scarf loosened and went flying. He spun around quickly to snatch it. The wind swirled, sending the scarf sailing the other way. And a torrent of rose petals rushed up to meet him.

He raised his hands to shield his face from the odd deluge. When he lowered them, he saw the woman standing on the curb, looking at him in dawning horror. Her peaches and cream complexion went white as Easter lilies as the petals winged away. "Oh, God," she uttered, the round box in her hands empty.

Byron reached out to grasp Roxie Honeycutt's arm. She looked dangerously close to falling to her knees. "Hey, hey. It's all right. They're just flowers."

Her gaze seized on his, her lips parting in shock. *Clearly not the right thing to say to a wedding planner*. He extricated the box from her gloved hand. "I meant there's probably more where those came from, right?" He tried smiling to draw her out of her blank stare. The woman he'd known for a little over a year was normally expressive. Bubbly, even. Sure, she'd been a thinner, quieter, more subdued version of Roxie over the last ten months thanks in large part to her husband's affair.

Idiot, Byron thought automatically whenever Richard Levy was mentioned. Make that her *ex*-husband, and rightly so. Any man who slept with one of his wife's sisters deserved to be kicked brusquely to the curb.

Roxie licked her lips. "I'm…so dead."

Her hand was in his. It was small, wrapped in cashmere. It folded into his big, icy fist like the wings of a jewel-breasted barbet. He moved his other palm over the back of it for friction. "Let's call Adrian," he said instantly. The florist was a mutual friend. She and Roxie often collaborated on events. "She'll get what you need."

Roxie blinked. "Adrian? She's doing flowers for a wedding in Mobile."

"Shit. Sorry." He shook his head. It was ridiculous. They were friends. He could curse in front of her.

She always put him on his toes. Not that she ever spared him the free-flowing tap of her amiability. There was just something about her… It didn't set him ill at ease. Not at all. It…brought him to attention. Close attention.

Kath would've said it was the "gentleman" in him responding to the lady in her.

"I'm sure there's a solution," he asserted, giving her hand a squeeze. He looked to her Lexus. There were boxes stacked neatly on the ground and more in the trunk. "First…why don't I help you get these where they need to go?"

She nodded. "That would be wonderful." Her gaze locked onto his again. Her mouth moved at the corners. "Thank you, Byron."

The first time he'd seen her smile, he'd stopped breathing. Actually stopped breathing. The zing of her exuberant blue eyes, her blinding white teeth—straight as Grecian pillars—had hit him square in the chest. Her beauty was impeccable. He remembered thinking that she was the most unspoiled thing he'd ever seen.

She was riveting. The kind of riveting that made a man stare a few seconds too long.

Carefully, he looked away from her warm round eyes. Growing up, his parents had lived in a house on the outskirts of Atlanta. Larkspur had grown there, blooming in blue-flamed spikes in high summer. When he looked into Roxie's eyes, he remembered just how blue those spikes were.

He bent to retrieve her packages. "Where're you headed?"

"Just around the corner," she told him, placing the empty box in the trunk as he gathered the others. "To the library."

"Fancy that," he said. "Me, too."

The small smile grew by a fraction. "That *is* fancy."

They crossed De La Mare, bound for the intersection of Section Street and Fairhope Avenue, the hub of downtown. On one corner was the white Fairhope Pharmacy. On the other was the city clock that chimed the hour. As they waited for traffic to move off so they could venture across, Byron saw that Roxie's pale cheeks were tinged pink. He might've thought it was the wind had her smile not grown into a full-fledged grin. "What?" he asked.

She shook her head. "It's nothing."

He nudged her arm with his. "Come on."

She licked her lips. Then she said, "You just always show up on my epic fail days."

He frowned. "That can't be true."

"It is," she insisted. Her stare flickered over his middle. "You remember last March."

He studied one of her gloved hands—the one that had wound up in his solar plexus that day in March. It had been an accident, of course. He'd stepped into the blow unwittingly and she'd apologized profusely...before crumbling on him and crying buckets. All as a result of finding Richard and her sister Cassandra in the middle of a tryst. "That?" He shrugged, dismissing the incident completely. "*That* was nothing."

"I hit you."

"You were having a bad day."

"When I break a nail, that's a bad day," she pointed out. "That one could only be deemed hellacious in the extreme."

"I wouldn't lose sleep over it," he advised. The light changed and they began to cross. "It's been a year."

"Eleven months, almost," she said thoughtfully.

He knew she was thinking about her divorce and not their exchange that day. He changed the subject in a hurry. "What's happening at the library?"

"There's a vow-renewal ceremony. Fifty years."

Byron whistled. "Impressive. Who're the lovebirds? Anybody I know?"

"Sal and Wanda Simkin. They're both retirees. They moved down south recently to be closer to their daughter and her family. They're from New York, where Wanda worked as a librarian and Sal as a janitor. She was working late one night while he was cleaning. She fell off a ladder. He was there to catch her."

"There's a happy accident for you," he mused as they crossed again, eastbound. The library was just ahead. When she pursed her lips, he asked, "What? You don't believe in accidents?"

She thought over it. "I don't know. A year ago, I would have said no, I don't believe in accidents, happy or otherwise."

"So you think it was what—kismet?" Byron asked, shifting the bulk in his arms from one side to the other.

"I'm not sure where I stand on all that anymore." At his curious gaze, she added, "Fate. Kismet. I used to be a big believer in serendipity. In signs. Now…?" She shook her head. Sniffing in the cold, she continued, "Anyway, Sal and Wanda wanted something small at the library. One officiant. Their daughter and her family as witnesses. But the daughter wanted to surprise them after the ceremony. As they exit onto the street, all their friends and extended family will be waiting outside."

He nodded understanding. "With the rose petals."

"That are halfway to Canada by now," Roxie noted as another gale blazed a trail through the tree-lined grove across the street where the college campus and amphitheater were located.

"It won't be hard to find more," he told her. "It *is* Valentine's Day."

"Yes. It is."

Ah, he thought, gauging the slight hint of her

displeasure. *A kindred spirit.* "After I use the Xerox machine here, I might have time to stop by the market, pick some up for you. Or I could try another florist. As long as you don't tell Adrian."

"My assistant will be here in a half hour or so. I'll have him stop by Flora and see if Penny can scrounge together some more petals." She stopped when Byron nudged the door open and stepped back to let her pass. Blinking at him, she gave a surprised smile. "Oh. Thank you."

Byron frowned as she brushed by him into the warmth of the hushed building. How little courtesy had she been shown through the last year that the simple opening of a door struck her off guard? Inhaling, he followed her subtle, sensory cloud of lilac that was florid and pristine.

Lilies. Larkspur. Lilacs. Could he be any lamer?

"Oh, my God!" Roxie exclaimed, bringing him to a halt behind her as she whirled around to face him in the lobby.

"Jesus," he muttered, bobbling the boxes at the renewed pallor on her face. "What?"

"Your scarf! It's—"

"Halfway to Canada?"

"It's my fault," she said ruefully. "We might still be able to find it—"

"Rox." Byron leaned toward her, lowering his voice as he cocked a brow. "It's a scarf."

"Yes, but it's yours," she lamented. "I'll get you a new one. I promise."

Byron nodded briefly to the woman sitting behind the information desk before setting the packages on the ledge. He relieved Roxie of hers to give her arms a break. "I'll do you one better. I'm picking up Olivia's tavern shift tonight. You could come by, buy me a beer, brighten my day."

"Oh." She stared at him, stunned. "I'd love to." She rubbed the cashmere gloves together. "But I actually have a date."

Byron didn't know why his spirits tanked at the news. Of course she had a date. It was frigging Valentine's. And she was Roxie Honeycutt. "Yeah? Who's the lucky guy?"

"Bertie Fledgewick," she said. "My sister Julianna knows his family. She set me up. You know how it is."

The only person either of his sisters had ever set him up with was Adrian. Adrian was now married to his friend James Bracken. "This isn't your first date since...?"

She lowered her eyes to somewhere in the vicinity of his knees and cocked her hand on her hip. "The second. Bertie took me out for martinis two weeks ago. Tonight's a little more formal. Dinner at Alabama Point."

"Sounds classy. You're still living in the apartment beside your shop, right? Above the tavern?"

"In Olivia's old bachelorette digs—" she nodded "—for the time being."

"Bring him by when he drops you off," Byron invited. "Drinks are on me."

She licked her lips to smooth a canny smile. "You want to buy our drinks or size him up?"

"I don't know if you know this, but I'm excellent at multitasking."

She laughed. It was like tinny bells on Christmas. It brought mirth and a pleasant flush to her face—a face he thought still a touch too thin after last year. It couldn't be her first good laugh since the divorce, could it?

She pressed her knuckle against the space beneath her nose as the laughter began to fizzle. She shook her head, eyes still sparkling. "I needed that."

Bertie, you lucky bastard. He picked up the boxes again. "Anytime. Tell me where these are going."

CHAPTER TWO

Wow. AND I THOUGHT chivalry was dead.

As Bertie helped her out of his car, Roxie pressed her lips together, remembering how Byron had opened the door to the library for her.

I guess, after everything, I might still be a sucker for a gentleman.

Bertie's hand squeezed hers as she stood in the parking lot of Tavern of the Graces, her friend Olivia's bouncing bayside bar. His hand lingered there, bringing her back again to the events of that morning when Byron had held it, too, tucking it against his middle as he comforted her.

She frowned. Looking up, she noted Bertie's presence. They'd had a pleasant evening. There had been wine, conversation, candlelight. He'd ordered the smoked oysters. She'd wondered at the selection...just as she'd wondered over the hand he'd let stray to her knee under the table as the appetizers passed into entrées and finally dessert.

He'd blazed through a bolero album all the way home.

His palm was a bit damp against hers. She

wished for her cashmere gloves, then dismissed the thought, pasting on her best smile. It had been so long since she'd dated. Had Richard's hand sweated when they'd first gone out all those years ago? They'd been married only three months before she'd caught him and Cassandra practicing their best wrestling moves on her Aubusson, but he and Roxie had been engaged for four years after dating since graduate school. So it had been almost a decade since she'd dipped her toe in the dating pool. Perhaps she'd just forgotten what it was like…

The first time, she'd thought she'd sluiced through the dating pool skillfully, hooking Richard along until the end of the meet. In the long run, though, she'd sunk. She'd sunk hard, dragged out by the unseen undertow.

Still, no matter how much had happened in the intervening years—no matter how much the dating world had changed with its Tinder apps and its trending hookup culture—Roxie Honeycutt did not put out on the second date. It made no difference how many glowing reviews Julianna had given on Bertie's behalf.

Bertie shut the car door. Roxie licked her lips when he stood close in the chilled night air. The wind shrieked off the bay, gaining strength. Bertie bounced at the knees, hissing through his teeth. "Let's get you out of the cold, sweetheart."

Sweetheart. He couldn't have known that was exactly what Richard had called her. Roxie's heart pounded, calling up the same restless ache she'd had trouble quelling since the divorce papers had been hastily drawn last spring. She eyed the lights in the windows above the tavern. The place had been her sanctuary. The thought of bringing a man into it…

Roxie tried to keep the smile. "I can walk up on my own," she told him. She saw the line dig in between his brows and misunderstanding glean. *Poor fella.* He wasn't used to rejection. Trying to ease the sting, she added, "I had a good time tonight, Bertie. Thank you so much for dinner."

He searched her briefly, before humor flashed across his face. "Is this you being a tease, Roxie?"

She felt his hand at the small of her back edging her toward him. Her hand flattened against him. Her smile fled. "I'm not a tease," she stated plainly. "I'm just not ready for you to walk me up to my place."

He bit off a sour laugh, clearly amused. "Julianna warned me about you."

"Did she?"

"She said you'd try to keep me at arm's length," Bertie said, the hand on her back lowering an inch. It pressed her middle against his. "Said you'd need a little encouragement."

Oh, double, double, toil and trouble. Why

wasn't anyone exiting the tavern? The parking lot was full up, yet not one patron had passed in or out of Olivia's bar from the time she and Bertie had driven up. He'd knocked back two martinis at the restaurant while they waited for the entrées. With the wine on top of it… He'd driven just fine, but had he had too much? "I'm certain this isn't what she meant."

"Ah, come on," he said, swaying against her, into her. The fingers of his other hand clamped on her forearm, as if he knew that her flight reflex was jumping into high gear. "You've strung me along too far."

Her voice clipped. "We've only been out twice, Bertie. Two dates isn't enough—"

"That's bullshit, Roxie. Complete and utter bullshit. And you know it." His mouth came crashing down onto hers.

Too hard, too hard! His mouth, his hands. Panic threatened to go on a tear inside her, buckling her at the knees.

She remembered vaguely the defense class she'd taken with Olivia, Briar and Adrian months ago. Olivia, pregnant at the time, hadn't been able to do much more than shout instructions. Roxie tried to summon her righteous words to mind now.

Get loud. Push back.

"Bertie!" She planted her arms between them,

trying to wedge space enough to at least breathe. "I'm warning you, back away!"

He laughed. Actually laughed at her. The grip of his arms didn't let up. Worse, his hand moved over her rear in a possessive sweep.

"Oh." Her hand came up. She meant to strike him flat across the cheek. Instead, her hand balled and she put more force behind it than perhaps necessary.

Her knuckles connected with his cheekbone. Pain flared down the back of her hand. He stumbled and she hissed, cradling the fist. "I did warn you," she reasoned when he looked flabbergasted. She hadn't broken the skin.

Seconds passed as he sized her up. Finally, he tilted his head in challenge. The wake-up call hadn't worked. If anything, she'd poked the snake with a stick and it was coiled to strike harder. "You think you can take a swing at me like that and walk away?" he asked, advancing.

"Yes," she said, putting her good hand out to shield herself. "It's called consent. I didn't give it."

"Come here."

He was used to giving orders. He was used to people following them. But Roxie wasn't one of his subordinates. When he reached for her, she blurted, "I don't want to hurt you again!" When he made a grab for her anyway, Olivia's voice filled her head once more.

Hurt or be hurt.

Where? Roxie thought wildly.

Olivia answered. *Go for the eyes. Gouge those suckers out. The groin's good, too. Knee to the groin, very effective. Or, if you have to, just—*

A long arm snatched Bertie away. His hold loosened, throwing Roxie off balance. She staggered, gaining her feet as an unmanned elbow came down against Bertie's neck. He crumbled, his face and hands close-encountering the gravel drive. It was then that Roxie saw Byron.

He'd loosened his tie. Reaching up, he tugged at his collar. His neck was red, his lips seamed tight. He eyed Bertie's prone form in a way that made the sea-tinged air go from chilly to glacial.

His eyes were blue. She knew that. Conversation with him was always very distracting with those midnight blues smiling back at her. However, under the low beam of the streetlight, they looked black. She wanted to reach out to him, soothe the deadly look on his face. Maybe assure herself he was still Byron. She'd never have guessed that behind the smiling eyes there was *this*.

"Get up," he sneered at Bertie. "Get the hell up."

"Byron," Roxie said. Damn it, her lips were quivering.

He held up a hand without turning his head to

her. "Just a second, duchess." When Bertie didn't rise quickly enough, Byron hauled him up by the back of his jacket. "Turn around," he warned, not raising his voice. *God.* Not that he had to.

Bertie lifted his face. There was blood in his nostrils. He sniffed wetly. "My nose. You goddamn broke it!" Scowling, he pinched the bridge. "I was just dropping the lady off. You don't know what's going on here, chuck."

"The hell I don't," Byron told him. "Now, judging by your breath, I'd say you've gone one too many rounds with the Grey Goose tonight. Maybe normally you're not the kind of guy who gets his jollies off feeling up a lady who in no way wants that type of attention. But, hey, what do I know? You could in fact be that pervert. So I'm going to give you one of two options…"

Bertie rolled his eyes. "For Christ's sake—"

Byron jerked a finger in Bertie's face. "Number one," he said, undeterred, "you call a nice cabbie to take you back to the hole you crawled out of. You put the tavern and Ms. Honeycutt here in your rearview and you approach neither of them ever again."

"You're out of your mind," Bertie remarked.

"Number two," Byron continued, "you keep acting like the vodka-soaked prick I just saw take advantage of my friend, and I put my fist in your mouth and call every single one of the rough-

and-tumble tavern regulars out from behind
those doors to join me. You leave in an ambulance and your sweet little Merc gets towed to
the garage with over a grand in damages. I testify
as a witness in the sexual harassment suit that'll
be brought against you and you go to jail long
enough at least for the other sex offenders to take
a shine to you."

Bertie's eyes darkened. Roxie saw his fist
come up and his body twist, coiled to strike. She
cried out. Before the sound was partway out of
her mouth, Byron quickly stepped into the space
Bertie opened up in the area of his shoulder. He
bent his arm and again the elbow came up against
the brunt of Bertie's head, snapping it back.

Bertie lost his footing, stumbling back to the
4x4 truck behind him. Byron's hands closed over
the other man's throat. The words that growled
low from within cut through Roxie as effectively
as the wolfish wind. "I'm getting real tired of your
attitude," he warned, "and I'm just mad enough to
knock out enough of those pearly whites to make
you look like a clown at the circus. You've got
exactly five seconds to change my mind. One…"

"Byron," Roxie said again, touching his arm.
"Really. He's not worth it."

"Two…"

Bertie's face was turning an alarming shade of

puce. His fingers clawed at Byron's hands over his throat.

"Three…"

"Byron, please," Roxie said, gripping the sleeve of his black shirt. *"Stop."*

"Four…"

"All righ'," Bertie wheezed. "All righ'. Lemme go."

Byron gave it another few seconds, his eyes drilling into Bertie's skull. Then he released him.

Roxie watched Bertie sink, gasping, to the ground. She felt sick.

Byron's frame swelled and released over several breaths. Then his brow arched and he reached up to straighten his tie. "Informed decision. There might be hope for you yet, Lothario. Now make the call."

"What about my car?" Bertie asked, his raspy voice carrying nothing more threatening than resentment. *Effectively cowed.*

Byron jerked a shrug. "A friend of yours can pick it up in the morning."

"It'll have to wait here?" Bertie asked. The incredulity shrank from his face when Byron tilted his head. A simple gesture with surprisingly lethal intent. "Okay," he said, taking a smartphone out of his jacket pocket. "Dialing."

They waited, none of them moving. Byron nodded from Roxie to the tavern doors. She shook her head. A stubborn move. Or maybe she just couldn't get her legs to move.

This was her mess. She'd see Bertie off, if for cognitive reassurance alone.

Not that he said so much as boo to her when, a half hour later, the transportation service arrived. On the way to the van he trampled over the handbag she had dropped when he'd started taking liberties with her. Byron went so far as to open the door for Bertie.

After Bertie climbed inside, Byron leaned in to deliver one last ultimatum. "If I get wind of you around here again, we'll assume you've forfeited the first option and there won't be a cop in town who's not on the lookout for your license plate and VIN number."

Bertie muttered something about good ol' boys. Byron rolled the taxi door into place and gave the window a few raps. It wasn't until dust rose in the van's taillights that Byron strolled to where the handbag lay and picked it up. It was beaded and yellow. In his hands, it looked as delicate as one of those Imperial Russian Fabergé eggs they kept behind glass in the Winter Palace. She focused on it, swallowing, as he dusted it off. Her throat was sore, strained by tension. She expelled a breath, reaching for clarity. "Was the choke hold really necessary?" she asked.

He turned to her. The streetlight fell over him

like a halo. His long, rich black hair was smoothed back from his face. It fell to the nape of his neck. It should be illegal to be so effortlessly handsome. In profile, his long face was a half-moon thanks to his large chin. He had an ever-present five-o'clock shadow. His proud aquiline nose was a touch overlong but it spoke of his Mediterranean heritage and suited him well.

At six-five, his broad frame saved him from being lanky despite his trim physique. His shoulders filled his button-up shirt.

It had been ten and a half months since she'd wept on him—and that long precisely since she abandoned any long-held notions of fairy-tale knights, whether they appeared in shining armor or tailored Brooks Brothers.

There was no chance she was going to start believing again. No matter how well he wore that Brooks Brothers.

He scanned her closely. She wished she was steadier. She was mussed—her dress, her hair… The glassy edge of fear was too close to the surface. She raised her chin again, locking her arms over her chest as he looked at her. Really looked at her.

He pushed the air through his nostrils and gave her a short nod. "Yes," he decided before returning to her, handing her the clutch.

"Thank you." She opened the handbag, letting

her hair fall across her cheek, shielding his view. She riffled through the contents. Everything was there, in place. As she checked that her smartphone was safe in the hidden pocket in the lining of the bag, her hand tweaked. Damn it, that *hurt*.

"Are you all right?" he asked.

"I'm fine," she said, clipped. She stopped, hearing the bite. She mirrored him, breathing deep, trying to unlock the tension. She closed her eyes and shook her head when it didn't work nearly as well as it had for him. "Really. I am."

"Yeah," he muttered. She could feel his eyes on her face, perusing. His hand lifted, as if he wanted to touch her. "Look," he said, lowering his head toward hers instead, "it's not your fault."

She felt something touch the corners of her lips. Something light. Humor? Fighting ghosts of aftershock and hysteria, she couldn't sort one emotion from another. "I know. I know that. It's just…a mess."

"The guy's a tool."

"He also happens to be the son of one of the wealthiest hoteliers from here to Fort Lauderdale," Roxie told him. "I'd be surprised if you didn't hear from his daddy's high-powered litigators by the end of the week."

Byron lifted a noncommittal shoulder. She'd forgotten he'd once been a high-powered litigator, too, and didn't seem at all concerned with the threat. "What kind of a name is Bertie anyway?" he asked.

"Short for Robert, apparently," she told him and rolled her eyes. "He'd do better to call himself that."

Byron scowled. "No, he'd do better to keep his hands to himself."

In the taut pause that followed the coarse words, Roxie saw him measuring her again. "I'm fine, Byron."

"Sure," he said, but closed the distance between them anyway. He reached up to take her elbow, making sure to keep his movements slow so she could track them. "Come on. I'll buy you that drink."

A laugh wavered out of her. "That's kind of you. But all I want to do is go upstairs, take a long shower and down half a bottle of moscato."

He glanced over her head to the apartment above. "All right. I'll call Adrian. Or would you prefer Briar?"

"Neither," she said quickly. When he looked at her in surprise, she shook her head firmly. "I'd rather they not know about this. Any of them."

"Why not?" he asked.

"I feel like I need to…absorb it before I get either of them involved," she told him. "Plus, if Liv finds out, she'll go chasing Bertie with her granddaddy's shotgun. I can't be responsible for her getting arrested after the babies."

He tipped his chin toward the windows. "Then let me walk you up." When her lips parted, hesitant, he spread his hands. "I'm already here. I'll just walk with you, see you inside."

Her mouth firmed. "But I'm fine."

"You keep saying that," he noted.

As he started walking, her steps fell into sync with his. It wasn't that she was afraid to be alone with him. There were few people she felt safer around than Byron Strong—though she didn't know why. But here he was again, witnessing another life fiasco.

His timing was horrendous. He'd borne witness to every low or ugly impasse of the last year. *Why is it always him?*

Still, she gave in. She wasn't steady. And she wasn't all right. It would be an hour, maybe two, before she could process anything. In the meantime, he was right. She might as well have company. And though she was desperate for the chilled wine in her refrigerator, she hated drinking alone… "Go around back. I have a key to the garden door."

The walk did her good, as did the shrill blast of icy air that knifed around the side of the tavern. Byron stepped in front of her, a solid wall that blocked the worst of the gale. She trudged along in his silent shadow. She needed that, too. Silence.

She rubbed her lips together. They felt bruised. Yes, she needed the moscato. To numb them. To mask the bitter taste of Bertie's mouth. She'd need more than one glass if she was going to sleep tonight.

When she fumbled with her keys, Byron smoothly took them from her hand and unlocked the private entrance. He ushered her inside. She led the way up the spiral stairs to the landing. Here she took the keys firmly in hand and thrust them into the lock. Her lips peeled back from her teeth as the pain in her hand shouted in red-hot abandon. *Ouch.* The deadbolt clicked. She pushed the door open, eyeing her current living quarters.

It was a small space. It had seemed a bit claustrophobic in the wake of the French Colonial that Richard's grandmother had gifted to the two of them upon their engagement. However, the apartment above the tavern had become that place she ran to for reprieve, for consolation and escape.

She needed the trio now. She needed them like moscato.

"Is there a glass of that wine for me?" he asked as she took a step over the jamb.

She stopped. His hand pressed against the frame of the door. He'd erected a smile. "You drink moscato?" she asked.

"Is it pink?" he asked with a slight wince.

Her smile grew genuinely. *Impossible*, she thought, bewildered. "No."

"Good." He grinned. "If the guys caught me drinking the pink stuff, I'm not sure I'd ever live it down."

She hid a laugh behind her lips. She sighed over it, over him. Then, without a word, she moved back against the open door. He gave a nod and brushed by her into her space. She took a moment, closing her eyes and letting his sweet, earthy scent of aged ambergris wash over her. It was the essence of calm, of strength.

Nodding to herself, she closed the door and made her way into the kitchen to pour two large glasses of wine.

"I NEVER THOUGHT I'd be back here again."

Byron refilled the glasses on the coffee table. He sat back on Roxie's purple velvet-upholstered couch. Or settee. It was way too fancy to be lumped as a couch. "Where's *here* exactly?" He handed her one glass.

Roxie lifted it by the stem. With her feet bare and her legs folded next to her, she looked relaxed. Not defeated. The wine might have had something to do with that. It had brought her color back, made her eyes lazy. The lids were at half-mast as she laid her head against the headrest.

She eyed the truffle in her hand. She'd already taken a bite and had been nursing the other half for some time. "Sitting here," she explained, "eating bonbons, drinking myself into a stupor, rehashing a bad date."

As she stuffed the rest into her mouth and reached for the tin on the coffee table, which held what remained of the exotic truffle collection they'd both foraged, Byron fought a smile. "It's not that bad." When she turned her head slowly to scrutinize him, he raised a shoulder. "I do it every other Friday."

It had the desired effect—her lips turned up in a smile. She pressed her fingers over them and the truffle behind them. The slender line of her shoulders shook with a silent laugh. As she tipped the wine to her mouth, she said, "I *highly* doubt that."

"Why? Guys don't eat bonbons?"

"Guys eat bonbons," Roxie asserted. "They just know them as megastuffed Oreos, honey buns and Cocoa Puffs."

Byron chuckled. "I'm pretty sure the last time I ate Cocoa Puffs I was in tighty-whities."

"But you *have* eaten them. Anyway, I'm willing to bet that no man who looks like—" she scanned his face closely before her eyes dipped over his torso, shying "—well, *you*…has ever had a date blow up in his face."

Byron contemplated that. "I can't say what happened with Bertie has ever happened to me, but I've had my share of bad dates."

"Name one," Roxie challenged. When he hesitated, she tilted her head. "Come on, let's hear it. If only to make me feel less like a loser."

"You're anything but a loser, duchess."

"I just keep picking losers?" she asked, brow arched. She sipped her wine. "I'm not sure that makes me feel any better."

"All right." Byron moved on the couch, bracing himself. "To make you feel better…"

"Please."

"I threw up on a woman once," he admitted.

"During a date?" Roxie asked, eyes round.

"Not just that." He grimaced. "It was *after* the date."

She gasped. "Oh, no. Not during—"

He downed the rest of his wine in answer.

"Wow, you're right," she said. "That is bad."

He sat forward over his knees and set the glass on the table with a clack. "Ah, it turned out okay. She was a friend."

"Not Adrian," Roxie said, alarmed.

"No, not Adrian," Byron said. "This was before I moved to Fairhope, back in Atlanta about—" he squinted, counting back "—four and a half years ago? And it was my first time…or my first *attempt* at intimacy since…" He forced the words out. "Since I lost her."

"Your friend?"

He let out a breath, feeling some nerves and a disturbed feeling in the pit of his stomach. "No. My wife."

She stared at him. Her larkspur eyes went round as bonbons. "You were married?" When he nodded, she asked, "How did I not know this?"

"I'm not sure a lot of people do," he considered. "That was the draw of Fairhope and life on the coast."

"To get away." Roxie nodded her understanding. Her throat moved on a swallow. "How did it happen? Can you talk about it?"

"Sure," he said, though he had to roll his shoulders back to cast off the ready pall. "Her name was Dani. Daniella Rosales. We met in college, freshman year. I saw her and...I was done."

A light wavered cautiously to life in Roxie's eyes. "Just like that?" she whispered.

"Just like that," he agreed. "When I was younger, around fourteen, my center of gravity couldn't keep up with my growth. I got clumsy. Really clumsy, and angry, too, because I was this big, goofy guy who couldn't walk across a room without knocking something over. It took me years to work out the clumsy and level the resentment. Then I got to college, I saw Dani and I tripped over her into the fountain outside our residence hall."

The light in Roxie's eyes strengthened. "That might be the cutest thing I've ever heard."

"I would've disagreed," he informed her. "On campus tours, the guides were adamant that nobody touch the water in the fountain. Because it was said that if you did, you'd never find true love."

"Did you prove them wrong?"

He grinned. "I was irate with myself—until Dani fished me out, led me back to her room and dried me off. You remember odd things through the years. I remember how her towels smelled. Not like laundry, but like that unknown thing that'd been missing. Only I didn't know it was missing until I found it…or smelled it." He rolled his eyes. "It's dumb—"

"No," Roxie said with a quick shake of her head. "It's not dumb."

"It's cheesy."

"There's nothing wrong with a little *cheesy*. It's the sort of thing I used to believe in. That I used to have. Or I *think* I had." A touch of confusion crossed her face. She dismissed it with a sweep and offered him a rueful grin. "It's nice, being reminded that it does happen. That it can be real."

"Real," Byron echoed. He nodded. "Yeah. It was that."

Roxie frowned. "You haven't told me—what happened to her."

Hadn't he? Byron shifted on the cushion. He poured more wine and picked up the glass by the stem. He used the thumb and forefinger of each hand to hold the delicate crystal shoot, spinning it slowly, watching each facet flash in the lamplight. "When Dani was little, she had a heart condition. The doctors fixed it when she was thirteen. Or so they thought. As an adult, she was healthy. Active. She was a photographer, so she was never still—on the job or off. My friend Grim used to call her the Dervish. Nothing slowed her down. Then a few years after the wedding we decided it was time to start a family."

Byron hesitated again. After a moment, Roxie reached out and touched his knee. He lifted one corner of his mouth, though he wasn't sure it could be deemed a smile. When he spoke, he was subdued. "After her doctors signed off on it, we tried for a while before it took. She was three and a half months along when she collapsed. She went into a coma and it was four weeks before those same doctors informed me and the rest of her family that she'd never surface."

Her hand stayed locked on his knee. He was grateful for the silence. He'd heard every condolence known to man. Before the move to Fairhope, it had seemed like he couldn't go anywhere without hearing how sorry everyone was for his loss. Like his clumsiness in youth, the condolences had awakened his ire. It had taken a while for that ire to simmer and for him to confront Dani's loss, and even longer for him to learn to wholly live life again.

He cleared his throat. "You know as well as I do that when you're at the altar pledging your life to someone, it's just that—your whole life. And even though you both say the words *till death*, you expect death to come later. Much later. It doesn't enter your mind that death's coming for you a mere six years, seven months and twenty-seven days later, or that it's not you it's coming for. It's the person standing next to you, the one you've promised to love every day that life gives you. And learning to live without that person… It feels so backwards and wrong. It unravels every bit of who you are."

"Your whole life," she echoed. She released a ragged breath. "The baby? They couldn't save it?"

He took a long glug of wine, shaking his head slightly as he did. As he lowered the glass back to the table, he ignored the bad feeling in his stomach that had grown into a full-on internal wail. "If she'd been further along, maybe. And when she fell…there was some internal damage." He laid his arm over the back of the sofa. There was a knot in the wood trim. He circled it with the pad of his thumb. "It was a girl. We'd only just stopped arguing over what to call her." At her questioning brow, he confided, "Maree Frances."

For a full minute, she said nothing. Thoughtfully, she edged closer. Shifting toward him, she fit into the groove under his arm next to his chest. The wail inside him was on the verge of a banshee scream. The wave of lilacs stopped it from reaching fever pitch, beating it back down where it belonged.

She spoke low, almost inaudibly. "Nothing I tell you could ever be enough to say how sorry I am for what you've been through. I can't imagine…" She sighed and pressed her cheek into his lapel. "So I'm just going to hug you."

"Okay," he said. It trembled out of him on a short laugh. It warmed him.

As he'd left the tavern after finishing his shift there, Byron had seen Bertie drop Roxie off. He hadn't liked the look of him—a knee-jerk and instant assessment. The guy drove a luxury Mercedes but ground the transmission when he shifted into Park. And he wore a three-piece suit that screamed *easy money*.

Byron had taken a moment, studying Roxie from a distance. He'd felt the warmth gathering over his sternum, remembering the sound of her laugh from earlier in the day. Tinny bells. The best kind.

Then Byron had seen the flash of Bertie's gold

signet ring move too quickly. He'd seen the guy's arms wind too hard around Roxie. He'd seen his body close in on hers and the hard lip-lock that came close on the heels of the not-so-nice embrace.

That's not the way, Byron had mused. Not with a woman like Roxie. Slow and smooth was more what a lady of her caliber deserved. Hell, it was what she'd need after everything she'd been through. The warmth over his sternum had hardened into a big, black ball of volcanic rock. The back of his neck had turned to fire as it always did when he felt the old anger, the ire, rising up from the black. He moved in, loosening his tie when Roxie's quick attempt at a punch failed and Bertie kept coming at her.

Was the choke hold really necessary? she'd asked after.

Byron had seen her fear and embarrassment, and the trampled strength behind it.

Yes, damn it, it had been necessary. A part of him still wished Bertie had taken the second option so Byron could've implemented a lesson with his fists.

He noted the place of her hand. Right over his sternum, where the warmth for her had built and shied and then built again. It was the same hand she'd plowed into Fledgewick's face. The same fist she'd given Byron nearly a year ago. The edge of his mouth curved as he touched it.

"Mm." She winced. The fingers stiffened under his.

Byron gentled his hold. Gingerly, he turned her knuckles toward the light and saw the bruising. "You should've let me hit him."

"What would that have solved?"

"Nothing. But it would've felt damn good."

"Didn't feel so great to me."

"Because you aimed for the face," Byron explained. "Suppose he'd raised his chin or you'd struck his jaw. Your hand would be flat broken."

"He was drunk," Roxie reminded him. "I wanted to sober him up."

"Next time, aim for the liver."

"I'm no good at this," she admitted as he caressed her knuckles. "I miss marriage."

His hand stilled on hers. "You do?"

"Yes. I miss the security of it. The comfort of knowing that I'm safe from all this, from the uncertainty."

"But that's all." Byron frowned. "Right?"

She paused. "I don't know."

Byron tried to read her. "Rox. The man failed you. He knowingly failed you."

"I know he did." She tipped her chin up and confronted him with a cool expression. "Trust

me. I was there. But we were together so long…
I don't know anything else. You and Dani were
together a long time. You said learning to live
without her unraveled you."

"It's apples and oranges," he noted.

"I know that, too," she said, tensing.

"Wait a minute," he said, straightening. She
sat up in response. He took a good look at her.
"You're not still in love with the guy, are you?"

Her mouth parted and her eyes glazed in
thought. "I don't know." She lifted her hands.
They were empty. "I know I hate being alone.
I know that when it was good, I loved the relationship, and not just the security of it—I loved
the unit we built. I know how much of ourselves
we put into it. And I know that Richard's sorry."

"He told you that?" he asked. "He got down on
his knees and begged?"

"No, he didn't get on his knees," Roxie dismissed. "But he did try to say he was sorry. The
mess was so fresh, the hurt, I couldn't listen even
if he was sincere." Before Byron could say anything, she quickly added, "What he did was dis-
graceful, and I haven't forgotten how it made me
feel. But you said it yourself—you pledge your
life to someone. Your whole life."

"He quit his vows," he said heatedly. "He quit
you the second he jumped on her." When her

eyes rounded in shock, he cursed. "I'm sorry. Damn it, I'm sorry." He pushed off the couch and left the room, taking his glass into her kitchen. He'd had enough to drink. Under the light of the stove, he rinsed the glass then used the tap filter to fill it. He tipped it up and downed the water quickly.

He was a damn fool.

Byron set the glass on the counter and braced his hands on the edge. Leaning into it, he ducked his head and breathed until he felt the heat in his neck subside. Why was the anger rising again? Was it Richard or was it pride?

Either way, he couldn't go back to her with ire. Even if it was his pride, she'd been through enough without him piling his bruised ego on the proverbial heap.

The small window above the sink drew his attention. He looked out on the listless bay. The lights of Mobile flickered far beyond the inky black waters broken only by the small bits of light from the tavern and the inn. The watery peaks were brushed with hushed gold filigree.

He did his best to absorb the calm and lulling placidity those waters brought with their small, whispering waves. This was why he'd gravitated to Fairhope in the wake of Dani's death—the serenity.

Calmer, he eyed the dishcloth beside the sink.

He grabbed it, balled it up and ran it under cold water for several seconds. He wrung it out and walked slowly back into the living room, where Roxie sat on the settee.

He extended the rolled-up cloth to her. "Here."

She narrowed her eyes on it as her hand lifted. Questioning, her gaze rose to his.

"Your hand," he said. He took her wrist and wrapped the cold cloth around her injured knuckles himself.

She sucked in a breath. A line dug in between her eyes.

After a moment, he asked, "Better?"

She gave a nod. "Thank you," she said quietly. "Do you...do you think that there's one great love for everyone? Just one?"

Byron lowered back to the settee. He reached up and loosened his tie, still a touch too warm. He thought about Dani. He thought about the doomed attempts at reconnecting with women since. The Strong family creed. "Yeah, I do," he answered truthfully. "And I believe you shouldn't settle for anything less than the extraordinary. Not when it comes to the rest of your life."

She fell silent and contemplative once more.

"Have you talked to Richard about this?" he asked.

"No," she said. "He's been away, somewhere.

His parents say he's 'working on himself.'" She used air quotes. The line was still entrenched between her eyes.

Byron weighed himself. He weighed her, their friendship. "Maybe you should contact him. Talking to him might give you the clarity you need." When she looked to him, he added, "You don't seem sure. And you need to be sure, duchess. Absolutely sure."

She nodded. Her chin lifted. He saw the poise, a shade of the confidence that had drawn him to her in the first place. "I will." She pressed her lips together. "How will I know if he's the one, do you think?"

"I only have one frame of reference," Byron admitted, "but I'm pretty sure when you love someone, you'll just know it."

Her mouth tipped down uncertainly again. "But if I love him, *really* love him, shouldn't I already know whether or not I want him? Do I really have to see him to be sure? Or is it just—"

It was impulse. Complete and utter impulse. But chances were, he'd never get to do it again.

He leaned in. She stilled. Her mouth stopped moving, her eyes went round. As he lessened the gap, he saw them begin to close. *There*, he thought.

His hand found its way into the dip of her waist.

It stayed there as he nudged her head back by fitting his mouth to hers.

It was simple. It was soft. For him, it was explosive.

He'd known there was *something* there. He'd known some part of him had wanted some part of her from the moment he'd laid eyes on her. Like all things unattainable, he'd ignored it.

It must've festered. Under cover of his ignorance, his attraction had bred on itself.

It had bred like bunnies. He couldn't count the stupid bunnies.

He broke away, stifling the protesting noise in his throat. It was his turn to press his lips together. She tasted like raspberries. Knowing that definitely wasn't going to lower the bunny quotient.

Are you happy now, Strong? He sat back. She stared at him, owl-eyed. She hadn't moved so much as an inch since he'd leaned in.

So much for their friendship. Byron cleared his throat and raised a brow. "Did that answer your question?"

Her round eyes shifted slightly. "Question?" she repeated in a scant voice.

"Who're you thinkin' about right now, duchess?" he asked. "Me or Richard?"

"Richard?" She lowered her face. There was color in it again. Lots of color. "Richard," she said once more without the question behind it.

He bobbed his head in an indicative nod. "Well, there you have it." When she didn't move, he lifted her glass from the table and extended it to her.

She took it. Drinking deep, she nursed the remainder as they sat in heavy silence.

CHAPTER THREE

"YOU'RE ALL GOING to hell," Roxie proclaimed. It was Wednesday morning, a brisk forty degrees. Not even the hearty bay pelicans had ventured out for their morning repast. And here she was chugging up the hill from the Fairhope Pier to the towering bluff that overlooked the Eastern Shore in all its splendor.

Adrian Bracken fell into step beside her, moving marginally faster, dressed in a gray hoodie and black yoga pants. A sun-battered baseball cap crowned her red bob. "This was Liv's idea. Not mine."

"Oh," Roxie said, her voice dropping a level. Her breath was whistling at the back of her throat and her calves were screaming. "There's a special place in hell for *you*, Liv."

The roar of a gas-powered motor crept up behind them. Roxie and Adrian glanced over in unison to the woman behind the wheel of a John Deere Gator. She had one UGG-clad foot propped up beside the steering wheel and a gloved claw wrapped around a chocolate éclair fresh from Briar's kitchen. "You know," Olivia Leighton said as she chowed down on the pastry. "If the two of you would stop squawking like seagulls, in all likelihood we'd be back home eating Briar's quiche by now..." She shrugged and stuffed the rest of the éclair into her mouth. "As it is..."

"Are you even allowed to operate an ATV on the open road?" Adrian wanted to know.

Olivia looked around, nonplussed. "Nobody's stopped me." She reached inside the box on the passenger seat for another pastry. "Come on, pick up the pace. I brought Gerald's Indiana Jones whip and I'm not afraid to use it."

Roxie groaned, falling behind Adrian a few more paces as the stitch in her side flared up and choked the wind out of her. "I'm sorry your doctor says you can't run yet because you just squeezed two babies out of you. But we don't deserve this."

"Huh," Olivia said with a smirk. "Bitter and out of shape. I'd feel a mite more friendly if I'd spent the night with a certain supersexy Greek man-cake."

Roxie stopped, planting her hands on her knees. Not for the first time since waking up to him in her apartment Tuesday morning, she felt the urge to wring Byron's foolish neck.

She'd insisted he sleep on a pallet in her living room, since they'd finished close to two bottles between them. The next morning he called down to the inn for coffee, meaning both Briar and her husband, Cole, knew that he was at her place early enough to be suspect. They'd informed Adrian and her husband, James. Who then told Olivia, who, of course, blabbed the news to everybody from here to the Flora-Bama. Roxie had half expected the stranger standing next to her at the grocery checkout yesterday to give her a sly thumbs-up. She'd tolerated as much from all three of her wedded friends.

When Roxie finally caught her breath, she lowered to the sidewalk, leaning back on her hands to ease the stitch in her ribs.

"Hey," Olivia said, the ATV coming to a halt as Adrian ran ahead to catch up with Briar. "Ass, elbows off the concrete. You're falling behind last week's time, which I'm sorry to say was shameful enough."

"Shush," Roxie said, too tired to raise her voice. She closed her eyes. *Breathe. Breathe.* "I'm trying not to envision man-cakes or any other type of Greek pastry."

"Why not?" Olivia asked, studying the éclair in her hand with a smug grin. "You still stuffed from Monday night?"

Roxie shook her head and fought hard not to laugh. At this point, it would hurt. Really hurt. "Nothing happened. In fact, I wish I could go back and make that whole twenty-four-hour period disappear forever."

Footsteps beat toward them. Roxie looked up to find Adrian returning, her high cheekbones pink from the February nip. "I can't catch Briar. She's like the female version of the Flash."

"My star pupil," Olivia said fondly, gaze combing the cliff above. Catching sight of the blonde along the sidewalk, she lifted the bullhorn from her lap. Her lurid voice boomed over the park, making Roxie grimace and Adrian plug her ears. "That's it, cuz! Boot and rally!"

"Wonderful," Roxie said, reaching for the side of her head. "I am now bitter, out of shape and one-hundred-percent deaf."

Olivia set the bullhorn down and reached back for the lid of the cooler in the Gator's cargo bed. She lobbed a bottle of water at Adrian's head. "Stretch and hydrate."

Adrian lifted her hands to block the bottle from hitting her square in the face. She bobbled it several times before catching it one-handed.

Roxie lazily watched the bottle meant for her sail clean over her head and bounce onto the grass beyond. "Thank you, Derek Jeter," she drawled. She retrieved the Dasani, cracked it open and frowned at the clear contents. "I'm thinking about getting back together with him."

Adrian stopped in the midst of a lunging stretch. *"Richard?"*

"No. Jose Conseco," Roxie said condescendingly. "Who else?"

"Go back," Adrian said, milling a hand. "What happened to Byron? Wait, go further back. What happened with Bertie?"

"Oh, right," Olivia said, leaning over the passenger seat in interest. "I forgot all about that yahoo."

Roxie scrubbed her hands back through her hair. "Julianna was wrong about him—to say the least. Luckily, as Bertie was dropping me off at the tavern on Monday night, Byron happened to be outside. He intervened when Bertie revealed his true colors. Very Perseus-type stuff."

"Byron?" Olivia cracked a laugh.

Adrian wrinkled her nose. "So you were the Andromeda?"

"Sort of," Roxie considered. "I was clothed but, still, humiliated. She was chained to a rock, though, so she wins."

"Ah, bondage," Olivia said reminiscently. "Didn't Andromeda get the man?"

"Yeah, but the damsel-in-distress thing," Adrian said. "Who wants it?"

A sly grin colored Olivia's face. "Clearly, you've never done role-play."

"Was Gerald the damsel?" Adrian asked, droll.

Roxie waved her hands. "No, no. No more unwanted pictures. Anyway, after the Perseus thing went down, I was a little shaken, so Byron walked me upstairs and kept me company for a while."

"Kept you company," Adrian said, picking through the words carefully.

Olivia coughed into her hand. "Man-cakes."

"There was wine," Roxie said, ignoring Olivia's pastry reference. "We both imbibed a little too much but not enough to lose our sensibilities." She refrained from mentioning his kiss. She was still trying to riddle through the consequences. Of Byron's mouth. On hers. "He wound up staying overnight, on the floor. Like a gentleman."

"Good," Adrian said. "Byron's a family friend, but I could still kick his ass. Or we could get Liv to sit on him. Either way."

Olivia cocked her head at Adrian. "He can get in line."

"What does any of this have to do with Richard, though?" Adrian asked.

"Before we went to bed—*separately*—I talked to him about maybe reconciling with Richard," Roxie explained. She tiptoed over any mention of Byron's marriage and his wife's death—it was clearly a part of his life he wanted to keep private. Respecting that was easy. If she could've found some way to keep the breakup of her own marriage less public, she'd have done it in a heartbeat.

"What did he have to say about it?" Adrian prompted.

"He cautioned me against it at first," Roxie said. "But in the end he suggested I speak to Richard about it in person."

"Will you?"

"Yes." Roxie nodded. "As soon as he gets back from…wherever it is he's been for the last few months."

"Why?" Olivia asked. She threw up her hands. "I'm sorry, but I'm not on board. The ink on the marriage license was hardly dry before he slept with someone else. Before he slept with *your sister*. That takes scumbaggery to a whole new level."

It had been the deepest betrayal Roxie could have ever imagined. She'd cried. For months, she'd cried alone in the apartment above the tavern. She'd taken little with her but the purple settee from their French Colonial after toying with the idea of setting fire to the whole thing. Dousing gasoline over the Aubusson rug where she'd found Richard and Cassandra coupling had been so tempting.

There was no way she could go back to that house. If they were going to start over…if they both wanted to start over and fight for all that they had built over the last decade, they would need a clean slate.

"Listen," Roxie said carefully, "I know you both think it's foolish." Adrian had said nothing but her reticence was answer enough. "And maybe it is. But I read this study recently about couples who decide to stay together and work for their relationship after a spouse strays once. Just once. The majority managed to make it stick."

"Once a cheat, always a cheat," Olivia opined.

Adrian sighed. "I'm sorry, but I agree with Liv for once. I always thought it was common sense that once someone cheated, they were likely to do it again."

"Richard was never a cheater, though," Roxie said.

"People change," Olivia told her. "I'm usually the one who would tell you to go for it, but, Roxie, we were all here last March. We saw how devastated you were."

"We just don't want that to happen to you again," Adrian added.

"If it does, we'll have to kill him," Olivia said. "Gerald hid my firearms after we found out about the babies, but I've still got my bat, and I think Richard could do without his kneecaps under the circumstances."

Roxie let out a laugh. "God, you're wonderful. You're all so wonderful. I love the concern and initiative. But you know what they say about regret. I can't go the rest of my life not knowing if I let go of the person I'm supposed to be with."

"Can I ask you?" Adrian said, narrowing her eyes. "Do you love him?"

"Byron asked me the same thing. And the answer is yes—on some level, I do. I can't be sure if it's enough to sustain us, *or* if he feels enough for me to want to start over."

"It's your call," Adrian determined. "Do what you have to do. Whichever way it goes, at least you'll finally have closure."

Roxie nodded. Closure. That was what she'd been missing for the last year. It was no good hanging in emotional limbo. No matter how often she'd told herself to move on, the hollowness inside had kept her tethered in the murky in-between.

Olivia frowned. "Well, damn. I had a whole list of ill-advised rebound candidates to throw at you."

Roxie arched a brow. "You weren't upset when you thought I'd rebounded with Byron. That was you playing Marvin Gaye on the jukebox after tavern hours all night last night. I know it was."

The Cheshire cat grin sat well on Olivia's face. "I do feel a bit bad now about telling everybody you two did the hot dog dance."

"Thanks for that," Roxie replied.

A Jeep pulled up next to the ATV. The driver's

window rolled down and James Bracken leaned out in dark sunglasses and a devastating grin. "Howdy."

"What are you doing here?" Olivia asked as Adrian softened. Every bit of her softened as she shaded her face with her hand against the brightening sun.

James jerked a shoulder. "I offered to head out and inform you that we menfolk have successfully thrown together a breakfast fit for a queen. Or four, in this case."

Adrian's smile turned knowing. She gave a laugh. "You bailed."

"Bailed?" James's grin faltered somewhat. "I don't know what you mean."

"Yeah, right!" Olivia said, catching on. She picked up another éclair. "You totally bailed on Cole and Gerald."

James pursed his lips. He took off his ball cap and combed his fingers back through his thick brown hair. His colorful sleeve of tattoos flashed vividly. "They've got it handled. Cole managed to fry up eggs and sausage and sweet-talk Harmony into staying at the table. She smeared bananas all over the place, but she ate and not one of us said a word about the mess." He pulled off his sunglasses and began to clean them with the edge of his shirt. "Then there's Gerald." He sent Olivia an impressive look. "It's only three weeks in, but the man's earned all the daddy badges there are to earn. Burping, changing, rocking. It's like watching the Daddy Olympic games."

"And Kyle?" Adrian asked, referring to her and James's eight-year-old son.

"I helped him and Gavin haul the crab traps out of the water," James told her, replacing his sunglasses and hooking a meaty arm through the open window. "Then I offered to let them tag along. But they wanted to stay behind and get to know their catch before we release them back into the wild. I expect all the crabs'll be named after Marvel villains before we get back."

"We?" Olivia asked. "Think again, mister. Your woman here doesn't need rescuing."

James tilted his head at his wife. The corner of his mouth moved. It was a nonverbal *come-hither* that nearly made Roxie's weary feet move in double-time. "I could persuade her. It's not rescuing if there's persuasion involved. Ain't that right, lil' mama?"

Adrian looked as if she were fighting laughter. Warmth flooded her features. She walked to the open window and angled her face up to his. "Any other day, you wouldn't have had to stop. You could've just slowed down, and Roxie and I would've jumped into the backseat and you'd be peeling out of here."

"Cheater, cheater, pumpkin eater," Olivia rhymed, polishing off the remnants of the éclair.

Though his chin came to rest on his folded arms, James eyed Olivia over the crown of Adrian's head. "Isn't it 'Peter, Peter?'"

"You need to take your peter home," Olivia informed him, crude. She brushed her hands together to remove the icing. "Save it for your red-head later."

"Hey," James said, feigning offense on behalf of his redhead and his privates.

The redhead in question grabbed him by the bill of his cap. "She's right. Get your fine ass back to the inn and stay there. A little baby time won't kill you."

James's jaw moved though he didn't look en-tirely dissatisfied. "The pink one puked on me."

"They're both pink." Adrian grinned.

"Okay, the loud one puked on me."

Roxie began to cross to the Jeep. "What's wrong, James? You don't like babies?"

"He loves babies," Adrian said, patting his arm. "He's just never been around them. Go. If you change one of them, I'll give you a cookie." Her brows quirked. "A very...hot...cookie."

His brows rose over the rim of his glasses and he reached over to put the Jeep in gear. "I heard that."

She leaned up to plant a kiss on him. Roxie

found herself sighing a little as the man kissed his wife with all the abandon of a person still completely and hopelessly lost over another. Apparently the romantic in her hadn't been completely ripped up from the roots. Perhaps she did still believe in love. Being surrounded by committed couples that had managed to find happiness despite daunting odds—Briar and Cole, Olivia and Gerald, Adrian and James—certainly helped.

She wasn't a quitter. She never had been. And she'd never *not* been a romantic. It was natural, even inevitable, that she'd reached the point of questioning whether she needed to explore an alternate ending for the marriage she'd desperately wanted in the first place—the marriage she'd idealized.

Olivia's voice pealed over the newlyweds' exchange. "Hey!" she said to Roxie. "Where're you going?"

Roxie dodged around the Jeep's grille. She wasn't a quitter. Nope. She wasn't a sprinter either. "Somebody's gotta ride shotgun." Lowering her voice through the passenger window, she added to James, "I change the diaper, you get the credit. Just get me out of here."

"I heard *that*," Adrian pointed out.

James reached over the passenger seat to pop the lock. "Hop in, sugar."

Roxie felt her phone vibrating on her hip. Holding up a finger for James, she pulled it from the waistband of her leggings. The caller ID was listed as unknown. She answered it anyway. "Hello?"

"Is this Roxie Honeycutt?"

"Speaking," Roxie replied.

"Hi! This is Vera Strong. I believe you know my son, Byron."

Oh, what fresh hell is this? The blood drained from Roxie's face. "I did not sleep with him!" she blurted then clamped her hand over her mouth.

There was a slight pause then a friendly chuckle. "I'm happy to hear it, dear. I'm calling because he's under the impression that you're looking for a new place to live."

For a moment, Roxie was confounded. Then she remembered the brief exchange she'd had with Byron before he left her apartment yesterday morning. He'd admired the view from the windows. She'd admitted that she was looking for a change of scenery. He'd had a hard time imagining better scenery than what she had already. Roxie had told him about her new mantra—New Year, New Roxie. Which all started with finding a new place to live. Something that might begin to erase the hollow feeling that had moved into the apartment with her and refused to depart despite repeated attempts at eviction.

What was wrong with the old Roxie? he'd asked. That had stuck with her. And the kiss.

It was difficult to forget a kiss, especially a kiss from someone…well, someone like Byron. She'd spent more time than she'd like to admit trying *not* to think about how sweet it was—she'd forgotten kisses could be so sweet. And she'd tried especially to forget how his lips had lingered. And how in lingering he'd awakened starbursts. Small starbursts of eternity.

Roxie frowned deeply. Being touched… It had been so long since she had *really* been touched. The emptiness in her had turned into a resounding ache at his contact, and for a few moments, she'd considered bringing Byron's mouth back down to hers. For a few moments, she'd craved more than his companionship. She'd craved the contact. The promise of heat that came with it.

But had she wanted it for the single reason that his heat could erode her loneliness? There was trust there. There was affection. For those small starbursts of eternity, there had been longing and the promise of flame. It had been so long since she'd felt the sheer electrical pulse of new chemistry.

But why did it seem like so long since she'd felt the flame? The passion?

Had she wanted Byron for the promise of passion? Had she wanted him because she was lonely—because she missed someone else?

She dispelled the riot of confusion left over

from that night. Byron wasn't the guy. He wasn't *her* guy. He'd admitted that there was only one great love in life. His words and the experience behind them had even gone so far as to convince her to give Richard another chance.

Of course, that was before the kiss. But that was beside the point.

"Hello?" Vera said.

"Yes," Roxie said, giving herself a quick, discerning shake. "Sorry. Yes, I am in the market for a new place."

"That's great," Vera said. "My husband, Constantine, and I are in the real estate business. We own a dozen or so homes in Baldwin County. Several of them are in the Fairhope and Point Clear area. Most are lease houses with a twelve-month contract. If you're interested, we could arrange a few showings. I understand you're a busy woman. We would be happy to meet you at your convenience."

Her heart began to beat a bit faster at the possibilities. *New Year. New Roxie.* This was exactly what she needed to get her life back on track. "I'm interested," Roxie told Vera. "Are you free late this afternoon?"

"Sure. Does five thirty work for you?"

"It does," Roxie said. She'd have to rush from the Hamilton wedding. It didn't start until three thirty, but she had her assistant, Yuri, to fall back on. And Adrian would be there to help. "Text me an address and I'll meet you."

"Fabulous," Vera cheered. "I'm looking forward to meeting the woman who didn't sleep with my son."

Roxie ended the call on a nervous chuckle. She stared at the screen for a moment, wondering if she should give Byron a call. As a thank-you.

No, Roxie. Nix the Perseus and Andromeda.

"Come on, Rox," James said. "Let's get goin'." As she hopped in, he flipped Olivia and Adrian a salute, shouted "Race you!" and with a mash of the accelerator, they were off.

"THE ONE ON Nichols wasn't so bad."

"None of the Strongs' houses have been bad so far," Roxie pointed out as she steered her Lexus through light evening traffic. "What I'm looking for, though, is something a little more... I don't know. Special."

In the passenger seat, Briar Savitt nodded. "You're waiting for something to jump out and take a bite out of you."

Roxie's lips twitched. "If Liv were here, it'd be Euphemism City. Though you're right. I want something I can be excited about coming home to."

At the sound of a squeal from the backseat, Briar turned and smiled at her daughter, Harmony, who was strapped into a car seat. "Almost there, baby girl." She groped for a toy Harmony had dropped on the floor and stretched to hand it back to her. "What do you think of Vera?"

"She's marvelous," Roxie said and meant it. "I don't know why I was worried." She had asked Briar to tag along. Vera and her husband, Constantine, had invested in Briar's bed-and-breakfast. The Strongs and Savitts were on first-name terms, and Roxie had hoped that having Briar around would help make the introduction to Byron's mother less uncomfortable after her awkward outburst over the phone.

In the end, Roxie hadn't had anything to worry about. Just as Briar had assured her, Vera was just as easy to get along with as Byron. Though hearing Byron's name in conjunction with the word *easy* made images come to Roxie's mind that would've made Olivia proud...

"Serendipity Lane?" Briar said as they passed the sign. "I've never heard of it."

"It's nice," Roxie acknowledged as they both took a look at the neighborhood. "Very nice." The area was clean and heavily residential. The trees were aged behemoths. Roxie could tell the homes were older. Most had been treated to modern face-lifts.

Vera's SUV pulled to the curb behind a mailbox

with the numbers 77 painted on it. "This must be the last one," Roxie said.

"Ooh," Briar said as Roxie parked behind Vera. "Would you look at that?"

Roxie's jaw dropped as she peered through the passenger window at the grand white Victorian. All the houses on the street were nice. But *this one*… It was like a celestial winter faerie palace, only more homey than extravagant. The front yard was large, rectangular. A picket fence framed annual springtime beds.

High on the second floor, there was a big round stained-glass window. The last light of day shined on it, making the wavy iridescent streaks of the orange sun hanging low over azure blue waves glow.

The breath rushed out of her. Her voice was scant when she finally found words. "Holy wow. It's like utopia." There was a wraparound porch with a large cushioned lay-back swing. She could imagine herself lounging there in the summer. She could hear the wind blowing through those ancient trees and the ice clinking against the sides of her tea glass.

The vision was so tangible, she had to blink to bring herself back to the wintry present. She barely remembered to grab her purse before joining Vera on the sidewalk, Briar right behind her with Harmony on her hip.

"What do you think?" Vera asked. The woman didn't look old enough to be the mother of a thirty-something-year-old man. Though one thing Byron and Vera did have in common was their striking good looks. With dark hair flowing down her back in waves, a tailored red dress cloaking her hourglass figure and towering Mary Jane heels, she looked more like one of the glossy coanchors of *Entertainment Tonight* than the low-key small-town real estate agent that she was. "I think we saved the best for last."

"You aren't kidding," Roxie murmured. "I've always had a thing for Victorians."

"Wait until you get a load of this one," Vera advised as she rooted through her purse for the key. She led them up the sidewalk to the porch steps. "It's a family house. Built in 1949 by Con's uncle for his wife when he brought her over from Greece to live out the rest of their lives here."

"How sweet," Briar said, peering through the glass surrounding the front door as Vera bowed to unlock it. "I love houses with a story behind them."

Vera swung the door open and turned back to them. "After you, dears."

"Thank you." Roxie stepped over the threshold. The flooring struck her first. It was spectacular. Walnut. There was crown molding. No doubt the interior had been updated within the last ten to fifteen years. The small cut-glass chandelier over the entry caught her eye. Drops of foggy sea glass dangled from the fringes. She had to stop herself from touching it.

"From the island of Santorini," Vera explained, "where Athena and her sister, Con's mother, immigrated from after the Second World War."

Beyond the foyer, she caught sight of the staircase in the living room. It arched to the right, and curlicue ironwork made up the banister. "Oh, my word." She lowered her voice in automatic reverence. "Vera, this is stunning!"

"It doesn't even have that old house smell," Vera boasted. "There're three bedrooms, an office, two full baths and one half bath. There's a full laundry service in the basement. The furnishings are optional. You can get rid of everything, keep everything, or pick and choose what you need until you get the desired result. Not to mention the detached garage. There is a tenant in the loft above…"

"That's fine," Roxie said automatically. She took a peek into the dining room on the right. More sea glass. And windows. Windows everywhere—thin, tall, lovingly trimmed in a fleur-de-lis motif. An archway led into the kitchen. "Would you look at this, Briar?" Roxie asked as she spun in a circle, taking it all in. "*Better Homes and Gardens* better watch its back."

"Glass-front cabinets." Briar sighed. "I've always wanted glass-front cabinets. And double ovens. And stone!" She ran her hand over the stonework surrounding what had likely once been a wood-burning hearth and stove. "I could die here."

Vera laughed. "You haven't seen the living room."

Here the clack of Roxie's heels echoed off high-arched ceilings. She'd thought old houses such as this were built tight with rooms closed off from one another under squatted ceilings. But this house breathed, the living room spilling up into the second-floor landing. More windows here, high and arched with transoms peering out onto a charming patio with a bricked fire pit. There was a fenced-in backyard that would be green and fragrant in spring and summer. Roxie stopped in front of the center window. Framed between the panes was one of those rare Japanese magnolias overflowing with plump pink blossoms.

Briar leaned toward Roxie's shoulder and lowered her voice. "If you get this house, I'll be insanely jealous, but at least I can visit. Or live in the kitchen. I'll cook. Cole can do yard work. We could make it work."

"It's mine," Roxie chanted. "All mine, I tell you." She blinked, cleared her throat and shook her head. "Sorry. Don't know where that came from. I haven't seen the upstairs and I know. I just *know*, Briar. It's like knowing you want to marry someone."

Briar smiled at her. "You're glowing. It's good to see your glow again, Roxie."

Roxie whirled around to Vera. "I'll take it. Can we sign now? I want to sign now."

Vera held up her hands. "Wait a second. You haven't seen the bedrooms or the basement. There could be leaks. Rats the size of armadillos... And I'm your Realtor."

"I'll call the roofers," Roxie claimed. "I'll call the Schwarzenegger of exterminators. I have to have this house, Vera. You tell me what we need to do to get this done tonight and we'll do it."

Vera opened her mouth to speak, but the faint sound of Jimi Hendrix's guitar wafted from her boho purse. She pulled out her cell phone and frowned at the caller ID screen. "So sorry. It's my youngest. She's flying in from Africa early tomorrow. Do you mind?"

"Of course not," Roxie said.

"Seriously," Vera cautioned, "take a walk upstairs. Leaks and rats excluding, I'll have the papers for you in the dining room ready to sign as soon as you're finished."

As Vera answered the call, Roxie and Briar gleefully sprinted up the stairs to find out what other treasures the house had to offer. The stained glass was even more exquisite up close as the last wavering light of the afternoon cast rioting crystalline swaths from floor to ceiling.

Roxie found a room to set up her sewing. Wide with the high boughs of the Japanese magnolia aligned in the single picture window, it was a creative space if she'd ever seen one. There were built-in shelves where she could arrange fabrics and an alcove perfect for her sewing and embroidery equipment.

In the master suite, she gawked at the turtle-back ceiling…and frowned over an overlarge television set up on an otherwise gorgeous antique dresser. The dresser could stay. The television… it stuck out like a sore thumb. The bed was built up on a platform to distinguish it from the sitting area. She'd trade the bed frame for the iron one she'd bought after the divorce. It would work well with the curlicue iron accents she'd seen throughout the house.

Briar, Harmony now snoozing on her shoulder, stepped out of the walk-in closet across the room. "There's enough room in here for the Duchess of Devonshire's trousseau. Wigs and all."

"Don't tease me," Roxie advised, moving toward the closet door to peek inside, too.

"Have you checked out the bathroom?" Briar asked, pointing to the closed pocket doors. She reached for the slight parting between them. "If there's a whirlpool tub, I might have to hate on you a little bit."

"Fair enough," Roxie said as she peered over Briar's shoulder.

Briar slid the pocket doors back. They whispered along the tracks in the wall. Steam greeted them. Roxie squinted through it. Just as Briar tensed beside her and reached out to grip her arm, a long form took shape before her. "Um, who…"

The intruder stood at one of the matching sinks, a razor raised to his chin. As the doors clacked against the jamb, he jerked and grunted a pained cry. He turned partway toward them, his hand clasped to his chin. Briar's gasp reverberated off the periwinkle tiles and Roxie exclaimed, "Byron!"

Shock and bemusement flashed across his face. He didn't say a word, just stared at them.

She stared back. He wasn't Byron. He was naked Byron. Or…almost-naked Byron. How could she not have known *all this* was under those suits and ties? His skin was the color of golden piecrust hot and fresh from the oven. There wasn't an ounce of body fat on him. The bastard. Everything was ripply and muscly, sprinkled with a fine dusting of dark hair that looked so soft that Roxie had the dubious urge to run her fingertips through it. He would have been bare if not for the black briefs hugging his… Roxie's cheeks heated quickly when words like *cruller*, *bear claw*, *sweet roll* rushed through her mind. *Damn it, Liv!*

Flustered, she balled her hands into fists, physically forcing her gaze anywhere but on his…accoutrements. "What are you doing here?" she asked.

"Me?" he asked. Before he could go further, he looked beyond her and Briar into the bedroom and paled considerably. "Ma?"

Vera's voice cracked like thunder. "Byron Atticus Strong!"

As if realizing he was bare as a bumpkin, he reached down to cover himself. Roxie's face flamed hotter at the move and she covered her mouth. "What is this, a town meeting?" he asked.

"Why the Dickens aren't you next door?" Vera said sharply.

"Next door?" Roxie asked. The truth hit her flat in the face. "You're the tenant?" Of course he was the tenant.

"I used to be," Byron answered. "Now I live *here*."

Briar's mouth formed into an intrigued O. She then cleared her throat and gestured toward the bedroom door. "Harmony and I will just tiptoe downstairs and wait." She cast her eyes in Byron's direction, fighting a grin. "Hi, Byron."

He pressed his lips together. "Briar."

Roxie waited until Briar was gone before lifting her shoulders. "What do you mean you live here now?"

Byron glanced around her to his mother. "By any chance, have you spoken with Pop about the house lately?"

"No," Vera said. "Why?"

Byron cursed under his breath. His gaze veered back to Roxie. "If you're interested in leasing the Victorian, you're going to be disappointed."

"Why?" Roxie asked, fearing she knew the answer already.

"Because it's mine," Byron finished. "Sorry, duchess."

CHAPTER FOUR

THE SOUND OF hushed arguing echoed into the dining room from the kitchen. Byron fought the urge to scrub his temples, where his irritation was starting to collect. Whatever satisfaction and tranquility he'd found under the rain showerhead in the master bath had vanished under storm clouds of hassle.

Byron pushed aside the spray of flowers in a beveled vase at the center of the table so that he could see Roxie sitting opposite him. She looked near perfection again in a navy blue dress belted in white sateen. Her hair was drawn back from her face at the nape. A string of pearls rested against her neck. Despite her polish, she couldn't hide the strain he saw around the lines of her mouth.

The voices in the kitchen rose several notches, his mother's whisper rising to a shriek as his father's exasperation rose to a muffled shout. Byron rolled his eyes toward them. "Sorry about this."

Roxie jerked a shoulder, glancing past him at

the archway through which his parents had disappeared. "Mistakes happen."

"Yeah. They do." When her gaze settled on him again, that unblinking stare of hers fixating on his face, Byron pushed up the sleeves of the denim button-up he'd donned quickly when he realized he had unwanted company. He and Roxie hadn't exactly parted under normal terms Tuesday morning. The whole thing had ridden on the back bumper of his mind—the kiss, the awkward lull that followed and the entire sleepless night he'd spent on her floor.

The wine hadn't been enough to forget her sleepy eyes, the lure behind them that had hooked him like a fish. He wished he didn't remember what it was like to kiss her. Every time he'd thought about it over the last two days, he'd felt that hook dig in a little further.

He stanched the flow of his thoughts, skimming the edge of his index finger under his nose. "Since the two of them aren't getting anywhere, maybe you and I could straighten this out."

Roxie's shoulders squared against the back of the chair. "Okay."

"My mother probably told you that this is my great-aunt and great-uncle's place. Since starting the accounting firm took a chunk out of my savings, I moved into the loft above the garage to build my savings back. On Monday, Athena gave my father the go-ahead to offer it to me outright."

Roxie's brows gathered. "But your mother thought the house was still available."

Byron wondered whether to tell her that the deal with Athena and his father wasn't concrete. Instead he said, "I figured word got around to my mother, seeing as she and Pop are still married and all." He stopped to let the spirited debate in the next room speak for itself.

Roxie fiddled with one of the pearl and diamond drops at her ears. "So I guess since you're practically moved in and the house is in your family, I don't stand much of a chance."

"Sorry," he said again and meant it when he saw the crestfallen look on her face. Guilt flared in the pit of his stomach and spread outward. He smoothed his hands over his knees when the urge to reach out to her nearly broke loose. He scanned her long lids as her gaze fell to the folder on the table in front of her.

The folder. Byron frowned at it and the family logo printed on the front. Inside would no doubt be the lease agreement. His brows came together. His agreement with his father was only verbal.

Suddenly, the heated debate between his parents began to add up. If Roxie had signed, then it was Byron's goose that was likely cooked. He cleared his throat. "Is that the, ah…" When her head lifted, he opened his hand to indicate the folder.

She glanced at it again. "The lease?" He made an affirmative sound in his throat and she nodded. "Of course it is."

"So you've already signed," Byron surmised, noting the pen clasped tight in her fingers.

Her hand spread across the top of the folder, as if she were prepared to guard its contents. "Why?" Her eyes rounded on his. "Didn't you sign one?"

Byron opened his mouth to respond. The sound of feet tapping against hardwood stopped him. His parents filed into the room, his mother straight-backed, tight-lipped. His father looked appropriately cowed, his shoulders slumped, hands buried deep in his pockets.

Vera stopped at the head of the table. When Constantine edged up beside her, she arched a brow at him. He lifted his hands in silent acquiescence and moved back behind her shoulder. It was like watching a skinny pine cower behind a brazen tulip. Vera turned back to Roxie and Byron and shook her head. "First of all, I'd like to apologize for the mix-up. It's an unprecedented predicament that could *easily* have been avoided."

Constantine coughed discreetly into his hand. Vera's lips folded in on themselves briefly before she gathered herself and continued. "It's difficult to settle on a fair arrangement for everyone.

Monday, Byron, you entered into a verbal agreement for the house with your father, and minutes ago, Roxie, you asked to sign before we were interrupted."

"Whoa, whoa," Byron said, holding up a hand. "She didn't sign?"

"Verbal agreement?" Roxie asked. "Then that means…"

"Legally, the house is still available," Vera announced.

Byron and Roxie looked at each other. In the space of the moment, one weighed the other. Byron's heart pounded when he saw the light of challenge flare into Roxie's eyes. His ambition, his desire for the house, the history he shared with it crescendoed. If he hadn't already, he would have rolled up his sleeves.

This was where six years of law school came in handy. "Ah, no, it isn't," he said.

"Excuse me?" Vera said.

"A verbal contract is binding in the state of Alabama," Byron pointed out. "So, technically, the house is mine. Plus…" He fished in the pocket of his slacks and tossed the key chain his father had given him onto the table between them. "Pop gave me this with Athena's blessing."

Vera lifted one discerning brow. "Your point being?"

"Evidence," Byron indicated.

"A verbal agreement with your father is hardly black-and-white."

"Legally speaking—"

"By," Constantine said and shook his head. "Let it go."

"Let it go?" Byron echoed, voice rising as anger seared up the column of his neck. "Why should I?"

"Because we raised you to fight for your rights, yes," Vera pointed out, "and we might have welcomed passionate debate at family dinners. But we also raised you to be a decent human being."

"Oh, come on," Byron said, exasperated. She'd said much the same thing when he was twelve and caught Priscilla and Vivienne coating his matchbox cars in purple nail polish. "We're all adults here."

"Yes, we are," Vera noted. "Which is why I hope you'll be agreeable when I ask you to stand down and let Roxie sign a lease for twelve months. When those twelve months have lapsed, you'll be in an even better position to buy the house and we'll let you make the first offer."

"It's me?" Roxie asked, her hopeful voice pealing into the tense void. She beamed at Vera and Constantine in turn. "You're…giving the house to me?"

"If Byron agrees to our terms," Constantine said, looking to his son with a measure of uncertainty.

Roxie looked to Byron, hesitant in her happiness.

Byron dug in his heels and clung. "I've wanted to live in this house since I was six."

"And another twelve months will not kill you," Vera added, astute. "They'll benefit you. You're too proud to pay anything below market value and in order to get the mortgage rate you want, the down payment will be substantial."

"Christ. Why do I tell you things?" He scrubbed his temples.

"Do we have an agreement?" Vera asked plainly.

Byron frowned at Roxie. He didn't like hurting women, particularly women like Roxie. He looked around at the cream-colored walls. The chair rail he'd nailed into place himself. The windows overlooking the porch. Outside, the swing was rocking gently, Briar and Harmony huddled there on the cushions, the light dying around them.

Son of a bitch. Trapped by his own budgetary constraints and the moral compass both his parents had winningly bestowed upon him, Byron gave in. But not without scruples.

He sniffed. "Twelve months," he agreed. "I'll give you the twelve months. But I won't move out of the loft and I still want access to the downstairs gym. After that, the house is mine. End of story."

Roxie's smile turned mischievous. "Unless I outbid you." She laughed as his face fell. "Kidding! I'm kidding!" She looked to Vera. "He gets flushed when he's agitated."

"He's one-eighth Italian," Vera said as she grinned affectionately at Byron. "Those chromosomes fought their way through." She leaned down and laid her lips against his hurting temple. "You should say thank-you."

"Me?" he asked. "For what? She got the house."

Vera frowned over him just as she had whenever he complained about his sisters. "For the common sense. A year isn't so hard considering how long you've waited to buy a house again. And you know rates will be down next year."

"You're right." He eyed her red dress. "Thanks, Satan."

She patted his cheek a touch too hard.

Roxie stood up from the table. "Thank you. All of you. You have no idea what this means to me." She looked to Byron, light beaming out of her.

It was a sight. *She* was a sight, but Byron still had a hard time generating any enthusiasm. He watched her hug his mother then his father. When she turned to him, Byron shrugged. "Looks like we're neighbors." Vera dug a subtle elbow into his ribs. He cleared his throat. "Congrats."

"I'll get the papers ready to sign," Constantine volunteered.

"Let me handle that," Vera spoke up quickly. "There's a bottle of champagne in the car." She placed her hand on her husband's lapel and angled her face up to his, raising a brow. "Be a good man and fetch it for us, won't you?"

"All right." Constantine's mouth softened into a tender smile. *"Matia mou."*

The stern set of Vera's face crumbled. She blinked. Byron looked away when her dark eyes grew wet and she began to reach for his father's face. He caught Roxie watching the exchange with a great deal of curiosity. Reaching back, he scrubbed his neck and cleared his throat once more. "I'll gather up my stuff."

"Okay," Roxie said. She stepped aside so he could pass through the archway leading into the den. "Byron." She waited until he glanced back. "I mean it. Thank you. Thank you so much—"

He held up a hand to stop her from going further. "It's no big deal." Grudgingly, he admitted, "My mother's right. She's always frigging right." He stopped talking when she moved toward him. Retreating back a step, he asked, "What're you doing?"

"Well, I *was* going to hug you again," she explained. "But I see now that might be awkward."

Byron jerked a nod. "A bit."

"Okay," she said, widening her eyes. "Is there anything I need to know about the house? Other than the fact that it's stunningly beautiful."

Stunningly beautiful. *Yeah.* "Mothballs," he

blurted. "The couple who lived here previously bombed the place with them when they moved in. You can still smell them here and there."

"Mothballs, check," she said. "Anything else?"

"The upstairs shower leaks," he said. "Oh, and watch out for the bunnies."

"The bunnies?" she asked, taken aback.

Did he say bunnies? "Squirrels," he back-pedaled with a quick shake of his head. "I meant squirrels. They used to nest in the walls. Not so much anymore but every now and then..."

"Squirrels," she finished with a knowing smile on her face when he trailed off. She rubbed her lips together, as if debating what she wanted to ask next. "Um, what did your father mean back there when he said mat—matea—"

Matia mou. "I'm not sure," he lied. "It's Greek. *Really* Greek."

"We're ready in here, Roxie," Vera called.

"I'll be upstairs," Byron announced. He scowled as he walked away and took the stairs two at a time, muttering to himself.

It was bad enough to have to take everything he'd filtered into the house over the last two days back to the loft. And coming to terms with the fact that he would have to wait an additional year to secure the Victorian as his own would take some getting used to.

Now he had to bargain with a new neighbor. And not any old neighbor…

He had work to do to get those stupid *bunnies* under control before he started rubbing elbows with Roxie Honeycutt on a more regular basis.

I COULD GET used to this.

Her boxes and furniture had been delivered. Her friends had brought her a large pot of winter soup to get her through until she filled the pantry. In the fridge, Vera and Constantine had left the bottle of Dom Pérignon to chill. Roxie didn't fight the inclination to take it and a champagne flute up to the master bathroom, where she kicked off her shoes and reclined in the empty whirlpool tub. She then did something she rarely had throughout the last year.

Indulge.

She sipped and smiled, smiled and sipped. Billie Holiday's bluesy voice poured through the small portable speaker on the counter several feet away and sieved its poignant way into her soul. Roxie waggled her foot, poured herself an additional dose of Dom and laid her head back against the lip, closing her eyes.

New Year. New Roxie. She could now officially tick *new living quarters* off her resolution to-do list.

What next?

Her smile slowly morphed into a thoughtful frown. She'd changed geography. That was an important step. One could even say a vital one. She couldn't start over with all those feelings of betrayal and anger, shame and despair, that had refused to be swept from the place she'd brought them into. Though Olivia had been generous to let her move into the apartment above the tavern on short notice. And being close to work and her friends had been instrumental in helping her heal to a certain degree.

As winter bore down belatedly on the Gulf Coast, however, nights grew long and the off-season quiet settled along the shore. Roxie had begun to see the puddles of tears piling up in corners, even if it had been some time since she'd stopped them from coming.

Puddles rose with the moon. On stormy nights, they'd threatened to drown her. She'd considered packing her bags and letting her flight reflex lead her away from the apartment, from Fairhope… On bad days, a transfer to the outer banks of Siberia hadn't seemed far enough away from the old Roxie—the solemn, low-spirited version of herself she no longer recognized and had no idea how to redeem.

As it turned out, all she'd needed was a Victorian. And time. Twelve months would be a satisfactory interval to get her thoughts in order. To figure out what it was she wanted. Who this new Roxie was.

Clarity. With the house, it was slowly coming back to her. She wouldn't leave Fairhope. She had a life here and a thriving business. Sure, people talked and she was constantly running into those who did. But she refused to be driven from the one place in the world she'd ever associated with home.

She'd contacted Richard's mother. He was still away. *On a spiritual retreat*, Lucinda Levy had stated matter-of-factly. The news had puzzled Roxie. Richard had always been pointedly intellectual, glossing over the spiritual with stoic reason and logic.

Maybe he was doing the same thing she was. Maybe this was what he needed to gain clarity, to come back and start over.

Why do I care?

Roxie tapped her finger against the side of the crystal flute. *Should I really still have feelings for him?* Her friends didn't seem to think so, but James had left Adrian years ago without a word about his whereabouts. He was gone for eight years. That hadn't stopped Adrian from loving him, even if it was, at first, against her own wishes.

Roxie had given Richard nearly ten years of her life—and she'd planned to give him the rest of it. She was a wedding planner. She staked her entire life on the concept of love everlasting, and she'd abandoned that concept in a rash of betrayal.

It was time to reevaluate the choice she'd made and whether or not she'd acted *too* rashly.

She needed to see him. The more she turned it over in her head, the more she knew that was what she had to do.

Until Richard came back, she had weddings to coordinate, a new line of bridal gowns and lingerie to put together, a house to play with and a new male neighbor to contend with.

A neighbor she'd practically seen in the buff.

Roxie tamped down the memory of Byron in punctuated briefs. It wasn't any easier than glossing over the kiss that had crowned an all-too-eventful Valentine's Day.

She caught herself eyeing the sink where she'd found him shaving. Was it just her or did it still smell like ambergris in here?

Shaking her head, she focused on other goals. She should learn to cook. She'd always wanted to. She and Richard had considering cooking classes at the local college. He'd hedged, blaming the constraints of his schedule for his reluctance.

If Roxie had pushed him to do it with her, would he have slept with Cassandra? Roxie tipped the champagne to her mouth, considering.

"Eh, duchess."

"Eep!" The glass upended, bathing her after all. Looking wildly around, she found her so-called knight staring at her from the pocket doors, one brow arched. Instead of the standard Brooks Brothers, he wore a sleeveless black T-shirt, blue basketball shorts and white sneakers that set off his tan limbs. "Sweet lord!" she exclaimed. She shook her dripping arms before gripping the edges of the tub and pulling herself to standing. "Did you just let yourself in?"

A scowl pulled at his mouth. It was the expression he'd worn since the day he'd agreed to let her live there. He hadn't stuck around to watch her move in her few belongings. In fact, he hadn't said more than two words to her since his parents left. "A little payback," he informed her.

This standoffish Byron was a stranger to her and more than a little off-putting. The way he looked at her had gone from warm and appreciative to as crisp as his work attire. "When the Goodchilds lived here, did you just come and go as you pleased?" she asked, reaching for a fluffy towel on the nearby rack. She dabbed at the stain on her dress.

"Pretty much." His gaze tipped over her torso, flickered over the mulberry midi dress and her bare, manicured toes. "Going somewhere?"

"No," she said, gathering a handful of skirt in her fist. "I was just having a glass or two of champagne."

"So?" he asked, pointedly looking at her attire.

She lifted a shoulder. "So I always get dressed up for champagne."

His brows came together.

She reached over and turned off the speaker, cutting off Billie's "Willow Weep for Me" just before the bridge. "I'd rather you knocked next time. Just for the record." She indicated the stain before veering around him into the bedroom.

He didn't follow her into the closet, where she'd already begun the process of unpacking and color coordinating. "I've come for my TV, Ms. Monroe," he called from the next room.

"Your TV?" she asked, choosing a silk kimono robe. She pulled the dress over her head, lamenting the newish purchase, and donned the silk before going out to face him again, belting it at her waist.

Byron's eyes did a sweep over her. Roxie felt it like a soft-bristled brush. She grabbed the belt of the robe, suddenly very aware that it was short and thin. She should've reached for the chenille she reserved for sick days. It came down to her ankles and had its own set of sexless slippers.

Thankfully, his eyes swung away and he lifted

a hand in the direction of the bureau. "The fifty-inch LCD. It's mine."

"Oh, thank goodness!" Roxie breathed. "I thought Colossus was here to stay."

"Okay, her name is Giselle," Byron told her. "And what've you got against fifty inches of technological goodness?"

"Well, for starters," she replied, crossing her arms over her chest, "nobody needs a TV that big. Aren't you worried about your eyesight?"

"I'll worry about cataracts later if it means watching *The Walking Dead* on a big screen," Byron replied. His hand glided along the top edge. "Don't you listen to her, baby. You're perfect."

Roxie fought the urge to laugh. "Whatever happened to the everyman claim 'size doesn't matter?'"

She thought she saw a smile work at the corners of his mouth. When he turned to face her, it was gone—though wicked promise gleamed there. "After your little peep show Wednesday night, you really think size is the issue here?"

Her jaw unhinged. Again, unbidden, the image of ripply arms, long hard thighs and all the lovely bits in between reemerged...as well as the mixed-up dream she'd thought she'd had in a fit of exhaustion involving a gleeful one-sided game of tic-tac-toe with mini-marshmallows and caramel syrup.

On his washboard abs.

Her eyes skirted him and she kept her lips shut.

She thought she heard him curse under his breath. "I usually work out around six during the week."

"Every weekday?" she asked.

"Yeah. Is that a problem?"

She shrugged. "No. We had an agreement. You could use the gym."

"I'm down there an hour tops."

"Fine."

"Oh, and my mom did mention that we share the washer and dryer in the basement, right?"

"Lord have mercy. I had roommates in college who weren't this intrusive."

"My college roommate slept with my sister," Byron pointed out. "When it comes to intrusion, you know nothing, Norma Jean."

"He slept with your sister?" Roxie asked, wide-eyed. "Oh, my God. What did you do?"

"We beat each other up for a good half hour after I found out," Byron considered. "Then he told me he was in love with her. We hugged it out. He's now my brother-in-law, work wife and business partner."

"Well. That's...tidy." Something told her this so-called living arrangement between them wouldn't be. It made her stomach tighten, the thought of their promising friendship rapidly falling through the cracks. *But why?*

"I can get everything washed in one day. Do Sundays work for you?"

She waved her hand in an absent motion. "Sure. Why not?"

His grunt rang through the room as he hefted the television. "I'll give you the cable info so you can set up your own system."

"I think I'll go without."

"Cable?"

"Television."

There was an "uff!" followed closely by a thud. He'd dropped the television on his foot. Grimacing, he looked at her as if she'd sprouted a tail. "You don't have a television?"

"No," she admitted. "You can stop looking at me like a leper. I like music. And I'm always too busy to keep up with anything on TV anyway."

"You don't watch *anything*?" he asked. "News? Shopping channel? Tim Gunn?"

"Not really." Her eyes narrowed on him. "How do you know who Tim Gunn is?"

He balked. "Sisters. I have two sisters. They're into *Project Runway.*"

"Sure, sure," she said smugly. "That leak in the shower...should I contact Vera about that or do you want to?"

Byron hefted the television with a look akin to

resentment. He began to maneuver it through the door. She took pity on him and grabbed one end. They made their way to the landing. She tried not to watch the way the muscles in his arms worked. They were ridiculous. And the sleeveless shirt did nothing to hide them.

"For the next twelve months per our agreement this house is yours," he told her. "If you've got problems, you can haggle with the landlords yourself."

She shook her head. "And here I was thinking you were a nice guy."

"Being nice has nothing to do with it," he groaned as he navigated the first few steps to the ground floor. "It's just business."

Was that how things were between them now? Just business?

She'd known the man a year and already she missed him and everything they'd shared in that small space of time. She missed the pieces of him that had retreated.

They reached the ground floor. Byron set his end of the television down and she followed suit. As he leaned against it, she couldn't hide a satisfied glint. "I bet you're wishing you bought a smaller one now."

He opened his mouth to argue but was cut off by the chirp of the doorbell.

Roxie peered into the foyer at the entry door.

She saw the knob turn, the door crack and the blond bouffant peeking through. "Yoo-hoo!" a voice pealed. "Roxanna, darling!"

"Oh," Roxie said, the one word dropping low in dread. "Oh, dear God, no." As Byron straightened, she saw the flash of concern on his face. She didn't give him a second to voice it, edging her shoulder against his chest and nudging him to the door under the stairs. "Hide, hide, hide!"

"What?" Byron asked, rivets digging into his forehead. "I don't have to hide."

"Yes, you do," she said with a definitive nod. She opened the door for him.

"Why?" he asked, incredulous. "Who is that?"

"My mother!" she hissed. "She cannot see you."

"Why?"

Marabella Honeycutt's voice rang pleasantly from afar. "I'm letting myself in!"

"Go!" Roxie coaxed. When he didn't move, she flattened her hands on his chest—his very hard chest—and shoved.

She might as well have tried to move one of the Parthenon's Doric columns. She dug her heels in, maneuvering him back through the door. At the sound of her mother's heels clacking against flooring, she went for the ear, grabbing him by the lobe.

"Ah!" he cried out. She shut the door on him, cutting him off as Marabella rounded the corner.

"There you are," Marabella said. She was regally turned out in an ermine-lined coat, kid gloves and Manolos. Her face was round, but the rest of her was sleek and slender. Contacts amped up her slate gray eyes to violet. Thanks to her active participation in the Botox movement, she always looked vaguely surprised. "Roxanna. I've been trying to reach you all day."

"Really?" Roxie could hear Byron's muttered cursing. She kept her hand on the door for good measure. "I've had my phone on me."

"It's a weekday," Marabella said. "I thought you were at your little shop."

Roxie might've rolled her eyes. Her mother and sisters had been referring to Belle Brides as her *little shop* since it opened for business. No matter that that *little shop* was a flyaway success or that she was the busiest wedding planner on the Alabama coast.

She lifted a hand to show her mother the moving boxes and haphazardly arranged furniture James and Cole had helped her move in. "I've been busy." As Marabella took a look around, Roxie fought the urge to straighten the lines of the chairs and settee. She folded her hands at her waist. "What do you think of the house, Mother?"

Marabella frowned...or her mouth frowned. Perpetual delight lived from the nose up. "It's lovely. But you're not planning on staying here, are you?"

"It's a year lease," Roxie explained. "I needed a house. More space to breathe. More room to think."

"You had a house," Marabella reminded her, frowning over the gargantuan television in the middle of the floor. "You couldn't do your thinking there?"

Her mother had voiced hearty rejection over Roxie's quick thinking surrounding the divorce and giving up the spacious French Colonial. "It was Richard's house," Roxie told her. "It was always Richard's."

Marabella gave a small sigh. She pulled her gloves off, one finger at a time. "Well. This one will do, I suppose. Just until you've sorted yourself out."

Roxie took a deep breath. "Actually, I have been doing some thinking already."

Marabella looked at her directly. "Yes?" Hope and anticipation lifted the word high.

"And…" It hurt but she said it anyway. "I think you might have been right. About Richard. Maybe even about the divorce."

A squeal launched from Marabella's throat. With a clap of her hands, she crossed the space between them, sidestepping Giselle, and pulled

Roxie tight to her. "Oh, *bébé*. You've finally come to your senses!"

Roxie smiled vaguely. "Mother. I said maybe. There's still a lot to figure—"

"Figure? What's to figure?" Marabella demanded, pulling back. The exuberance was caked on her features as heavily as the Elizabeth Arden. "You should've patched things up months ago. Think of all the time you could've been in counseling together. Think of all the time you've wasted living in that shoebox on the bay."

"I needed time," Roxie said, defensive. "I still need to think about what I'm going to do going forward—"

"Well, that's simple," Marabella said lightly. "Get Richard on the phone. Tell him to come home. Tell him you've forgiven him."

"I'm not sure I have," Roxie blurted.

Marabella faltered, falling back a step. "What do you mean, you're not sure?"

"He slept with Cassandra," Roxie said plainly.

"It was once," Marabella said. "Now the both of them have admitted their mistake, and you've seen Cassandra and Jefferson. They're doing better."

Roxie had seen Cassandra, once or twice. Neither of them had breached the gap and actually spoken. "I thought you said they were in marriage counseling," Roxie said.

Marabella waved a hand. "They're working through it. They're actively mending what needs fixin'. And you should already be doing the same. The doctor they're seeing…she's a real wonder. They say she can fix anything with time."

And the right amount of money, Roxie thought, then quelled the ready cynicism. "I don't know—"

"I ran into Lucinda the other day at the store. She says Richard's a mess. A fine mess."

"A mess?" Roxie asked. Richard had long been the epitome of still waters. During fights, he would maintain a stubborn thread of reason-ableness. Whenever Roxie raised her voice or brought even a hint of intensity to the scene, Rich-ard called her on it. *There's no need for dramatics here, Roxie. Your mother's hysterics are enough to deal with, wouldn't you agree?*

Sometimes she had absurdly wished that they could fight like everyone else—shout, curse, call each other names. They'd never even had make-up sex. They'd never needed it. What was there to make up when their arguments were as organized as their individual planners?

So Richard was a mess, Roxie mused. She found the idea somewhat amusing… Okay, she found it *very* amusing. Did he miss their life as much as she thought she might?

"You should call Cassandra," Marabella maintained, eyes widening at the prospect. "Call her now. She can give you the doctor's name and number. Get the ball rolling. When Richard gets back, you can dive straight into the healing."

"Mother," Roxie said. She shook her head. "I'm not going to call Cassandra."

Every trace of exuberance vanished from Marabella's face as she planted her hands on her hips. "Now, Roxanna. I have been patient. I have stood by like a good mama and I've left the two of you to your own ends. But this is getting silly. If you can forgive Richard, you can forgive your sister."

Hadn't Roxie told her she wasn't sure about the forgiveness part? Breathing carefully through the minefield of her exasperation, Roxie counted to ten.

Marabella went on unhindered. "Forget the phone. One of you has got to take the first step. You should just go by her house. Drop in for a visit and get it all out in the open. It's time to move on. You have no idea how taxing all this avoidance is on my nerves."

"Thank you, Mrs. Bennet," Roxie muttered.

"What was that?"

"Nothing," Roxie said quickly.

"This last year has been so difficult." Marabella's voice began to lift and crack. Her eyes grew damp. She fanned herself with her hand. "My girls. My eldest and my youngest, in such a state of estrangement. I can't tell you how terrible it's been."

Roxie closed her eyes as Marabella dabbed at her own. She combed the sour notes from her voice and said, ever the dutiful daughter, "I'm dearly sorry for your inconvenience, Mother."

"Please, *bébé*," Marabella said, reaching out to squeeze Roxie's hand. "Go see Cassandra. She needs to be refitted for her bridesmaid dress anyway."

"What's wrong with it?"

"I think she's gaining weight," she said in scandalized tones. "You didn't hear it from me. But her gown will have to be taken out. Let's just hope she doesn't gain any more before the ceremony. I gave her some new diet pills. We'll see how she responds to them. Bless her heart. She's got the Walton waist but the Honeycutt hips."

Roxie cringed. Her mother and her diet pills. The combo was a cocktail for calamity.

Marabella scanned Roxie's figure more closely. "Turn for me, *bébé*."

Roxie resisted the command. The silk robe suddenly felt like a brown paper sack. *Nope. Not this game.* She began to bounce on her feet instead. Toe, heel. Toe, heel. An old habit, one of the few she'd retained from years of ballet.

"Have *you* been gaining weight, Roxanna?" Marabella asked, stricken with horror at the prospect.

Yes, she'd gained weight. She'd worked to put back some of the twenty pounds she'd lost following Richard and Cassandra's betrayal. "I've gained a few pounds," she admitted.

"Oh," Marabella said, disappointment a well-hewed knife. "Oh, dear. You were looking so well. Just as you did in New York. Don't you remember how well you looked then?"

You mean when I was unhealthy, Mother? When I was a slave to bulimia and your diet pills? Her mother's obsession with weight had landed Roxie in the emergency room. Sadly, she wasn't the last of Marabella Honeycutt's daughters to have her stomach pumped. "Let's move on," she pleaded. "Is there a reason you stopped by?"

Marabella continued to eye her for a moment more before she remembered. "It was for Cassandra. The dress. Have you finished all the dresses? Georgiana's wedding is only three weeks away…"

"The wedding is four weeks from Saturday," Roxie corrected, struggling to adopt a reasonable tone amid mounting inner tension. "And the gowns will be done by Monday. Just measure Cassandra yourself. She can call me."

"I'm not a tailor like you. I could be doing it wrong."

"It's pretty straightforward."

"I think my measuring tape's wrong."

Roxie moaned. To laugh? To scream? To scream with laughter? "Just measure again. If the numbers are off, I'll take the dress out."

"I'll have her come by the shop. You can measure her there. Don't allow that assistant of yours to do it. It was him who measured me for the Mardi Gras ball. I've never had a thirty-three-inch waist in my life. He *is* European. Maybe he's still on that metric system."

Give me strength, Roxie pleaded. She heard a thud behind the basement door and cleared her throat. "Thank you for stopping by, Mother. I'm glad you got to see the house."

"Why is there a television in the middle of your living room?" Marabella asked in bewilderment as Roxie ushered her toward the foyer. "Don't you think this one's a little excessive?"

"Hmm," Roxie said in answer.

"You should rethink the housing situation. Really, there's nothing wrong with the French Colonial. If we must, we'll have someone come in and cleanse the place. That's apparently a thing now. Something to do with chakras...?"

"I'll think about it," Roxie lied as they reached the door. Marabella took her time putting on her gloves and Chanel sunglasses. They kissed each other, once on each cheek, and said goodbye.

Roxie locked the door behind her. She heard another thump and went quickly back to the basement door. No sooner had she opened it than Byron stumbled out.

"I'm sorry," she said instantly.

"What just happened here?"

"I'm sorry, I'm sorry," she said again, shutting the door behind him. "She doesn't know I'm living with someone like you, and I didn't have time to arrange the fainting couch."

"What's 'someone like me?'" he asked.

"You know," she said. When he only scowled at her, she waved a hand to indicate his physique. "A man. Another man who's…" Tall? Dark? Toned? Attractive? Flipping gorgeous. Much more than any card-carrying member of the male species had a right to be. *Hello, Mother. This is Byron, my sexy man-friend who lives next door. I've seen him naked. But I don't think about it. Absolutely do not think about it. Tee-hee.*

She trailed off when he sniffed and dabbed at his nose. "What're you… Are you *bleeding*?"

"Apparently," he groaned, turning partially away from her when he saw the blood on his knuckles.

"Why are you bleeding?" she asked, distressed. She bent at the waist, trying to get a look up his nostrils.

"I don't know," he replied, droll. "Maybe my schnoz got in the way of that door you slammed."

"It hit you in the face?" she asked.

"I'm trying to think if it was before or after it knocked me down the stairs…"

"Oh, my God." She grabbed him by the hand and marched him forcefully into the kitchen. Pulling out a chair, she nudged him back again. "Sit. I'll get you something."

"Amaretto on the rocks," he said, sprawling into the spindly Queen Anne. It creaked beneath him and looked miniaturized. "Double tall."

"Would you like a cherry?" When he only eyed her, she sighed and went to the sink. Did she mention hating that they weren't friends anymore?

"So," he said as she filled a washcloth with ice cubes and balled it up tight. *"Roxanna."*

She stopped. The muscles in her stomach tightened in defense even as his voice stretched the long *a* in the middle of her given name like a favorite chord in a song. "Don't," she said in simple warning as she went back to him. Encouraged by the slight grin on his face, she pressed the balled-up ice gently to his nose. "Atticus."

His shoulders moved on a silent laugh as he tipped his head back. He winced but only slightly.

She stood over him in silence for several moments before he spoke again. "It's a family name."

"How about the nose?" she asked. "Does that run in the family, too?"

He chuckled. Quietly, but out loud.

The sound was a relief. When genuine, his laugh trebled over the surface, like a rock skipping on water, leaving ripples behind. She welcomed the rings, licking her lips to keep the relief from curving them too widely. "Truce?" she whispered.

The stolid lines fell upon his features and his gaze turned thoughtful as he scanned hers. "She's wrong."

"Who?"

"Your mother."

"Oh." Sighing, she asked, "What about?"

"Everything, now that you mention it."

"You still don't think I should give Richard another chance," she assumed.

"I don't like the guy," he said, pulling the ice away from his nose. He took it from her to wipe some of the mess on the edge of the cloth. "But I'm not the one who was married to him."

"No, you aren't."

He frowned. "It was what she said about your weight."

Again, the muscles in her stomach knotted. Her voice dropped back. "What about it?"

"It looks good on you."

The ice was dripping through the cloth. She

didn't look at him as she took it away. "I know. But she's my mother."

"She's a Hun." At her shocked glance, he raised his brows. "She is."

"No," Roxie said. "She's just a silly woman who likes to micromanage everything and everyone. Especially her children."

"Do you let her?"

"Not anymore."

"Good." His mouth moved warmly again and, this time, his eyes smiled up at her, as well. "I still think she's a Hun."

Roxie considered. "If your mother was a Hun, wouldn't you defend her?"

"Yes," Byron answered in a ready way that spoke volumes about his feelings toward Vera.

Lifting her thumb, she grazed the pad over the space above his top lip, wiping away the last watery smear of blood. There was a dip there, pronounced and perfect. "You love them very much, don't you?"

"Yes," he said again.

"I envy you," she realized. She felt the entrenched line work its way between her eyes. "I envy you your family." When he only looked at her, she realized that her thumb had lingered above his lip. She pulled it away quickly and busied herself wrapping up the ice once more to keep it from dripping across the floor. She carried it back to the sink. "Feel better?"

There was a long pause. The Queen Anne whined as he pushed to his feet. "I need to get Giselle home."

"Does she turn into a pumpkin," Roxie asked, "or is *Project Runway* on tonight?"

"Hardy-har-har."

"Byron," she called to him. He paused in the arch leading into the den. She smiled when he glanced back over his shoulder. "Can we call it a truce?"

He returned a half smile. It looked stilted, but nonetheless he said, "We're all right, duchess." Tapping his balled-up fist against the wall, he moved away from her.

CHAPTER FIVE

"THERE'S A WOMAN living in my house." Byron glanced up from the caramel cube he'd been unwrapping from cellophane. "Sorry. Your house." He held the cube out.

Diminutive and wise-eyed, Athena Papadakis took the caramel between her fingers. Her nails were shiny and kempt, her gold rings and bangles on display even here in the retirement village where she'd decided to live out the rest of her days. Her skin was white, nearly translucent, giving way to capillaries. Veins pushed up from underneath in blue-ridged chains.

Those channels of blood looked vibrant and coursing, like the woman herself. It was the outer layer that was beginning to fray. A life force like Athena's was too much for the outside to contain, anyway, Byron mused, watching her press one of her beloved caramels between thin, papery lips. She regarded him and his conundrum through exotic dark eyes. "Is she pretty?"

Byron chuckled, stuffing a caramel into his

mouth and reaching for another. "I should've known you'd ask."

"Well. Is she?"

"On a scale of one to ten," he asked, "or one to Athena?"

Those dark irises warmed over his charm. She tutted at him and reached over to the small table between the needlepoint chairs for the blue-and-white teacup with its Greek key motif. He beat her to it, bringing it up to her lips. Her hands followed his. She sipped, waved the cup away and waited as he set it back down to rest in its saucer. "How are her hips? Not too narrow?"

Byron hissed. He pointedly took a drink from his own cup. He liked tea one way and that was sweet and ice-cold in the summer. Since always, though, Athena had made it warm and herbal and, even as a boy, he'd drunk it without exception. Running his tongue over his teeth, he propped his elbow on the arm of the chair and canted his head against his hand. "Athena, Athena."

She chuckled. The sound was a deep, satisfactory rumble. She reached out again, patting his knee. "The minute I stop teasing the men in this family is the minute I'm dead." She let out another laugh but it died in a blaze of chest-deep coughing. Byron shifted toward her as she shook with it, her posture caving.

"I'm all right," she said. Hoarse, she took a

drink from the teacup when again he offered it, sipping to sooth her throat. "Get back to the girl," she said, waving off any concern for herself. "Will you stop beating around the bush and marry this one already? I'm getting old, nephew. I'd like to see you settled again before my time."

"She's just a neighbor," he told her.

"Let me tell you something, Byron Atticus," Athena said. "Your name may be Strong but you're Maragos to the bone. Strong-willed, thick-skinned. And this 'just a neighbor' lady has dug her a place beneath it."

"Has not."

That deep chuckle galled the truth at him. "You play pretend and tell yourself it's irritation that put her there. It was the same with Ari when I first came over."

He lifted his cup again to sip, frowning at her over the rim. Athena was his great-aunt on his father's side. She'd traveled over with her sister, Byron's grandmother, to enter into prearranged matrimony with a man she'd never met.

Byron's grandmother Fillipa had married a Swiss émigré by the name of Nils Strong and moved to the suburbs of Atlanta while Athena traveled to the Eastern Shore to marry a Greek expat, Ari Papadakis. While Fillipa and Nils's relationship had proved just as lasting as Athena and Ari's, theirs wasn't near the love affair that the latter turned out to be. "He told me he fell in love with you on sight," Byron recalled. "The liar."

"He did not lie," Athena asserted, lifting a finger. "Ari did love me, from the first time we met. But he didn't want a wife. It was his family, you see. His family forced him into marriage, just as mine forced me to come to America and marry him. We weren't pleased with the arrangement, but we pleased each other. It just took some time for him to admit as much. He tried to make me and himself believe that I was little more than a burden to him. In close quarters, it didn't take long for the tension to drain and for the love to shine through."

Byron lifted his brows knowingly. "Yeah. I think the house is proof of that."

Remembrance and tender affection lifted the corners of Athena's mouth in a wavering smile. "Yes," she whispered. "He did build me a good house."

Ari had built his Athena a masterpiece, and Byron couldn't pretend that he wasn't still irritated that the Victorian was another twelve months out of his reach. "Why me?" When Athena blinked her way out of a bittersweet reverie, Byron added, "Why give me the house? 'Cilla and Vivi love it every bit as much as I do."

"Priscilla has her own home," Athena reminded

him. "She takes pride in it and her family, as she should. And you know as well as I do that Vivienne and her man will never be able to stay here when they know there is suffering elsewhere. They will live where they are called. Do you remember how you used to stare at the walls? You always had this look of wonderment. I knew they would be yours somewhere down the road. Ari knew, too."

He unwrapped a caramel and passed it to her.

Athena chewed it thoughtfully in the meaningful, companionable silence that followed. "So you won't marry her?"

Laughter bolted out of him. He pinched the bridge of his nose between two fingers and let it roll through him. "I love you," he said. The words and the sentiment behind them came easily to him. "God help me but I love you."

"He's laying it on thick," said Grim's baritone as he entered Athena's room. He carried with him a bouquet of fresh tulips.

"What are you doing here?" Byron asked in mock wariness.

"Trying to edge you out as the favorite man," Grim pointed out. He knelt next to Athena's chair and laid the flowers on her lap. "Hello, beautiful."

Athena beamed. "Hello, Tobias. How are my odds looking?"

Grim pulled a small notebook from the breast

pocket of his sports coat. He flipped the cover back and wet his fingertips as he thumbed through the pages. Finally, he found what he was looking for. "You're sitting pretty. Everybody's betting the baby's a boy, including Byron. So far only you, Con and 'Cilla think it's a girl. If you're right, you'll have a nice new roll for your cash jar."

"You're wrong this time, Athena," Byron wagered. "Grim here's got five brothers back in Arkansas. Odds are it's a boy."

"Never bet against Athena," Priscilla warned as she entered the room a step behind her enlarged belly. "Sorry. Potty break." She leaned over and kissed Athena on the temple. "How are you today, Auntie?"

"Crowded," Byron muttered, pushing up from the chair.

As Byron guided her to the seat, Priscilla threw him a look that was identical to the one their mother gave him when he was being less than generous. "You can't have her all to yourself."

"With the rest of you lurking, certainly not," Byron said as he went to stand at Athena's shoulder. Bending at the waist, he touched her arm and muttered in private fashion, "You let me know if these kids bother you." He jerked his thumb toward the door. "We'll kick them right out."

Athena was nothing short of glowing. She laid

a hand on top of Priscilla's baby bump. "Is she moving?"

"Nonstop," Priscilla replied, shifting Athena's palm around slowly until she found the right spot. "She's been battering away at my ribs there. The way she kicks... I think she's going to be a soccer star." Both women smiled when something happened on the other side of the belly. Athena began to murmur a blessing in Greek, the hand rubbing now in small, maternal circles. When she was done, the hand lifted to Priscilla's cheek, doting. "You look so beautiful. Tobias, isn't your wife *oraia*?"

"She's a regular Sofia Loren," Grim said, his attention seized on Priscilla's face. "If it's a girl, she might give her great-great auntie a run for her money."

Athena chuckled once more. "Where's my Vivienne? Why hasn't she come to see me?"

"She flies in tomorrow," Priscilla said, lifting what was left of Byron's tea. She tipped it to her mouth and drained it.

"Don't count on seeing her much once she does come home," Byron advised. "The watchman on the door has her picture. He won't let her in."

Grim nodded agreement. "Yeah, once the baby of the family gets here, none of the rest of us have a chance."

"The baby might be coming home," Priscilla

noted. She patted her belly. "But this one's going to edge her out in a month."

"Children, children," Athena cooed. "Tell me about the wedding. The arrangements are coming along?"

Priscilla eyed Byron over Athena's head. "I need to talk to you about that."

"Me?" Byron asked. The thought of joining the mad torrent of wedding preparations made him more than a little ill. His mother and sister were sticklers for perfection. Vivienne's nuptials were turning out to be a breeding ground for their detailed obsessiveness. "Why me?"

"Donatella quit," Priscilla said, setting the cup back in the saucer with a clipped rattle.

"She *quit*?" Byron asked. "She can't just quit. She's the wedding planner."

"Mm." Rubbing her belly, Priscilla jerked a shoulder in a shrug. "Her husband ran off to the Caymans. Apparently, there was some legal trouble. He took the nest egg and hightailed it."

"Prig," Grim said.

"So we're down one wedding planner," Priscilla continued, "and a venue."

"Why the venue?" Athena asked.

"The club's exclusive to members," Priscilla explained. "Donatella was our in. With her out of the country for the foreseeable future, we don't have a venue."

"The wedding's right around the corner," Byron realized. "Has anyone told Vivi?"

Priscilla was never not solid. She rarely showed the smallest weakness or fissure. He saw the anxiety lurking beneath the surface and it hit him like a ton of bricks. "I wasn't able to tell her. Not on the phone."

"Let her come," Athena advised. "Let her get settled. The family should tell her, as one."

Priscilla dropped her face into her hand. "Oh, Vivi. Vivi, Vivi."

Byron scowled. Vivienne had trusted the planning to the family. Now she was coming home to disappointment. "Son of a bitch," he muttered low so Athena wouldn't hear.

"Athena's right," Grim agreed. "We should tell her as a team."

"What can Byron do?" Athena asked after a contemplative pause.

"I'm actually ashamed he hasn't thought of it already." At his blank stare, Priscilla rolled her eyes. "Oh, come on, By. You're living with wedding planner extraordinaire Roxie Honeycutt."

"*The* Roxie Honeycutt?" Intrigued, Grim smirked. "Nice."

"Hang on," Byron said. "I'm not living with anybody. And the wedding's in two weeks. Who says she's available?"

"Nobody says that," Priscilla noted. "That's why the next time you see her, you're going to ask her. Sweetly. You might even think about groveling, need be."

"Huh."

Priscilla narrowed her eyes. "'Huh' is guy-speak for 'yes, sister dear, I'll take care of it, no problem.' Right?"

"He likes her," Athena noted in an undertone, while taking her time unwrapping a caramel.

Priscilla's brows arched high as she homed in on the roll of her brother's eyes. *"Does he?"*

"Quite a lot, I think," Athena added.

"Okay, you two," Byron intruded.

It was no use. Priscilla asked, "She's divorced, isn't she?"

"He wouldn't tell me about her," Athena told her.

Priscilla's mouth dropped. "Oh, my God. He *does* like her."

"I'll do it," Byron blurted, raising his voice over the ill-fated exchange. "I'll ask her. But I won't grovel."

"Not even for Vivi?" Priscilla asked, incisive as always.

Vivi. Byron let his eyes close. *Damn that Donatella.* He gave Athena's shoulder a pat, leaning down to kiss her cheek. "I won't grovel," he decided. He gave his sister's cheek a pinch on the way out. *Much*, he thought silently.

"THIS SAUCE WILL make your grandmamma dance the jitterbug," Olivia said, handing a recipe card over the glass display counter of Belle Brides.

Roxie read the ingredients and skimmed the instructions. Looked easy enough. She studied the neat, compact handwriting. "Gerald won't mind me stealing his recipe?" she asked.

"If you'd asked him first, he would've handed it over in a flash himself," Olivia replied. From the large double stroller she'd pushed up the long wheelchair ramp came a whine. Her attention strayed to the twins snuggled up under plaid blankets. "Shhh," she soothed, gripping the handle and rocking the stroller back and forth on its all-terrain tires.

Roxie watched Olivia radiate with maternal strength. Motherhood suited Olivia more than any of them could ever have fathomed. Watching her transition so naturally into parenthood had been a fascination for all. "I can turn the music down," Roxie murmured, leaning over the counter to get a better look at the young Leightons with their sweet red lips and tiny long-fingered hands.

"The music's fine," Olivia claimed, brushing a fine blond lock under the brim of one of their stocking caps and adjusting it so that it covered the boy's ears. "It's Finnian. He gets feisty near feeding time. William would sleep through the day if we let him. But Finnian…he's a rascal."

By the look on Olivia's face, Finnian could have no finer ambition in life than being a rascal. Roxie shuffled through the remaining cards. "These two are from the girls?"

"Adrian says the rosemary chicken is easy prep," Olivia explained, "but it looks and tastes fancy. Cook that one when you want to impress someone. And Briar said you wanted her piecrust."

"Oh, *yes*." Roxie held the last card close. Nobody baked like Briar. And for some reason, lately Roxie had been craving gold-flaked piecrust with a vengeance. She couldn't wait for spring when the garden berries at Hanna's Inn ripened and Briar started turning out delicious home-baked pies by the dozen.

"Have you heard from Richard?"

The question sounded more ominous than inquisitive. Roxie licked her lips. "His father reached out to him. He and Lucinda expect him back sooner than later."

"Well, that's something at least," Olivia said with a shrug. Then she frowned over her own crumbly tone. "If he comes back soon, it's a sign, I guess, that he's not willing to let everything fall through the cracks. Right?"

"We'll see."

Olivia's expression lightened considerably after a moment. "I hear you and Briar saw Byron in the skinny."

The sly remark made Roxie think carefully as she set aside the recipe cards. She dialed back the volume for the speakers, dimming the sound of Charles Trenet's luscious "Verlaine." She couldn't have him parlaying in romantic tones when she thought about Byron. In or out of the skinny. "I'm sure you pried all details from her."

"She offered up some." Olivia's brows wiggled. "Is it true about the sex lines?"

"The what?"

"You know." Olivia angled her hands at her hips. "They arrow like this, pointing you down to all the hairy goods."

Roxie snorted. She pressed her fingers beneath her nose, stopping the noise. She tried not to meet Olivia's gaze. "Oh, God. I can't…" She snorted again and broke into shrieks of laughter. "I can't even."

"Who knew Byron looked like a legitimate Perseus under the threads?" Olivia said, eyes widening. "This whole time!"

"He works out," Roxie reasoned. Every other day he showed up at her back door in workout clothes that revealed more man muscles. She'd never thought she could be as aware of a man's deltoids…let alone that they could make her want to sink her teeth into them.

"And while we're on the subject of hairy goods—"

"You really should stop," Roxie advised.

Olivia would not be deterred. "He might be Perseus on the streets, but from the sounds of it, he could be Zeus in the sheets. Va-va-voom."

So much for not thinking about Byron and romance in the same breath. Roxie tamped down on all the hot, fuzzy feelings she'd had much practice suppressing anytime he appeared from the basement panting and sweat sheened.

The bells above the entry door clattered musically as it opened. Roxie looked over to greet the customers. In a flash, the flushed feeling left her, and cold and tension locked her up like an underground vault.

"Roxie," Georgiana cooed on sight. She was wearing a leopard-print ensemble that was too trim to look overtly tacky. "You're here!"

Roxie's gaze landed on the person who accompanied Georgiana into the shop. The glass door closed at Cassandra's back and the music died. She took off her dark designer shades slowly, matching Roxie stare for stare. She looked smart and polished, as ever, in a black business suit tailored to perfection. The jacket was cut low. Several tiers of pearls spilled into the void. She stood with her feet braced apart, knees straight, hips over center, back perfectly in line, chin high.

"Oh, brother," Olivia said, not bothering to lower her voice.

Roxie darted a glance at her. *I'll handle this*, she transmuted silently. Dear God, she hoped she could handle it. She inhaled carefully and said, "What are you doing here?"

Georgiana answered readily. "Mother sent us. I wanted a peek at the bridesmaids' dresses. And mine, of course!" She giggled at her own anticipation. "Cassie needs to be fitted again for her gown. But you already know that."

Of all the Honeycutt girls, only Georgiana had mastered Marabella's flair for flippancy. She was silly and sweet. Sweet enough for a toothache. She bypassed Olivia and the stroller and walked to the far side of the display counter that shined with diamonds. "Ooh. Look at this tiara! I like the diamond headpiece I found, but this is so regal! Can I try it on, Roxie? Roxie?"

Neither Cassandra nor Roxie moved for a minute. Then two. Georgiana looked around at the silence. Her nervous giggle filled the air. "Cassie, put your bag down and go change. And, Roxie, could you brew a pot of tea? We might be here for a while. Might as well get comfy. Right, Cassie?"

"I need to speak to Roxie," Cassandra said. She winged a pointed glance at Olivia. "Privately."

Olivia's frown mirrored the one Roxie felt. Drawing her mouth into a deep downhill slant, she looked to Roxie, questioning. Roxie nodded silently and again when Olivia's frown deepened.

Olivia gripped the handle of the stroller. "I guess I'll take Finny and Shooks downstairs to see Auntie Adrian. Holler if you need us," she added.

Roxie brushed her fingers across William's cheek as the stroller rolled past. She wished she could gather some serenity from his sleeping face. "Thanks for the recipes."

Olivia wheeled the stroller to the door and bumped it open with the front wheel. "Don't worry, *Angelina*," she drawled to Cassandra close to the entrance. "Mama's on the door." She rolled her eyes back at Roxie before making her way out onto the landing and pushing the stroller down the ramp out of sight.

Minutes later, the two sisters left Georgiana in front of a mirror with an assortment of gems. Feeling suddenly claustrophobic, Roxie sought the outdoors. The February wind was still bracing. There were clouds, but they trapped a bit of warmth between earth and ozone, heating things enough for Roxie to seek the refuge of the inn garden. She spotted the gazebo Cole had built for Briar after the last busy season ended. Wrapping her cardigan against her, she lowered to the bench inside as Cassandra mounted the steps.

Cassandra was the tallest of the Honeycutt girls. She, Julianna and Carolina had several inches in leg on the others. Cassandra moved like a giraffe, rod backed and oddly at ease with her height and bearing. She and Roxie shared the same hair and eyes but not much else to speak of.

Except Richard. Roxie chewed over the bitter thought then turned her mind elsewhere.

Leverett Honeycutt had only ever shown polite interest in his five daughters. Then Cassandra had expressed interest and acumen for the business world and he'd taken great care in grooming her for it. An executive in the Mobile shipping company that had been passed to Leverett from his father and grandfather, Cassandra was poised to inherit a great deal of the Honeycutt trust. Roxie had spent most of her life envying more than just her eldest sister's looks. She'd envied Cassandra's close bond with the father who'd managed to attend every milestone in his eldest daughter's life—to the point that there was little left for the rest of them.

Folding her arms over her middle, Roxie waited for Cassandra to circle the deck, her expensive ankle boots tapping against the wooden planks. Her sister went to the rail and stood, looking out at the white chop off the gray bay. Her dark hair blew back from a rigid jaw as she put her sunglasses back on. "Mother thinks you and I should bury the hatchet," she said finally.

Roxie said nothing. A sailboat cut across the water, racing the wind.

A cheerless smile galvanized Cassandra's mouth. "In her head, I think she still sees us as girls and all I'm guilty of is stealing your pageant sash again." When once more Roxie said nothing, Cassandra's chest rose on a long sigh. "If you're just going to listen, I might as well start from the beginning."

Roxie shook her head. "I don't want—"

"You can rake me over the coals however much you want," Cassandra interrupted, "but first I'd like to explain." Their mother had played her hand. There would be no more avoidance or withholding, for either of them.

It took a moment but Cassandra spoke with decisive care. "Three years ago, I found out Jefferson had been having a little fling on the side."

Roxie's brows crowded inward.

Acid dripped from every syllable out of Cassandra's mouth. "We started therapy a lot sooner than everyone thinks we did. Through it, he admitted that he'd had the affair because he thought I'd grown too hard. And Trudie… That was the tart's name. *Trudie*. He sought Trudie's company because he needed a 'softer touch.'"

Roxie struggled with what to do with the new, torrid wave of information. It gathered at the apex of her mind. A headache began to thump behind it. She tucked the hair behind her ears. "Am I supposed to feel sorry for you?"

Cassandra's head snatched her way. "No, I don't expect pity. Not from you."

"Then why are you telling me this?"

"Because it's the same thing I told Richard," Cassandra claimed. "We bumped into each other in Galveston when I was there on business and he was at a conference. We had drinks. Just drinks. It was all innocent. But we talked. It was the first time I told anybody, other than the damn therapist, about Trudie and Jefferson. He was kind. I never really understood your pull toward Richard. He always seemed so... I don't know, *vanilla*. He was so kind, though. He helped me talk it out better than the therapist had. We started texting. Again, innocent. He would check in to make sure Jefferson and I were doing okay. I would make sure you and Mother weren't driving him too crazy with wedding plans..."

Roxie didn't want to hear any more. She *really* didn't want to hear any more.

But Cassandra was on a roll now. "Then... somehow it happened. I was frustrated because therapy had taken a bad turn, because Jefferson and I were fighting again... We rowed like we'd never rowed before and I walked out. And the first person I thought of going to was Richard. I expected you to be there and that was okay. I just needed to vent, just to get it out. You know?"

"But I wasn't," Roxie muttered. "I wasn't there."

Cassandra hesitated a long time, as if choosing her words with consideration. "I don't know how it happened, exactly. That's such a cliché thing to say in situations like this, but that's just the way it was. One minute I was talking and pacing. I think I might have been crying." She said *crying* like it was distasteful. Roxie had never seen Cassandra cry and had often wondered if she knew how. "He stopped me, tried to calm me down and…" She trailed off.

Roxie was very glad that she'd come to the end of the confessional. "I've heard enough," she said, fingers biting into the edge of the bench on either side of her.

"We felt terrible," Cassandra said. "Immediately after, we stopped."

"Well, I should hardly expect you to finish," Roxie said and it was the first jab she'd taken.

"I meant we stopped whatever was happening between us," Cassandra clarified. "No texts. No calls. Nothing. I know less about his whereabouts than you do and, frankly, I think it's better. For him, for you, for me and Jefferson—especially since we're back in therapy."

"Why?" Roxie asked. "Why are you and Jefferson still fighting for each other? You've both been unfaithful. You apparently make each other miserable—"

"Why do you want to patch things up with Richard?" Cassandra asked. She lifted a shoulder. "Because you love him?"

Roxie licked her lips. They'd gone dry from the wind. Passing a hand over her brow, she went forward again with the safe nonreply.

"We weren't always miserable," Cassandra admitted. "Before there was a Trudie or Richard, there was love. There was tenderness. I fell in love with Jefferson because I thought he made me a softer person. And I've never quit anything in my life. Marriage certainly isn't going to be the first."

Cassandra's reasoning was sounding more and more like Roxie's own. "I don't know what's worse," Roxie said quietly, "the whole thing being revenge sex…or more."

"Why would you want it to be more?"

"Because then at least it meant something," Roxie said, coming quickly to her feet. "Then at least it would've mattered. You threw away my marriage along with, potentially, your own without an ounce of feeling? What kind of bullshit is that, Cassandra?"

Cassandra lifted a brow over the edge of her shades. She looked more impressed than critical.

Roxie came to the rail, too, and scowled out over the bay. "Knowing your excuses doesn't make it any easier to forgive you."

"Did I ask for forgiveness?"

"Did you ever figure Jefferson's right?" Roxie asked experimentally. "That maybe you have grown hard?"

"You've always seen everything in black-and-white," Cassandra accused. "Mother told me to bury the hatchet. I don't have a hatchet to bury with you. Mine's with Jefferson and Trudie, the cheap masseuse from Beaumont. If you want to keep carrying your own hatchet, that's fine. Maybe things will change when Richard gets back." She reached into her purse and pulled out a card. "Here. This is the number for the new therapist Jefferson and I are seeing, the one we're actually making progress with. Believe me when I say that I hope it works out for the best." She took out a cigarette and a lighter and turned out of the wind. "And I am not hard."

Roxie frowned at the name printed on glossy cardstock. What her mother thought of as a life-line felt more like a fuse. What kind of saving grace was it if it was handed to her by the cata-lyst of her destruction?

Where was Sophocles? He could sign the whole family up as tragic muses.

Waving at the smoke from Cassandra's Lucky Strike, Roxie tucked the card into the pocket of her cardigan. "Come back to the shop," she said solemnly, "and let's get this over with."

CHAPTER SIX

THAT EVENING, BYRON walked around to the back door of the Victorian. He lifted his hand to the knob to enter then hesitated. Loosening a sigh, he let it fall. Making an effort to relax his stance, he rolled his shoulders and rotated his head on his neck to align it. He cleared his throat and shifted his feet apart on the welcome mat before rapping a knock on the glass.

There was a clatter on the other side, a muted exclamation. Byron squinted, trying to see through the lacy curtain Roxie had fixed into place for privacy. *A load of good it's done her*, he thought. He'd contemplated investing in a gym membership for the next twelve months just so he wouldn't have to breeze in and out of her soft lilac cloud every day. She'd lived in the house that should've been his for merely a week and already the walls breathed with the scent…

He wasn't here for a workout, though. He'd done little but shed his coat and tie, and roll up the cuffs of his business shirt since returning from work. Priscilla had called him on the way home, nagging him to bring along some sort of offering. A bottle of wine, she'd suggested, or chocolate.

He could've picked up a bottle of moscato. Alternately, he'd helped Roxie clean up the last of her truffles on Valentine's Day—it would have been easy to replenish them. In the end, though, he'd shown up empty-handed. He would ask Roxie to help his family and, yes, he might grovel. But he wouldn't butter her up with gifts.

And the idea of giving a woman something as suggestive as wine and chocolates had nearly made him break into hives.

Strong, it really has been a long time since you treated a woman, huh? Not that he was treating Roxie. "Hell," he muttered, rapping again on the pane. "Would you open the door, duchess?" *Put me out of my misery.*

He heard the lock click. The door shied from the jamb. Byron pressed his hand against the wood, pushing it further in. Instantly, a bevy of nongardeny smells assaulted his nose. "Rox?" he asked, peering into the kitchen.

"I'm here, I'm here!" she said from the stove.

Byron stood for a moment, taking in the scene. She had an irritating habit of being perfect all the time, so he noticed her messy ponytail straight off. There was a large copper pot on the range in front of her. She was stirring it with a wooden spoon and muttering a colorful soliloquy. She'd kicked off her shoes but was still wearing the mint-colored day dress he'd seen her leave the house in for work that morning. It was what was tied over the dress that gave him pause.

Roxie glanced back, face flushed, eyes a bit wild. They flicked over him in an irritated manner. "What?" she asked when he just raised a brow at her.

He cleared his throat again. "You're wearing an apron."

She looked down at the black hostess-style apron. There was a red bow on the front that made it look more like something from a French maid costume. "Yeah, so?" she challenged.

Clearing his throat for what he realized was the third time, he trained his gaze instead on her legs. Bad idea, he thought. He'd always liked her gams. Her toenails were painted Lick Me pink and he actually thought about licking them. "Ahhh…" What had he come here for? "I need to ask you something?"

"Can it wait?" Pushing at the lock falling from her scrubbed-up queue, she said, "Kind of in the middle of something."

"What are you doing, exactly?" he asked, hesitant. His hand was still on the door and he was considering using it as an escape route.

"What does it look like I'm doing?" The words were clipped. Where usually her movements were graceful and practical, they were chopped and tetchy. They broadened as she continued. "You're a smart man, Byron. Make an educated guess."

"Okay." There was some sort of sauce bubbling close to the lip of the copper pot. So close that it was splashing specks of red on the rest of the stove as it rolled into a boil. By the color and smell, he guessed tomato but didn't step closer to investigate. He was distracted by what he saw in the sink. A chicken. A whole chicken, its white flanks wet with perspiration as it defrosted. On the prep counter, there were mangled tomato parts and sprigs of basil and thyme. A mushroom cap had rolled onto the floor. There were several knives displayed helter-skelter on the countertop amid the veggies and a small bushel of shining Gala apples.

Knowing he risked coming up on the bad end of one of those knives, Byron shrugged and asked again, "Roxie, what are you doing?"

"I'm cooking, damn it!" she answered, picking up a spice jar and shaking it brusquely over the pot.

"No, really," he said, the corner of his mouth lifting. If he laughed, he would definitely meet a bloody end.

Roxie set the jar down. Seeming to cave in on herself, she lowered her head into her hands. "Oh, God. Oh, God. This is a disaster. *I* am a disaster."

"Hey, take it easy." It wasn't until he'd closed the door and started to cross the tiles to the stove that he realized he was staying. He reached for the wooden spoon still gripped in her fist, only then noticing the bandages on her fingers. "Jesus," he muttered, folding his fingers around her wrist and lifting hers to the light. "I never figured you for a cutter."

"It was the knives," Roxie said. "The girls gave me some recipes to try because I want to cook more at home." She tossed the spoon onto the counter. "Today was one of those days I could've used a personal victory. Congratulations. You've caught me in yet another splendid epic fail."

He frowned at her and the mess. Making a decision, he expulsed a breath. "Fix yourself a tall glass of wine and cop a squat somewhere that hasn't been hit by the small foodie tornado. I'll try and clean this up."

She eyed him uncertainly. "You want my apron?"

He made the mistake of scanning it from top to bottom. It hit her midthigh and he contemplated what she'd look like in it. Just it. "Keep it." *Throw it out. Burn the devil.* As she turned away to reach into the cupboard, he bent his head to sniff the substance in the pot. It didn't *smell* like an epic fail. "Marinara?"

"Gerald's recipe," she confirmed, pulling moscato from the fridge. "Spaghetti."

"Uh-huh. And why are you making enough for Patton's army?"

"Because that's how much the recipe said to cook." She produced a card from a pocket hidden beneath the bow and offered it to him.

It was sauce smudged. Byron was able to read enough of the ingredients to guess where her problem was. "This is bulk. You make it, you store it."

"Well, how was I supposed to know that?"

"A pound and a half of tomatoes didn't tip you off?" He dipped the wooden spoon into the vat and lifted it to his mouth.

"Oh no, don't!" she shrieked as he tasted it. "Oh, my God, I just poisoned you. I'm a murderess!"

Byron licked his lips, swallowed, tilted his head. "Not the worst poison I've ever tasted."

She paused as he went back for another spoonful. "Really?" she asked, almost whispering in surprise.

"Mm," he said. "Mushrooms. I taste the mushrooms. And something smoky. It's good."

"It is?" Hope was born somewhere underneath a blanket of larkspur.

"I'd eat it," he said. "But we've established that I eat honey buns and Cocoa Puffs, so I wouldn't apply to the Olive Garden just yet." Using a fork, he nabbed one of the green beans floating with diced onions around a small pan. "Hmm. What'd you put in these?"

"Comin'."

He nearly dropped the fork. "Do what?"

"Comin'?" When he eyed her, askance, she lifted a bottle of seasoning for him to see.

The effort not to laugh at her again nearly drove him to his knees. "Cumin, you mean?"

Roxie turned the label toward her and read it once more. "Cumin." She pressed her lips together and avoided his stare altogether. "Don't say a word," she warned.

"Wasn't gonna," he said carefully. "What's with the bird?"

"I was going to make Adrian's chicken. She said it was easy. But the thing's frozen solid."

"When you buy your chickens from the freezer section, they have a tendency to remain solid."

"No kidding," she said and drank. "I thought the defrosting process would be quick."

"Do me a favor. Don't offer to do a turkey for Thanksgiving. Stick with dressing. Wait, no. Cranberries. *Just* cranberries."

"Fine," she said wearily. "What do I do now about this mess?"

Byron spotted the trash pail next to the counter with the cutting board, herbs and veggies. He slid it over with the toe of his shoe, lifted the chicken with a set of metal tongs and dropped it into the disposal with a satisfying *plop*. "Next?"

She stared at the pail with a dejected look. Then she turned her head to the stove once more and said, "Spaghetti." When she made a move for the range, he stopped her by tugging at the apron tie at the small of her back. "Sit down," he said. When she frowned at him, he lifted his brows. "I got this."

He spent the next ten minutes cleaning the unused elements. He burned the side of his hand on the edge of the copper pot. He brushed her off when she came at him with the first-aid kit. Putting the sauce on simmer, he boiled water for pasta then worked on cleaning the prep counter, salvaging what he could of the leftover ingredients. As he started to wash the knives, he asked, "What's wrong?"

"Whatever do you mean?" She'd been leaning on the counter, watching him and sipping her wine, for several minutes.

"Something's wrong," he said knowingly. "You're not exactly yourself."

She counted the Galas he'd left on the counter. She picked one up, frowning over its smooth surface. "You mean for once I'm not pleasing? Nobody can be pleasin' all the time. No matter how hard they try." She took a bite out of the apple and chewed it slowly. "What do you think happened to the old Roxie?"

Byron set a clean knife in the dish drain and started on the next. "I guess you're right. Nobody gets mowed down by a Mack truck and walks away unbroken."

"I spoke to Cassandra today." When he looked around, she nodded. "My mother arranged it. Cassandra conveyed to me matter-of-factly how her own marriage fell apart, how it drove her into Richard's arms."

Tossing the towel onto the dish rack, Byron crossed back to the stove to check the pasta. "So what's the verdict? Is all healed and forgiven, hallelujah, amen?"

Roxie set the Gala back down and straightened, moving away from the glass that was now empty. "I want to be the bigger person. I want to move on like she says she's done. But I don't know if I'll ever be able to look her in the face again... and not see her beneath him."

"Then good riddance."

"She's my sister," Roxie said with a helpless lift of her arms.

"You deserve better," he told her, turning to her on an indignant burst. "Just because her relationship went to shit didn't mean she had to come after yours to make herself feel better."

"She said it was an accident."

"Isn't it always?" he noted, sardonic. "You're right. You can't be pleasin' all the time and when it comes to Cassandra you don't have to be ever again. That's your right, duchess."

After a moment's stillness, Roxie grabbed the neck of the bottle and poured herself another glass of wine. "*Is* the world so black-and-white?"

"It is to me," he said, switching the heat off the pasta. It always had been. "Christ. Marriage might not be a simple affair but fidelity is. End of story." He transferred the pot to the sink, where he drained the pasta in the colander, shaking and rinsing. He heard a *thunk* behind him and looked around to see her at the cutting board, handling one of the last knives she'd left alone in the butcher block. "Nuh-uh," he said, moving to her back and making a grab for the knife handle. "Give me that."

"I need it," she argued, pulling it out of his reach. "I have to peel and slice the apples for pie."

"Look at your hand." He closed his hand over hers and pried the handle from her fingers with the other. "Not just no, but *hell no*."

"Give it to me!"

"Step aside, Rox," he said firmly.

"No, *I'm* doing this! I want to do it."

"Fine, but you're going to learn to do it right first."

"Byron. I've got it. Okay?"

"The only thing you've got is bad technique. And here's your first problem—you're using a steak knife."

"What's wrong with that?" she asked as he tossed the knife back into the sink with a clatter.

"Not sharp enough." He took one of the clean knives out of the dish drainer and returned to her. "The duller the blade, the more dangerous it is because of the resistance you get when cutting. What you need is a good paring knife."

She eyed the blade he held up. "And the difference is...?"

"It's shorter, gives you more control. It might be sharper, but with the shorter blade there's less room for incident." He held it high, out of her reach when she fumbled for it again. "*If* you know what you're doing."

She rolled her eyes. "Paring knife. Check. Now gimme."

"Take a seat. School's in session."

"I need to do this myself," she insisted, trying for a reasonable tone. "That's what this whole thing is about. Learning to cook for myself."

"Explain something to me, duchess," he said. "I get that you're no cook, but veggie and fruit slicing is rudimentary. How have you managed to go through life without a lesson? Did you have a nanny who did everything for you until you left home?"

She reached for the knife again. "Just give me the thing."

His brow lowered. "You did, didn't you?"

"She was an au pair."

"Did you have a pony, too, Bonnie Blue?"

"No, I didn't." She lowered her head slightly. "I was allergic." When he only stared, she gave in. "All right. Teach me." His eyes narrowed and she clapped her hand over her heart. "I promise not to hack off one of my fingers."

"I'm more worried about my own." He stepped in behind her, up close. He fitted the Gala against her cupped palm, then handed her the knife. "Show me how you'd hold this."

She showed him. He made a discouraging noise in the back of his throat. Reaching around her, he repositioned her fingers to strengthen her grip. "Tight. Confident. But not overconfident." Because his nose was all but in her hair and it threatened to shepherd him into a lilac-induced stupor, he moved so that his cheek was next to hers. Angling her wrist, he directed her into cutting the peel in a fine strip, circling the Gala so that it shed its outer layer in one curly ribbon. Her hands, wrists, arms looked pale under his, and delicate, too, especially with her manicured fingers wrapped in bandages and a vintage diamond ring with small marquise-cut emeralds twining the silver band like leaves on a vine.

"Is this right?" she asked after he'd let go, allowing her to finish.

"Hmm," he said. He'd shifted his hands to her waist without realizing. Instead of removing them promptly, he contemplated nosing around her throat until he found the pulse point where she dabbed her perfume.

She stilled, as if attuned to his thought process. The peel fell to the cutting board. Slowly, she turned her face up to his.

It would've been wise to turn away but her eyes passed from one of his to the other, looking. Looking deep and searching.

What are you looking for, duchess? he wondered.

Maybe if he showed her…would she keep guessing?

It wasn't impulse this time. His hand moved up to grab the ponytail on the back of her head in a gentle hold and he kissed her like that was the solution.

THE PARING KNIFE clattered to the cutting board. The apple, bald, rolled off the edge of the counter. Roxie's head dipped back as Byron's hold slipped from the mess of her hair and cupped the nape of her neck. Her hands flailed in reaction as his mouth took hers. Otherwise, she stood stock-still, absorbing the impact. *Oh.*

Oh. Oh. Oh.

It wasn't a question this time. It wasn't an experiment, like the last kiss. It wasn't curiosity or even an idle whim.

Byron was kissing her. *Kissing* her. And he meant it. She knew it when his head tilted slightly, just enough to kick the kiss up a notch from something stolen to something designed to tease yummy noises out of her. Her heart beat like a bodhran, up-tempo and all over the place.

Yes, he meant it.

Oh. That need. The drilling, pulsating need to be touched fired inside of her as it had before. It blazed high and hot, striking her off guard. She reached back to fit her palm over the back of his neck, breaking the kiss long enough to shift around so her body confronted his. Lost, she kept her eyes closed.

His mouth found hers again. She felt a tug at the tie on her back as his hand slid home beneath it. One of the yummy noises she'd been trying to lock down found a hatch. It sounded needy, plaintive in the air. His lips lifted from hers and he nudged the end of his nose against hers, raising his chin by a fraction. Her mouth parted in response and he went back to kissing her silly, his tongue sliding past her lips to graze the tip of hers.

"Ah," she gasped. The atmosphere had become thick as a sauna. Bracing herself against him, she pressed a hand to one of the deltoids she'd fantasized about. Even through the crisp shirt, it felt as solid as a rock.

He released his hold on her neck.

She dragged out a ragged breath. "You keep kissing me," she said on a whisper, nearly inaudible.

"Yeah." He paused. "Maybe you should hit me."

She shook her head after a few seconds' consideration. "You're so good at it, I don't want to hit you."

"Once." When she refused, he took her fist, balled it up and placed it low over his ribs. "Clean shot. Right here. Just like I showed you. Remember?"

Her mouth was sealed but it spread into a wide, warm curve. Her hand splayed beneath his and she cradled the space above his liver. The smile drifted off slowly as his eyes reached for hers then dipped over her features, coming to rest on her mouth again. His lips parted. They were such good lips. Soft for a man's yet sure. Definitely sure.

When they began to tilt toward hers again, her grip went from his deltoid to the collar of his shirt and she tensed, bringing him up just shy of the mark. "I…" She squeezed her eyes closed. A grimace worked through her.

She felt him give, shifting to his heels in retreat. "Say no more, duchess."

"Richard," she said anyway. She felt Byron stiffen at her ex's name. "Richard's coming home." Opening her eyes, she watched the inflexible shield lock down his visage like a foxhole. "I'm sorry," she whispered.

His mouth didn't look soft anymore. He dropped his hand from the small of her back and his fists clenched at his sides. "Richard." He gave an acquiescing nod. Or was it one of defeat? Before she could gauge him properly, he walked toward the exit.

"Byron," she said to his back. "I'm sorry."

"Wanna know the first step to bringing the old Roxie back?" he asked. "Stop apologizing. That's twice now I've crossed the line. I'm responsible. Both times I knew full well that you are not, never have been nor ever will be mine."

She scrubbed her hand over the center of her chest. His intensity was palpable, startling, mesmerizing. A little heartbreaking. "What's the second?" she asked.

His shoulders dropped, angling down. "There is no second. You put one foot in front of the other and, if you can't find what makes you happy, you ‸‿ what you can to get by until you do."

‸‿‸ cooking?" she said with a nod to the

mess around them. When he said nothing, she asked quietly, "What was it for you?"

When he'd talked of Dani before, she'd seen something grim take over. Then, it was only a matter of seconds before he blinked and there was Byron again. Now she saw the shadow come over him. It lingered as he reached back into the past. "I worked like a son of a bitch. When I wasn't working, I threw myself into physical fitness. I worked on my great-uncle's Camaro. I pounded music into the quiet. I binge-watched television. I dove headlong into books." Crossing his arms over his chest, he shifted his feet, bracing them apart. "Quiet drove me crazy. Even when I read, I'd have noise in the background. Even when I slept. *Especially* when I slept."

"And how long did it take you—to find what made you happy?"

"A while," he said honestly. "It took a while to even want to be happy. Getting out of Atlanta helped, and so did starting from scratch. The town, the bay—they helped, too. Quitting law and becoming an accountant like I was supposed to from the start…that was the first thing I remember that made me happy."

"The house," she said with a small sigh and a glance at the interior, seeing him clearly through it. "It makes you happy, too."

"Yeah," he said, his eyes going dead as he

jerked his shoulder in a shrug. "Just find what makes you happy, duchess. Stop listening to your family's expectations and everybody else, and ask yourself what it's going to take for you to make a new normal. If it's not the same thing it was before, that's fine. Sometimes finding that something new is all it takes to get you going in the right direction."

Roxie soaked in the lesson that he'd come by the hard way. When he walked the rest of the way to the door, it struck her. "You said you needed something, when you came in."

He muttered. Relinquishing his hold on the knob, he said, "It's my family. They need the favor. My sister Vivi is getting married in two weeks and the wedding planner just dropped out. We're down a coordinator and a venue, apparently. The family wanted me to ask you if there's any way you can fit us into your schedule."

"Two weeks?" she asked, stunned.

"Yeah," he said. His jaw tensed. "We're desperate."

"I've got several events lined up," she contemplated, trying to remember what her calendar looked like exactly. "And my sister Georgiana is getting married, too, in a month. To say she and my mother aren't stalking me with details is an understatement."

"All right," he accepted. "I'll tell them."

"I didn't say no."

"Vivi wouldn't want to overburden you," he said. "Don't worry about it."

"Byron, I'll help," she told him. "But…only under one condition."

"What's that?" he asked.

She thought about it quickly. "I'll waive the last-minute fees because I need a favor, too." Swallowing, she didn't choose her next words lightly. She needed to be careful here, in light of what had happened between them. "Richard might be coming home, but I don't have a definite as to when. It could be before Georgiana's wedding or after. And even if he does come back, there's no guarantee he and I will be on the same page. I might still be out a plus one when the wedding rolls around and I can't show up alone."

"Why not?"

"Because it's a masked ball," she pointed out. "And… Well, there might be a waltz."

He frowned. "Who does that?"

"It's a Mardi Gras wedding," she told him. "And it's Georgiana. We're lucky she's not making everyone wear hoop skirts."

"Just cummerbunds?" he asked condescendingly. "I don't dance."

"But you go to weddings all the time," she recalled.

"Have you ever seen me dance?"

Come to think of it, she hadn't. "So you won't dance with your own sister at her wedding?"

What little life there was left in his eyes fizzled completely as he retreated behind that curt shell once more. "No."

"Is it a family thing?"

"Please give me an answer," Byron requested. "Ever seen lionesses hunt baby elephants on the nature channel?"

"Okay," she said with a half laugh. She thought of him. Of Vera and Constantine and how generous they had been. "I'll do it."

"Even if I don't dance?"

"We'll see," she replied.

He shifted from one foot to the other. "I'm behooved to say thank-you."

"I'll tell the lionesses you did," she assured him. Then she felt humor finally blinking back. "Was the kissing part of this?"

"No," he said, seriously. "Kissing was a mistake. *Clearly* a mistake."

"I got it," she said quickly, sorry she'd asked. The humor fled her in an instant and she felt empty in the absence of warmth, his and hers. Absolutely empty.

CHAPTER SEVEN

ARMED WITH HER planner and a pie tin, Roxie rushed into Hanna's Inn, where she had arranged for the evening's consultation. As the entry door closed behind her, Briar breezed into the foyer, a tray of canapés balanced on one hand. "Oh, good. You're here."

"I'm late, I know," Roxie said as she shrugged out of her coat. One-handed, Briar hung it on the peg by the door. "Are they—"

"Yes, but don't worry. I gave them some refreshments and seated them in the sunroom."

"Great," Roxie said, moving down the hall past the stairway that led up to the guest suites. The den was empty. Roxie and her guests had the inn to themselves for a few hours. "Just in time for sunset." Roxie handed the pie to Briar and fidgeted with her blouse's jabot, slowing her steps as she heard the chatter from the sunroom.

Briar stopped and stared at her. "Roxie. You're nervous."

Roxie blinked. "Nuh-uh."

"Yes, you are." Briar smiled, straightening the

edge of Roxie's stand collar herself. "I know your schedule's tight, but we can pull this off without a glitch. Especially if they go with the Bridal Suite."

Roxie wasn't worried about pulling off Vivienne Strong's wedding. But she was nervous. Her stomach was in knots and her breathing wasn't right. She hadn't felt this fretful since signing divorce papers. "I'm fine." Hearing communal laughter, she asked Briar in an undertone, "How do they seem to you? Byron's sisters? Are they—"

"Lovely. Just like Vera and Constantine. And Byron, of course."

Byron, lovely. Roxie pressed the heel of her hand against her stomach. Those were not butterflies. "Right." She nodded toward the pie. "I brought that for you and Cole."

Briar took a peek under the foil's edge. "Smells fantastic. You outdid yourself for a first timer."

"That's my sixth attempt. Didn't sleep a wink last night. Couldn't rest until I got it right."

"I'll serve coffee next," Briar said knowingly. "Go on in. Give the word and we'll start the tour."

Roxie veered into the sunroom, appropriately named with floor-to-ceiling panoramic windows, potted plants of a tropical variety and a row of cushioned lounges. The view was spectacular: Cole's trim green lawn, Briar's gardens overflowing with perennial greenery, and the bay. Today it was moody brown. The winter sun was hanging low in the west over Mobile. As the waves rolled lazily into shore, they caught the light, burning amber for a stolen moment before bubbling and foaming into shore.

Briar had given Vera, Priscilla and Vivienne the settee on the far side of the room. They drank the famous inn tea from tall glasses and were passing Briar's madeleines from one to the next as they admired the baker's touch and the seascape outside by turn. Roxie took a second to size up the company.

Priscilla had a striking resemblance to her mother but was taller, much taller. Amazonian almost. She was also hugely pregnant. Her eyes were dark. Roxie detected some of Byron's shrewdness there.

Vivienne was the flip side of the coin. Where everyone else in the Strong family seemed to be dark haired, she was vividly blonde. Her eyes were blue, bluer than Byron's, and they shared a nose, though Vivienne's face was more Greek. She held her shoulders high and had the distinctive glow of a prospective bride with more than a dash of added vitality.

Stifling what remained of her nerves, Roxie approached them, apologizing when they stopped speaking as one. Vera rose to greet her, introducing her daughters. Roxie shook each of their hands as Vera explained, "Roxie's one of the best wedding planners in the state, I've heard. And it's lucky for us she's living in the same house as Byron. Though she's *not* sleeping with him."

Roxie laughed lightly. "No, I'm not," she said as she sat in a wicker chair.

"Well, why not?" Vivienne asked, bright eyes latching on.

"Yeah, we hear he's pretty good in the sack," Priscilla contemplated, polishing off a madeleine.

"No teasing, girls," Vera warned them. "We need this one."

"But, Ma, it's okay," Priscilla said lightly. "Byron likes her."

"He does?" Vivienne asked, complicit.

"Athena said so."

"*Athena* said?" Vivienne looked at Roxie in a new light. "You could be my new sister!"

"I—" Roxie fumbled.

Vera took pity on her. "I'm sorry. These two do whatever they can to make their brother cringe, even when he isn't present and accounted for."

Vivienne gave a good-natured laugh. "It's true. But you have to understand, Roxie. The first time Athena met Ma—"

Vera rolled her eyes heavenward. "Here we go."

"—she told our father, and I quote—"

Priscilla intervened smoothly. "'Nephew, she'll give you three golden children and you'll spend the rest of your life in worship of her.'"

"And when she met Toby…" Vivienne continued.

"My husband, Tobias," Priscilla explained quickly.

"…she said, 'Priscilla, that man is going to ask you to marry him and you'd be a fool to resist,'" Vivienne regaled. "And when she met Byron's college girlfriend Dani…you do remember what she said about Dani, don't you, Ma?"

Vera sighed a little as Priscilla sobered. "'You'll love this one so much it'll break your heart…'"

"'…but you'll never be whole without her,'" Priscilla finished. She hid the sad lines around her mouth by taking an extended gulp of tea.

Vivienne leaned forward to grasp Roxie's hand. "Athena's coming to the wedding. You simply have to meet her. I'm anxious to see what she says about *you*."

Roxie could hardly catch her breath. She hadn't expected the familiar greeting. Nor had she expected the open emotions. Though Priscilla was watching her intently for a response and Vivienne was still smiling, Roxie couldn't give them what she should have—an automatic denial over anything romantic with their brother. "Your aunt sounds like a remarkable woman."

With perfect timing, Briar arrived with the carafe. She passed around china cups and dessert plates. "Vera, you have to try this pie Roxie made. You'll never believe it's one of her first." Briar looked to Roxie. "Vera owned her own bakery in Atlanta."

"Oh," Roxie said and her eyes widened as Vera didn't hesitate to take up the dessert fork Briar offered on a napkin and cut the corner off a slice. "Goodness, I hope it's edible."

"Mm." Vera's eyes widened as she savored a bite on her tongue. "Oh, this is fine! Better than my grandmother's apple pie. 'Cilla, try some."

Priscilla took a bite and Vivienne did, too. Roxie tried not to agonize over the potential of food poisoning.

"They should serve this at the wedding," Priscilla decided, going back for another bite. "Not that flaming flan business you discovered in Antigua."

"It was Argentina," Vivienne informed her, "and it's Sid's favorite. But maybe we could put this on the dessert table, too. Mini apple pies." She giggled over the idea. "We have cultural flavors from everywhere Sid and I have traveled. This could be our something American. What's your secret, Roxie?"

Sin. Roxie shook her head, trying not to think of Byron kissing her over the Galas. It was a lost cause. *Sinny sin sin.* "Luck," she said instead. "My kitchen experiments have mostly turned foul, but the baking thing… There might be something to it. It makes me feel accomplished in some way."

"You're more than accomplished." Priscilla lifted her half-finished plate in indication. "You've perfected apple pie and you've managed to make my dill weed brother silly over you."

Vivienne grinned around a bite. "At last."

"Enough about Byron," Vera said. "Vivi, do you have the folder? We put together a comprehensive list of everything that was planned so far for the ceremony at the club."

"It's in my chair," Vivienne said, pointing toward something in the corner.

It was then Roxie realized why Vivienne hadn't risen to greet her. She'd thought it was due to Priscilla's pregnancy.

In truth, it was the other way around—Priscilla hadn't risen because Vivienne couldn't. Roxie leapt quickly to her feet and went to the folded wheelchair. She found the binder in the bag hanging from the handle. Handing the binder to Vivienne, she noted that Vivienne's smile had lost some its luster.

Vivienne was handicapped. Roxie never would have guessed. She wore a maxi dress with an exotic print so Roxie couldn't see her legs, but her feet laid flat against the floor in flip-flops. They were tan, the nails pristinely tipped, one graced with a toe ring.

Byron hadn't mentioned a disability or an accident that would prevent the bride from walking down the aisle…

But he'd told her something else, hadn't he? She'd asked him if he would dance with his sister at her wedding. *No*, he'd said and the light had gone out in him.

Feeling foolish, Roxie did her best to fan over her shock as Vivienne showed her pictures of the gown, a charming Grecian design she'd picked up on a weekend jaunt to Corfu. Priscilla told her how her own gown had had to be changed after they found out she was pregnant two months after Vivienne and Sidney set a date. "She wouldn't let me change it," Vivienne noted. Vera explained that they wanted to keep it outdoors, if possible. The club had had an open conservatory. "But I suppose that's out the window now," she added.

"I have some news there," Roxie said, glancing over the printouts from the club's website on the tabletop. "I spoke to the manager of the club. After some cajoling, they offered back the deposit, but they've already booked the conservatory."

Vivienne lifted a shoulder. "Just as well. It was too perfect, wasn't it? I don't believe in complete perfection, not even on my wedding day. Though Ma's right. I have always wanted an outdoor ceremony."

"Well," Roxie said, "I might have a solution.

How would you feel about the ceremony and reception taking place at Hanna's Inn?"

Vivienne gazed out the windows, seeing the grounds from a new perspective. "They do that here?"

"Sure," Roxie said. "Briar and her husband were married in the garden. It was a beautiful affair, very intimate."

"But the guest list," Vera said as she took a leaf of paper out of the binder. "There's two hundred names on here."

"And they've already received invitations," Priscilla added. "Two hundred isn't what I'd call intimate."

"I was thinking the lawn itself," Roxie said, gesturing to the grass outside. "We can bring in a tent and space heaters to keep everyone warm but still have it open, inviting the outdoors in. We can bring in greenery to enhance the natural aesthetic. Flora will provide the flowers. And the owner of Tavern of the Graces has offered to provide you with one of her professional bartenders and a custom bar for the reception."

"Sounds like a package," Vivienne said, brightening once more.

"We call it the Bridal Suite." Roxie grinned. "And, yes, it does come with the actual honeymoon suite here at Hanna's, which is nothing short of dazzling. If you're open to it, Briar has arranged for a tour of the house and gardens."

"Yes, yes." Vivienne nodded. "I want to see the suite."

"The stairs," Priscilla said, glancing quickly to Vivienne. "There's no elevator."

"Sid!" Vivienne burst forth. "He's having drinks with By and Toby at the tavern. He could carry me up. I *have* to see the suite, 'Cilla. And it'll be good practice." She winked. "For the wedding night."

"He needs practice?"

"I'll call him," Vera said, pulling her phone from her purse. She began to dial.

Vivienne spoke to Roxie in an undertone. "You're sure the guest list won't be a problem?"

"Olivia, who owns the tavern, and Briar have both informed me that we'll be able to accommodate all two hundred," Roxie assured her with confidence.

"I tried to cut out most of the Delacroixes, but they hold grudges like nobody else."

"I'm sorry, who are the Delacroixes?" Roxie asked.

"Ma's family," Vivienne said, rolling her eyes much in the way Vera had. "Wait till you meet them. They're a hoot."

Priscilla cut in. "What she means to say is they're a bunch of pious bigmouths who hate our father."

"Hate him?" Roxie said, taken aback. "Who could possibly hate Constantine?"

"The Delacroixes," Vivienne and Priscilla said as one. Priscilla continued, "They think he stole Ma away from them."

Vera finished the call. "Sidney's rushing over. And I mean rushing. And your father did steal me away from the Delacroixes. Thank heaven." As the girls giggled, Vera explained to Roxie, "Con and I eloped. My family was nothing short of scandalized."

"Ma," Priscilla said, "I'm not sure it was so much that you ran away with him as the fact that when you made it to the altar, you were as big as me. You were barefoot on a beach in Jamaica *and* the ceremony was presided over by a Buddhist monk."

"I can't help that I looked as far along as you are. Your brother sat completely out in front, nearly broke my back. As for the monk, it was better than the family priest who informed me and your father in dire tones that our child would be born both a bastard and a heathen."

"Byron is a bastard," Priscilla opined. "He pushed me out of a tree once, and I hold as good a grudge as any Delacroix."

The sound of running feet brought their heads around. Vivienne's lit up like a theme park and Roxie turned to get her first impression of the

groom. Panting, charmingly rumpled, Sidney responded in kind, grinning broadly as he crossed
in a wide gait to his bride. "I came as fast as I
could. Your brothers are trying to get me trashed."

"You know you didn't actually have to run,"
Priscilla drawled. She couldn't quite manage a
disparaging tone as Vivienne reached up in a
loving habit to finger-comb Sidney's curly mop.
"She's not going anywhere."

"He's running from Byron and Tobias," Vera
surmised. "They're hell-bent on some sort of
primitive initiation rite. If they tell you to do oys-
ter shooters, *don't*."

"Fair warning," Priscilla chimed in, "or you'll
wind up in a shipping container bound back for
Mozambique."

"They wouldn't," Vivienne said offhandedly,
though Sidney didn't look entirely convinced
himself.

As for the tour, it went off without a hitch with
both Adrian and Olivia joining in to detail how
their sides of the Bridal Suite worked. And before it was over, Vivienne and Sidney happily
agreed to a wedding on the lawn in front of the
inn, welcoming the collaboration of the Savitts,
Belle Brides, Flora and Tavern of the Graces.

They saved the viewing of the honeymoon
suite for last. Roxie trailed behind as Sidney lifted
Vivienne from her wheelchair and carried her up

the stairs. They took a peek into the room and master bath. On the private balcony, Briar served mimosas and they all sipped their drinks, watching night fall over the Eastern Shore.

It wasn't until after Sidney went to bring the car around to the entrance that Roxie began to see fatigue wavering on the fringes of Vivienne's smile.

"I'm glad I have you alone for a minute," Vivienne said. "There's one more thing you should know before the ceremony. I've been working with a physical therapist. He's a friend. One of the best in the field. He's part of our team. Sidney's the builder. He builds hospitals and easy access points to schools and homes for the disabled. I'm the speaker. I try to motivate those who're disadvantaged and educate their families, friends and communities on their significance. Ike does PT, helping the children, especially, gain strength. He even helps some of them walk again, on their own or with the aid of prosthetics."

"It's incredible what you're doing," Roxie said. "And very brave."

"The people we serve are just like me," Vivienne said modestly. "Every single one of them is vital and strong. They just need someone in their corner to shine a light on them, to help and encourage." She shrugged. "Anyway, Ike and I started working together on the QT after Sid proposed. All the doctors here said I'd never walk again. But if Byron, 'Cilla and I have anything in common, it's that we're stubborn. With Ike's help, in three months I was standing and in a handful of others I took my first steps again."

Roxie's lips parted. "Vivi, that's fantastic!"

"Shh," Vivienne said, lifting a finger to her lips. "No one knows. Not yet. When I walk down the aisle, I want it to be a surprise."

"It'll be the highlight of the night," Roxie told her. "I'm just happy to be a part of it. Thank you so much for taking me on, and the others, too."

"No. *Thank you.* I think it was fate that brought us all together." Vivienne narrowed her eyes. "Do you believe in things like that? Fate and destiny? Byron and 'Cilla think I'm fanciful."

"I…I used to," Roxie admitted. "Either way, we're going to make this every bit the wedding of your dreams."

Vivienne lifted what remained of her mimosa. "Cheers to that." She clinked her flute to Roxie's as her grin turned mischievous. "Now. What do you *really* think of my brother?"

Roxie laughed freely. "I think he's lucky to have a sister like you."

Vivienne's expression changed. Reflective, she breathed the briny air and gazed over the water. "I'm luckier."

"WE CAN MOVE this inside," Roxie offered. She hoped the offer didn't sound too plaintive.

How were they supposed to focus as a group here on the front porch of the Victorian with the men over there playing a spirited bout of basketball on the driveway?

"Give him the elbow, Gerald!" Olivia hollered as Gerald came up on the wrong end of a foul from James. "Bless him. He's too British for basketball."

"Whoop!" Vivienne shrieked, clapping her hands when Sidney intercepted the ball. "You go, hon... Oh." She pressed a hand to the lower half of her face, fighting a laugh when her intended went down under a defensive play from Byron and Cole that won them the ball. "Oh, shoot. That was dirty."

"Byron, stop hogging the damn ball!" Priscilla instructed. She shook her head when her brother answered by charging the goal for an impressive jump shot. "Shouldn't count. Tobias was wide open."

Answer: we aren't *supposed to focus.* Roxie cleared her throat. "Briar. Do you have the menu? We can go over that now."

Even Briar, smooth and businesslike, kept one eye on the game as she shuffled through her papers. *Heaven's sake*, Roxie thought. The wedding was in a week.

"Mm," Briar muttered. "Must've left it in the car."

"I'll get it," Roxie said, rising from the fold-out table where she and the girls had laid out their lists and some refreshments. "Olivia, go over the wine list while I'm gone. Please."

Olivia bit a baby carrot in half. "He's too polite," she mused, still watching Gerald with intent. "That's his problem."

Roxie sighed. She made sure to give the men a rigid glare as she passed by the makeshift court. From what she'd been able to discern as she led the girls through a review of the wedding plans thus far, what had started out as a friendly game of horse had progressed into bragging and trash-talking. Even Constantine had chosen to partake in the contest.

She quickly retrieved the menu from the passenger seat of the truck Briar and Cole had arrived in. Glancing over Briar's notations, she clacked back to the house, making mental notes of her own...

"Heads up, Roxie!" someone shouted from the porch.

The alarm brought her head up just in time to take a blinding sideswipe from a sweaty-T-shirt-clad player.

Down she went tumbling, or crumbling, to the lawn. The weight knocked the breath out of her as he landed solidly on top.

A torrent of running feet beat down on them. Byron's voice thundered down from the melee. "Pop!"

"I'm all right, I'm all right," Constantine said, waving them away as he crawled off Roxie and hunkered in the grass on hands and knees. He eyed Roxie. "You okay, Ms. Honeycutt?"

"I'm fine," Roxie wheezed, peeling herself off the lawn. She brushed the grass from the heels of her hands.

Byron cursed. "Clumsy old man." Then he swooped, scooping her up like something small and fragile.

"I..." Roxie began. Then, "O-oh."

"Is she all right?" Vera asked as she and the girls jogged toward them, Priscilla holding her swollen baby bump firmly in place.

"Out of the way," Byron said, curt, as he cut a swath through them. He wasn't slowing. If anything, he sped up. She could feel the strength in his arms, cupping her shoulders and under her knees. Belatedly, she reached with conservative effort for the hem of her business skirt, smoothing it flush against the back of her thigh. Behind them, she could hear Vera tearing verbal rifts into Constantine and the rest of the players.

Vivienne called out to them, concerned, from her seat on the porch as Byron mounted the steps.

He didn't answer and all but kicked the door in to carry Roxie over the threshold.

It was only after the warmth of the Victorian made her realize how overheated she was that Roxie found her voice again. "Put me down?" she suggested.

"Yeah," he said. But, of course, he didn't. He carried her to the back of the house to her purple settee in the den. He set her there like a vintage dolly, splaying a hand firmly over her middle and taking a good look.

She blinked under the survey. She meant to push his hand away but wound up cupping the back of it instead. Just as she had in the kitchen a week ago.

"What hurts?" he asked, eyes scanning her face, looking for breaks in the skin.

"Nothing," she said truthfully, for she felt nothing. She might've been floating. She couldn't quite say. "Nothing hurts."

"What hurts?" he asked, persistent.

"Nothing!"

"*Don't* lie to me."

"I'm not lying," she said with a touch of affront. She swallowed. Her mouth was dry as dust. Still, he looked unconvinced. "I don't. Lie."

His free hand wrapped gently beneath her chin and tilted her head back so he could scan her more closely, homing in on the eyes.

She went very still. All except her pulse. It careened wildly, out of control, very aware of his proximity. She knew what it was like to have him close. She'd tried very hard not to think about what it was like over the last seven days. Out of respect for the house. Out of respect for his sister whose wedding she should be focusing on. But here he was leaning over her, looking her over, so close she could feel the heat and concern pouring off him, and she wanted him to be closer. So much so that she was afraid her gaze whispered exactly that back to his.

Closer. A little closer.

"What are you doing?" she asked in a voice that sounded almost choked.

He blinked. Finally. "Checking for concussion."

She tried swallowing again. Was she dehydrated? Where was her saliva? "Are...are you sure?"

He blinked again. She saw that there was a red tinge to the skin of his neck again. It rouged when he was angry, she noticed. But he wasn't angry now...

He held her by the chin, under his gaze, until the others rushed as one into the room, a whole wave of them. Even then, he didn't leave her. He folded to the couch next to her. Someone pushed a cool glass of water into her hands. Someone brought her a damp cloth for the potential head injury she hadn't experienced.

Or had she? She felt woozy. Breathless, woozy… Still floating.

"Back off," Byron bit out, waving them away. "Don't hound her. Let the woman breathe."

"You're the one who needs to breathe," Priscilla suggested, eyeing him with a great deal of interest. "Here, you ninny." She took the cloth from Roxie's hand and pushed it at him. "You need this more than she does."

He pushed it back. "Do not."

Vivienne rolled into the scene with Sidney behind her at the handles of her wheelchair. She craned her neck to get a look at her brother and tried to stifle a smile. She failed. "Look. Look how worried he is. Isn't he cute?"

Byron grew rigid next to her. Roxie reached out and placed a hand on his knee. The edge in him had been born out of concern for her. It was quickly warping into irritation—and anger was surely close behind. "It's okay. I'm okay," she announced to the general audience. Everyone was crowded into her living room. The space had never felt so small. Airless. She looked around and found Constantine, leaning on Vera and cradling his ribs. "Did I break *any* of the fall?" she asked, trying for humor.

The man smiled, chuckled. "Why do you think

I'm still standing?" He tilted his head. "More than we can say for my son."

"Okay," Byron said. He rose to his feet, letting her touch slide from his leg. "You've all had your fun?" Turning to her, his eyes circled her features again. He raised his brows. "You sure you're okay?"

No, she thought, fighting her reaction to him—to what worry had done to him. His face was cloaked in perspiration, and not just from the game. *Are* you *going to be?* she wanted to ask. Knowing the question would irritate him further, she simply nodded. When he offered her his hand, she took it and let him bring her to her feet once more. She saw it as a personal victory when she didn't waver there next to him. Brushing her hand along the outer seam of her blouse, she felt a tear in her sleeve. "Oh, no," she said, twisting her arm around to see the damage.

"Can you fix it?" he asked.

Why was his head bent down so close to hers in front of everyone else? Especially when they were both doing their best to convince the lot that there was no spectacle to see here?

"It's a lost cause, I'm afraid," she answered. Her eyes rose halfway to his then fell. She stepped back. "Excuse me," she said to the ladies. "I'll throw something else on. Then we can finish."

"We'll go with you," Olivia said on her heels, with Adrian and Briar behind her.

Roxie moved quickly up to her room, leaving the door open for them. She went into her closet, riffling through the blouses hanging to the left. Scrupulously organized. She wasn't sure she saw even one.

Briar entered and laid a hand on her arm. "Are you sure you're all right?"

Roxie smiled breezily then all but tore a midnight blue number off the hanger. She realized too late the significance behind the color then went against her code by abandoning it on the closet floor. "Constantine might be tall. But he's hardly a linebacker."

"And Byron?" Briar asked.

Roxie heard more than curiosity behind the query. She chose a Kerry-green option this time. She shrugged it on and buttoned it quickly up the front. "I'm sure he'll be all right, too."

"You did see him," Briar noted. "Didn't you?"

How could she stop seeing him? She'd asked the question of herself a number of times since Valentine's Day. She hadn't seen him before that point—not like this. Now she couldn't *stop* seeing him.

It was adding to her confusion. If she truly loved Richard, would she be thinking about someone else this way? Was she angry enough, desperate enough, to want to be close to Byron because she could still feel the hand of betrayal?

Or did she want Byron simply because he was Byron? Moody, peevish, lovely, wonderful Byron?

As always, she fell back to the standard *stop thinking about it. Stop thinking about* him. "The menu," she said as she and Briar reemerged from the closet to join the others. "Let's get on with things and go over the menu."

Briar paused before taking the discarded piece of paper from the pocket of her slacks. "The menu, then." She gave the others a pointed glance before joining Roxie in the trek back down the stairs.

CHAPTER EIGHT

"Byron. Vivi would like to see you."

Byron turned away from the window in the bay-view suite where the groom and groomsmen had been given strict instructions to wait until further notice. His fingers fell away from the cuffs of his sleeves where the cufflinks Sidney had given him were secured. Sid had bought them in Africa, jewel-backed sea turtles. Not exactly Byron's style. But neither was the lavender bow tie he'd struggled with, or the matching striped suspenders. However, it was Sid's day and he'd wear the ensemble without too much complaint.

At the sight of Roxie peering through the door, he asked, "Everything okay?"

She smiled a reassuring smile he was sure every wedding planner learned from day one on the job.

Hers was breathtaking, though. As breathtaking as it had been the day he met her. He could no longer deny or hinder the added stimulating effect it had on him.

"We're on schedule," she said. "The bride's insisting, though."

He glanced to the other side of the room, where Grim was helping Sidney deal with his nerves with a well-concealed bottle of ouzo. Grim gave him a nod. "I'll take care of Sid."

Byron finished fastening the cufflinks and walked to the door. As he moved past Roxie into the hall, he heard her hiss into the room, "One shot each of the contraband then hand it to Father Constantine when he comes 'round. All right, fellas?"

"Yes'm," they muttered apiece and she closed the door.

Byron cleared his throat, fidgeting with his collar. "Heads up. Father Constantine comes with his own set of vittles."

Roxie stepped to him, close in the dimly lit hall. She rose up to the toe of her high heels and fussed with his bow tie. He kept his gaze studiously on her face as she straightened it, lifting his chin to give her better vantage. Trying hard not to imagine burying his face in her hair or touching her in her plum-colored sheath and nude-toned blazer.

When she was done, she dusted off the shoulder of his shirt, smoothed the wrinkles. Clearing her throat, she lowered back to the heels of her shoes and her hands fell pointedly away from him. "Sorry," she muttered. "Habit. Anyway, I heard your dad clinking past me in the hall earlier. Vera and I gave him a joint scolding."

"You and Ma could open a ball-busting business. Hire 'Cilla and Olivia. They could be your enforcers."

Roxie didn't laugh. Lifting a hand to his chest, she looked at him closely. "Tell me how you're holding up, tiger."

"Aren't you supposed to save the 'tigers' for ring bearers?"

"Byron."

He let out a small sigh. "I'm fine. Don't I look fine?"

Wrong question, he realized belatedly as her gaze, round and blue, softened significantly— becoming somehow rounder and bluer as it passed over his features. *Ah, hell,* he thought, swallowing as the hand on his chest lifted, fingers grazing his shirtfront as they fell away. She eyed the buckle of one of his suspenders and assembled a smile. "Very fine... You look pretty dapper, actually."

"I don't know about that," he said, fiddling with the strap that was snug over his left shoulder. "You're sure Vivi's okay?"

Roxie's smile morphed into something meaningful and his heart gave a great yank. "I'll let you see for yourself. This way."

He followed her down the stairs to the first level. The evening was mild for winter. Briar and

Cole had opened the doors and cracked some of the windows of the inn to invite the fresh air inside. Byron heard the hum of activity as the strings of the quartet warmed up and the guests began to trickle toward the tent on the lawn. At the paneled doors to the dining room, where the bridal party was encased, she stopped and asked him, "Ready?"

Byron eyed the doors. He nodded mutely.

Roxie's hand found his as she parted the doors. She tugged him inside, letting them whisper closed behind them. "Vivi," she called. "I found him."

Though the chaos of the bridal party was evident with makeup and garments thrown over every surface, the room was now empty. From the office access on the other side, Vivienne called out, "Okay. I'm ready."

Ready for what? Byron wanted to ask. When Roxie let go of his hand and said, "Wait here," he had to stop himself from reaching out to grasp her again. He watched her go through the door, throwing a wink at him over her shoulder. Trying to prepare himself for the unknown, Byron went to the wide window across the room, twitching back the curtain to get a glimpse of those arriving. It wouldn't be long now.

"By?"

It was Vivienne. He looked away from the window. His hand flattened against the cool pane.

She was standing in the doorway, wearing something long and white. He had a vague notion of her slender silhouette and translucent draping over one shoulder as well as a halo of purple-and-green flowers. All he could really see was Vivienne standing unsupported on her own feet.

She laced her hands together. "Well? What do you think?"

"Viv," he said in a hushed tone. Damn if he hadn't lost his voice. He thought to close his mouth but his jaw muscles had gone slack. The vision of her began to waver and he blinked several times.

Her smile fled and her lips trembled. "Oh, Byron. You can't do that."

"Do what?" He sniffed. *Damn it. Damn it all to hell.*

"You're my Tin Man," she murmured. "You can't..."

He gave a stiff nod, doing his best to even his breathing. "Yeah. Okay." He cursed under his breath. *Oil can.* Lifting his hand and shoulder as one, he asked, "How, uh... How did you—"

"Ike," she said by way of reply. "Everybody said I couldn't do it. There was only one person before him who thought I could and I wanted you to be the first to see." She beamed. "You were right, By."

"Tell 'Cilla that, what you just said."

Vivienne laughed. "I'll tell her." She gestured to the table. "Will you sit with me for a while?"

"Of course," he said and took a step forward to help her.

She held up a hand. "Wait." Glancing back to the office door, she called, "Roxie?"

Byron watched as Roxie came into the room again. She took his sister's elbow. "Slowly," she whispered, guiding her to the closest chair. "Let's not tire your legs out before your walk. Byron, would you be so kind as to pull out a chair?"

He leapt to. Grabbing the chair by the top rail, he slid it out and stood readily by as Roxie helped Vivienne lower herself to the seat. As she knelt to straighten the train and keep it from wrinkling, Byron watched Vivienne's hands smooth the skirt over her lap. "You're going to call me a liar," he told her. He didn't think his voice would ever recover. "But you're the most beautiful frigging bride I've ever seen."

"Oh, poop," Vivienne said though she beamed once more. Roxie smiled, too, as she rose. She took Byron's elbow now, guiding him to the next chair. She pulled it out for him and pointed at it. Vivienne grinned as Byron folded into the seat. "Isn't our Roxie a dream?"

Roxie's hair had fallen over her face, cloaking most of it from view. Byron saw her lips pressed taut together and when her eyes rose to his for a brief second, he saw that the larkspur had gone damp. He fought the urge to pull her down to his lap before she clattered to the door in her heels, talking quietly into an earpiece.

Vivienne's smile bloomed wide when the door closed behind Roxie. "Admitting it's the first step, big brother."

He reached for his tie then stopped himself. "I don't know what you're talking about, baby sister."

She laughed, small. "Fine. I have some things to say to you."

"Warning. Even men in hard metal jackets have their limits."

"Noted," she allowed, dropping her chin in confidante fashion. "How are your knees?"

Byron frowned at them. It was a miracle he hadn't fallen on them when he'd seen her standing there. "They're all right."

"Good." She smiled. "Because, in a few minutes, I'd like you to walk me down the aisle."

His mouth opened but nothing escaped. When he only stared, she spread her fingers on her lap, turning them up to the ceiling. "I've already spoken to Pop. He liked the idea, too."

He racked his brain for an answer. She'd

knocked him senseless. She and Roxie were making an art of it. "I'm honored. But why me?"

"Because I never would have done this without you," she told him. "Because I never would have done any of it without you. I never would have gotten out of bed after the accident if you hadn't told me to and then dragged me out of the covers when I refused. I never would have gotten strong again or moved on with my life, finished school, much less traveled or discovered the thing I was supposed to do with my life. And I definitely never would have met that person I'm supposed to spend the rest of my life with, just like you said I still could. You'll have to tell me how you're always right about things, By."

He shook his head. Something was working at his throat. He couldn't open his mouth until it stopped.

"So…" She sighed and it came out tremulous. Her eyes shined with emotion. "I'll ask again. Will you let me lean on you one last time before I become Mrs. Sidney Hewes?"

"Yes," he said, taking the hand she extended to him. "After I beat myself on the chest and man up a little to the task. But, hey, it doesn't matter what your name is, Viv. You can lean on me from now until the hereafter."

Her fingers gripped his, squeezing. "Okay,

good," she breathed. "Because there's one last thing I need to say to you while we're both still Strongs."

"Oil," he wheezed.

She giggled. "It'll be quick. You know that I love you and I'd never dream of telling you how to live your life, but Ma tells me that you'll be buying the Victorian soon."

"You're okay with that?"

"More than. I always saw you there. Of course, I never saw you there alone."

His good-natured expression fled. "Viv."

"No, let me say this," she said, gripping his hand tight when he would've let go. "When Dani died, it killed me to see you down. It took some time, but then *you* got out of bed. You went back to work. You came here and started over. You walked away from a partnership in the firm in Atlanta and started a new business with Toby. And now you're buying a house again for the first time after Dani…" She trailed off. "Byron, you've been *so* strong. You've moved on in every way. Except one."

"I've moved on," he claimed.

"I don't think so," she disagreed. "I think you've put on a good face, gone on dates, maybe even been intimate with a woman or two, but deep down, I don't think you've really tried to find anyone else."

"Look," he said carefully, "I get that it's your

wedding day. I get the inclination to throw happiness around like confetti. But I'm okay where I am. I swear to you—"

"Don't," she interrupted, gently stern. "You're an open book. I know when you lie. Don't lie to me, By."

He focused on the gold cuff spiraling up her arm from wrist to elbow. It was something borrowed, their mother's. "This is about Roxie, isn't it?"

"You like her," Vivienne surmised. "You really like her."

"I like her," he admitted out loud for the first time. "All right? But she's hung up on someone else. Her ex."

"And if it weren't for him…?" Vivienne asked.

"If it weren't for him," Byron said, taking the cue, "not a lot would've stopped me from trying… well, *trying*." He lifted his shoulders, at a loss. "But she can't help the fact that she still wants him any more than I can help the fact that I've spent the last five years wanting my wife back."

Vivienne stared at him unblinkingly. There was no pity. Just kindness. Just love. "If, in the future, you find somebody else, will you try again?"

"Yes," he said with some reluctance. "I will, for you."

"Not me," she said with a shake of her head. "It should be for yourself and…whoever she is.

She's lucky, so lucky. Roxie doesn't know what she's missing."

Byron cleared his throat, releasing her hand so he could dry his palms on his slacks. "Sid'll be missing you if I don't get you to the altar soon." A quick knock came at the door and he stood. "Shall we?"

CHAPTER NINE

"LOOK AT THEM," Briar said wistfully, nursing a flute of champagne.

"I'm going to have to stop looking at them," Adrian admitted, "before I start blubbering like a baby." She glanced sideways at Roxie. Her eyes widened. "Ah, crap. They broke Roxie."

Something escaped Roxie. A laugh or a sob, something in between. In vain, she tried to reel back the tears into their ducts and away from her makeup. In her white gown, the bride circled one spot on the dance floor slowly, leaning largely on the solid line of her brother. Her cheek was pressed to his lapel. His head was low over hers and shaded. They swayed gently in the protective circle of each other's arms, and Roxie didn't think her heart would survive the last refrain of Dave Matthews's "Sister."

She'd done countless weddings. Her soul had been touched in many ways through the years...

But then there was Byron. She'd watched him walk Vivienne down the aisle, glowing nearly as brightly as she did. And something inside Roxie had cracked when a stunned Sidney overcame his shock and met the pair halfway down the aisle, offering to take his bride the rest of the way. Roxie had watched Byron follow, offering a ready handkerchief to his mother and father in the front row before taking his place at Sidney's back.

The cracks had begun to web when, alongside Priscilla—stalwart Priscilla, who had been weeping openly—he'd bound their hands for the Celtic-style handfasting. *By the knots of these cords your love is united*, they'd spoken together before taking turns reading the blessing itself.

These are the hands, Byron had read alone, *that will comfort you in illness and trials, and share the joy and happiness of life together...*

Roxie's professional composure had fissured well before the start of the reception, when again Vivienne rose to towering applause to share her first dance with her husband, then partake in a father-daughter dance with Constantine and, finally, a dance with Byron.

"Here, honey," Olivia said, handing Roxie her own champagne. "You need this more than I do."

Roxie took it. She sniffed, swiping her fingers as discreetly as possible underneath her eyes as she tipped the bubbly substance to her mouth.

She felt Olivia's pat on the back. "Hell of a wedding."

"Absolutely," Adrian added while Briar simply

pressed her fingers to her lips and gazed out over the dance floor.

"I'm not sure I'm responsible for any of it." Roxie's voice lagged when Byron lifted his cheek from Vivienne's. His head turned slowly and his eyes found her. All the fissures and cracks exploded, leaving nothing behind to shield the light that had been burning behind them unbeknownst to her. She sucked in a breath, stunned at the aching.

Oh, God, what do I do about this? What do I do about this man and the way I feel about him?

All three girls looked from Byron to Roxie. Adrian smiled and went back to sipping her champagne. Olivia raised a brow and exchanged perceptive glances with Briar. None of them said a word, though, and Roxie couldn't look away as Byron's mouth tipped into a rueful smile. He lifted his shoulder the slightest inch, a helpless posture that made her own smile bloom. She shook with quiet laughter and felt it color and warm her cheeks.

Briar cleared her throat. "You should cue the band." When Roxie looked at her, blank, she said, "For toasts."

Roxie snapped to. "Yes. Yes, of course." She searched for a place to set her glass.

Adrian took it. "I've got it."

She handed the glass back to Olivia, who told

Roxie plainly, "Don't worry. You'll get your cake later." She smirked.

Roxie's lips turned inward and she shook her head at Olivia's throwback to Byron's man-cakes. Still, she said nothing as she walked away, unsure how to shrug off the speculation when she was as translucent as the Cristal buzzing through her system.

As the reception wore on, she milled between various stations and tables while keeping tabs on the happy couple. She let Vivienne and Sidney linger with each other and their guests as the party swung on into the night, guiding them gradually from the toasts to the cake cutting. She made sure Vivienne had a plate of food from the banquet tables, assigning Constantine to supply his new son-in-law with one, too. It was her job to ensure that everyone was enjoying themselves. With the Strongs at the celebration helm, that was an easy feat.

Midway through the reception, she caught the ring bearer leading the flower girl by the hand from the garden, where she'd scraped her knee. Roxie took them both into the inn's kitchen and sat the girl on the stool, wiped away the blood and talked to both in happy tones as she applied a bandage from her emergency kit. She was leading them back through the screen door when she saw Byron coming toward the house. He found her and his eyes stopped roving. *Looking for me, hmm?* she mused, squeezing the flower girl's hand before sending her off to her mother.

"Trouble?" he asked as the children capered off.

"Nothing an Olaf Band-Aid couldn't fix," Roxie explained.

He held out his hand for hers. "Come on," he said when she stared. "There's someone who wants to meet you."

She lifted her hand to his. He kept it there as they meandered through the crowd on the fringes of the dance floor. Vivienne had declared that even if she could only stand up for three dances there would be nonstop dancing at her wedding. The lively band and guests weren't disappointing her.

Cole and James had put several sofas on various parts of the lawn near the space heaters designed for comfort against the cool night air. Byron led her to a plush green antique sofa where Vivienne had parked her wheelchair and was sitting next to a woman late in years. A faux-fur blanket covered both their laps and they were speaking in secretive tones, hands clasped. Byron let go of Roxie's hand as they neared. "Athena?"

The woman's fond smile was like a joyous whisper. "Byron." She gripped his wrist and cast a curious glance at Roxie. "Did you bring her?"

"This is Roxie Honeycutt," Byron confirmed. "Roxie, this is the goddess Athena."

As Athena bade her to come closer, Roxie knelt before the sofa and took Athena's crepe-skinned hands. "Your family speaks of you so often, I was hoping to get a chance to meet you in person."

Athena studied her face, not as judge or jury, but with all the wisdom of a lifetime and perhaps something more sentient. Goose bumps sprung along Roxie's arms as Athena made her quiet verdict. She looked to Byron and said something unintelligible.

"Oh, my," Vivienne purred, grinning widely at her brother and Roxie in turn.

"Greek?" Roxie guessed.

Byron shook his head. "Senile."

Athena tutted at him as Vivienne belted a laugh. The older woman didn't let go of Roxie's hands. "My great-nephew tells me you are living in the Victorian."

"Yes," Roxie nodded. "It's a spectacular home—"

"Is he treating you well?" Athena asked.

Roxie cut her eyes to Byron, a sly conspiratorial grin pulling at her mouth. "He has his moments."

"Avoid him in the mornings," Vivienne suggested. "He's Henry VIII until he gets a shot or two of espresso. Before that point, he'll say snarky things in Greek that would normally doom him to Hades."

"So he *does* know Greek," Roxie realized. "I wondered."

"Of course," Athena said. "He spent a summer on Santorini, where my sister and I lived. She and I came to America at the same time, but she never applied herself to English."

"Mm, that's because Grandpa Strong never spoke anything but French with her," Byron noted, his statement laden with accusation. "She lived with us for a while after he died, when I was younger."

"Taught you much Greek, didn't Fillipa?" Athena said.

"Except how to say... What was it?" Roxie asked Byron. "What your father called your mother the other day."

Vivienne gasped. *"Matia mou?"*

"Yes!" Roxie said. "Vera melted into a puddle when he said it. It melted me a little, too. I asked Byron what it meant..."

Athena frowned. "And he told you he did not know," she said, turning to him for answers instead of Roxie.

When Roxie, too, frowned at him, Byron shifted on the spot. "It's just a phrase. A common endearment."

"Common endearment," Athena muttered. She waved her hand from Byron to Roxie. "Tell her, Byron. Tell Roxie what it means."

He sighed then faced Roxie fully and admitted, *"Matia mou* means 'my eyes.'"

"Oh," she breathed.

Athena leaned forward to explain. "It means romance. Something only lovers say to one another." She pressed a hand to her heart. "You understand?"

"Yes."

"It's kind of like being called 'precious,'" Vivienne pointed out. "Because sight is precious. Right, Athena?"

"Exactly, Vivienne. Exactly."

"It doesn't mean what it used to." When both his great-aunt and sister frowned at him again, Byron said, "It doesn't. It's too familiar now. A girl sold me a map on the roadside in Messaria and called me *matia*."

Athena scoffed. "In my day, it meant something. The first time Ari Papadakis called me *matia mou*, I knew what he was really saying was 'I love you, Athena Maragos. I want you here with me in this life in America.' And so I stayed. I stayed with him, for all the time we had left."

"Athena," Byron murmured, bending to the arm of the couch. He put his arm around her shoulders as her bottom lip quavered and she lowered her face. Tenderly, he touched the top of her head. "I'm sorry." He pulled her to him. "Come here, Auntie. You know I didn't mean to upset you."

Vivienne stroked her arm. "No, no, he didn't mean it, Auntie. I know he didn't."

Athena breathed carefully into Byron's shirt for a moment before she straightened, fluttering her hands at the fuss. She stopped when Roxie offered her an embroidered hanky. "Thank you," she said sincerely. She dabbed her eyes. Then she looked at Byron. "Look at you, Byron Atticus. Look at your face." She reached for him, patting his chin and clucking maternally. "It's all right, *paidi mou*. Auntie's all right."

"I'm sorry," he said again, raising her hand to his lips for a kiss. "Forgive me."

Athena offered him a good-natured chuckle and waved the hanky like a flag. "The way you speak sometimes…so offhand. So cynical, so male. It's like Ari's speaking to me all over again. It's why it gets under my skin." Dipping her chin, she added a significant "We know how people get under our skin, Byron, no?"

He smiled and lied, "No. Athena, tell me what to do for you. I'll do anything you need me to do."

"Ask Roxie to dance. It will do me good to see you two dance."

"It will, huh?" Byron asked.

Roxie's pulse did a funny pirouette as he looked to her, debating. To ask a woman to dance at a wedding—a woman who wasn't his sister—was he ready for that? Was Roxie ready to be that woman?

She was afraid she wanted to be. Very much

afraid. Standing and brushing off her knees, she said, "I'd love nothing more than to dance. But I'm afraid I need to steal Vivi for the bouquet toss." Gripping Athena's fragile fingers once more, she added, "It was lovely to meet you, Athena, finally."

"Bless you, child," Athena said, patting the back of Roxie's hand. "We'll meet again. Until that time, don't let Byron here give you too much grief. If he does, you come see me."

"Most definitely," she said with a wink, narrowing her eyes on Byron in mock suspicion.

He smiled back with a softness that betrayed that light inside her again.

BYRON SPENT THE rest of the night debating with himself. As the reception rolled on into the late night, he danced with Priscilla. He danced with his mother. He saw Athena off with his father soon after Vivienne and Sidney's exit to the honeymoon suite. The band had packed up and left, leaving an iPod playlist for everyone who lingered and the cleanup that followed. Grim insisted on taking a resistant Priscilla home because she was sore and tired. Byron stayed with his mother, the Savitts, Roxie and her few hired helpers to break down the tent, tables, and chairs and pack up everything else.

The music played all the while and his periph-

ery was involuntarily tuned to Roxie's movements.

It was soon after midnight when he'd finished
taking three trash bags to the parking lot, where
he and Cole had loaded them into the bed of his
truck to be hauled off the next morning. He looked
around. He didn't see Roxie buzzing around like
the bee she'd been for the last ten hours.

He felt a tap on his shoulder and found Briar
behind him. "Down by the water," she indicated.
Her hands were full of platters, so she nodded toward the shore.

Byron looked and saw Roxie's slender silhouette close to the dock. Briar began to walk back
to the kitchen door. He stopped her. "Let me help
you with those."

"No, I've got it," she assured him. "She might
need some help, though."

He caught the knowing gleam. Vivienne was
right when she'd called him an open book. He'd
figure out what to do about that later. Sucking it
up, he walked to the water.

Roxie carried a trash bag and a prod and was
combing the shoreline for discarded plates. She'd
taken off her heels and was walking tippy-toe
across the sand, moving with uncommon grace
on the uneven ground.

The music changed. From "Boogie Shoes" to
something slow and brooding. A sign.

Since when did he believe in signs?

So cynical...

I heard that, Athena, he thought. Taking his cues from his great-aunt and Ed Sheeran, Byron stopped hovering in the shadows. "Almost done for the night?" he asked, sidestepping a large rock smoothed by years of bay tide.

Her head snapped around and she stopped what she was doing. "Almost. I thought you'd gone home." When he shook his head, she added, "Byron, I appreciate your help tonight. You didn't have to stay."

"Yeah, I did," he replied.

"That breeding of yours," she said with a shake of her head as she went back to picking up waste.

Byron mused that it wasn't so much his breeding this time. "You got a minute?"

"Just that. We still have to get the speakers in. There's a rainstorm coming tomorrow. And the sofas, too."

"Cole and the rest of the guys said they'd take care of that." For the second time that night, he held out his hand to her.

She stared at his fingers.

"I can understand your confusion, but this is me asking you to dance, duchess. I owe you one."

Her eyes widened. He could see them even in the dark. Her head began to shake. "You don't have to—"

"I've gone over it in my head through most of the evening," he informed her. "And, as it turns out, I do."

"You *want* to dance with me?" she asked skeptically. "This isn't just about Athena?"

"You're a hard sell." When she tilted her head, he released a breath. "Yes. I want to dance with you."

Finally he saw the corners of her lips twitch in amusement. "Did that hurt?"

He thought about it for a split second before taking the bag and prod. "Surprisingly, no."

"Oh," she said as he set the items aside. She rubbed her palms on the hips of her dress in a nervous motion before taking the hand he was holding out again.

Tugging, he coaxed her out of the sand onto the dock. Without the aid of her heels, she could've laid her head comfortably on his breastbone, he realized as he drew her close enough to slide his arm around her waist, fitting it in the exact spot he had the last time he'd kissed her. She draped her arm over his shoulder and, as one, they clasped hands, raised them and began to sway in the night.

As if on cue, the lights on the inn facade, and those that had been put up for the event, flickered out. All that remained were the twinkly lights from Briar's garden, the stars and the lights of Mobile on the far side of the bay. The music remained, as well. Had it not, the whisper of waves might've been enough to dance by. As the water rolled into the sand beneath the planks below their feet, it was as rhythmic and lulling as any tune.

They said nothing for a minute. Two. Until he let go with one hand. She stepped back briefly, paused before he brought her back against him and they circled some more.

"Not bad," she murmured.

"I didn't say I couldn't dance. I only said I didn't."

Roxie licked her lips. "About the *matia mou* thing…"

"Yeah?"

"Is that what you called her?" she asked. "Dani?"

His brows came together. "No."

"What did you call her?"

The quicksilver jet of a falling star caught his eye. "'Spanish eyes,'" he said clearly. "Dani was always 'Spanish eyes.'"

Roxie smiled as she turned her face into the lavender boutonniere Adrian had fastened to one of Byron's suspender straps. "You're not going to tell me what your auntie said about me, are you?"

Athena's words came back to him. He let out a half laugh. "I'll tell you she's a piece of work."

"Was it good at least?"

You two would have siren children. Now what are you going to do about it, nephew? "My

Greek's a little rusty," he claimed, "but I'm pretty sure she likes you better than me."

"That couldn't possibly be true." The smile melted away by gradual degrees before she asked, almost whispering, "What happened to Vivi?"

He'd known she would ask. He answered readily, staring over her head at the Fairhope Pier visible in the distance. "Bicycle accident. A drunk driver went off the road and clipped her. She was nine."

Her grip on his shoulder tightened. "My God, Byron."

"Yeah, when some intoxicated jack-hole breaks your sister's spinal cord, you get angry," he acknowledged. "Instead of wrestling with the anger like I did when I was younger, I decided to channel it into something constructive. So I dropped my accounting major and went to law school."

"That's why you became a lawyer," she said, comprehending. "Will she and Sidney ever be able to…?"

"Have a family?" he asked when she couldn't. At her nod, his face hardened. He gave the tension a moment to fall away. Regret and more than a little anguish stirred in its wake. "Not by traditional means, no."

"Vivi's wonderful. They're all so wonderful. I'm so glad you asked me to do this."

"Vivi's the best of us," Byron told her. "She's

the strongest. And you made my sister happy tonight. You made my whole family happy. I'm
grateful, Rox."

Her smile returned, feather-soft and true.
"You're softening me up so you don't have to
waltz or wear a cummerbund at my sister's wedding."

"I wasn't," he said, "but since you're the one
who brought it up, how 'bout it?"

She deliberated as they swayed some more.
"Perhaps." She touched the tip of her nose to the
lavender, smelling it. Her cheek came to rest on
his chest, right where he thought it would. Too
close to his heart, he pondered.

Ed stopped crooning. Silence trickled over
the landscape, then the familiar notes of a Marvin Gaye song convened. Byron stopped circling
abruptly as Roxie stiffened. She was the first to
let go, reaching up for her hair. "Ah…" she said,
her gaze skimming up to his and away. "And here
I'd thought Liv had gone home."

"Olivia's here?"

She shook her head, flustered. "Never mind."
She stared at a button on his shirtfront. "I guess
I'll finish cleaning up down here."

"No. You go on up to the inn and regroup with
the others." When she refused, he said, "Go in,
Roxie. You're cold."

"I am?" Her arms crossed over her chest. "I

am," she said. Her hands skimmed her arms, up and down. "My blazer…"

"You took it off." He'd noticed. He fought the urge to warm her himself. He could think of four or five ways to manage it, none of which were technically legal in a public venue. "It's on the banquet table."

"You're sure—"

"Go, duchess," he said, not looking at her so much now. He sounded stern, but, damn it, even men accused of gentlemanly behavior had only so much self-control.

She waited a beat, then, "Okay. Good night, Byron."

"'Night." As he watched her bend to grab her heels from the grassy hill, he repeated what he'd told Vivienne before the ceremony. That she belonged to somebody else. That, regardless of where she stood with Richard—the pissant—she didn't feel the same way Byron did. Letting the cold seep in, he waited until she'd found her blazer and was at the inn door before he picked up the bag and finished what she'd started.

A DAY OFF was rare during wedding season, particularly during weekends. Since spring would be starting in a handful of weeks, Roxie decided to do something she rarely did and take the next day, Sunday, for herself. She got up early, as always, brewed tea and took it out onto the patio with a blanket to watch the wind stir the Japanese magnolia. Back indoors, she put three fat pink blossoms in a bowl of water where they could float face-up. She ate avocado on toast before padding back upstairs. She put on work clothes and tied her hair back with a patterned handkerchief.

She'd set the paint cans by the back door. She rolled out covers for the floors and furniture, pulled the furnishings away from the walls and pulled a ladder from storage. She fixed painter's tape along the edges of the room and windowsills. Music flowed from the speaker on the coffee table as she began to paint the den of the Victorian the eggplant shade Vera had personally okayed.

It was one more step in making the house feel like hers, Roxie had thought. She'd painted the rooms of her and Richard's French Colonial, one by one, with infinite care, selecting the various hues throughout the house meticulously. There was something therapeutic about painting a room, she'd learned through the experience. It was often a slow, delicate process, but it helped her balance and center.

Roxie had wanted to wait until after Georgiana's wedding to start painting the Victorian, until her sister and mother stopped blowing up her phone. Until the stress of the family event was behind her. However, as wonderful as Vivienne and Sidney's wedding had been, it had forced her to confront one big truth.

She didn't know what she wanted anymore. Had she ever known? Would she have ever questioned it if she had?

Byron in his suspenders, leaning over his aunt, caring for his sisters, dancing with his mother… She couldn't get the images out of her mind. They'd followed her home. They'd stayed with her as she drifted off to sleep, visiting her in dreams. She'd woken up with him on her mind, unable to shake him. Not wanting to shake him.

What do you want, Roxie? She mulled the question as Ella and Satchmo crooned together about dancing cheek to cheek and her painter's brush cut in what the roller had missed.

She was balancing on top of the ladder to finish work around the first transom when a knock clattered against the door. She'd opened the windows to let the paint fumes out and the freshness of the midmorning in. Setting her brush on top of the bucket, she glanced at her hands. She picked up a cloth, then descended the ladder and made her way to the front door. She rubbed her hands as dry as she could make them, then swung the door open.

"Roxie," Richard greeted. He began to offer her a smile then stopped when he saw her paint-flecked outfit. "You're busy."

"No," she said automatically. She gripped the door and tried to collect herself. "I—" Dear God, it was him. He looked rested and relaxed, even trim. He'd barely had time to maintain his medium build over the last few years. He usually wore tweed jackets and khaki pants and the same pair of eyeglasses—rimless, rectangular and titanium.

The glasses were the same but the cut of his hair was a touch different, more stylish. His oxford shirt was untucked from his khakis, no jacket, and sneakers covered his feet instead of the usual loafers.

His eyes were brown and intelligent. Never acerbic, they carried with them a tinge of boredom even when he was engaged in in-depth conversation. His was the male equivalent of resting bitch-face. He smiled quietly, but it was hard to make him laugh. She was one of the few who could.

Or she *had* been in the early years when such things were more natural.

He was attractive. She'd always thought him so. But now he looked as he had when she'd first met him—his laser focus intent on her instead of ungraded papers, lectures or case notes…

Roxie took a breath. "When did you get back?" she asked, trying for an easy tone. It sounded more like rain boots plodding egg shells.

He offered a quick nod, moving his hands into the pockets of his slacks. "This morning. I came straight here."

"You did?" she asked, surprised.

"Well, yes," he said. "My father said you needed to speak with me. My retreat ended yesterday. I would've left sooner but the place was up in the mountains and there's no way to get down without a shuttle."

"Oh." She caught herself shifting onto the balls of her feet. "You're...you're different somehow."

"Good. That was the intent when I left." When she only stared at him, blank, he asked, "May I come inside?"

She hadn't asked him, she realized. In fact, she stood with her feet planted on the entry rug. As if guarding the threshold.

She frowned. She hadn't wanted Bertie to come upstairs to her place above the tavern. It had felt... wrong. Similarly, she didn't want Richard inside the Victorian. Numerous people had made themselves at home since she moved in. Constantine and Vera. Briar, Adrian, Olivia, their husbands, their children... Her mother had forced her way in a time or two.

Byron had been in and out daily with the gym downstairs and his Perseus-like gestures— "rescuing" her from the lawn, playing doctor on her settee...

She licked her lips, wondering over her hesitation. She couldn't let Richard in. Not yet. Clearing her throat, she said, "It's a bit of a mess. I'm a mess." She passed a hand over the handkerchief knotted on her head. "Why don't we meet somewhere later?"

"For dinner." Richard nodded. "We could go to that place in Montrose. The one we both like so much."

Again, she hesitated, frozen by indecision. Why did she feel so cold?

"It *is* still there," Richard said. "Isn't it?"

Roxie snapped to. "Yes. Yes, of course." She lifted her shoulders. "I suppose it's a date."

"I'll pick you up."

"No," she said with a shake of her head. "I'll meet you there. Around six?"

Richard's shoulders moved as a puzzled frown touched his features. "A little early for dinner, but it's your call. Six. See you there?" he added, obviously a bit unsure about the formality of meeting her. He took a moment, lingering. His gaze touched her face, admiring. "It's good to see you. I'm…I'm happy to see you."

He'd never been good at expressing things verbally. Knowing how much it had likely taken for him to drum up the words, she offered him a kind smile. "I'll see you later." The four words held all the promise she could give.

He seemed to seek more as he searched her, silent. Then he backed away, turned and walked down the front steps.

She waited until he was in his car and out of the driveway before she closed the door. Resting her hand on its warm wood, she did her best to sort some clarity from her emotions. She'd done it. She'd seen him again. How did she feel about it? How would she feel going forward, starting with dinner? A formal dinner at their favorite restaurant.

The confusion was still as heavy as ever. She squeezed her eyes closed, looking inward. Looking hard. Nothing lifted. Nothing lightened. It was just...blank uncertainty.

Sighing, she pushed away from the jamb, hoping after dinner tonight she'd know what she wanted at last.

CHAPTER TEN

"SO YOU'VE BEEN COOKING." Richard's mouth smoothed into a wide grin, amused, as he forked a bite of his blackened salmon entrée. "Really cooking."

"Well, baking mostly," Roxie admitted, shrugging one shoulder. She felt a bit easier here in the familiar setting. On even turf. At the table they'd always reserved. It overlooked the restaurant's portico with its orange-spiked birds-of-paradise and tropical palms. In summer, there were honeybees there buzzing lackadaisically from flower to flower.

"In an apron," Richard surmised, laughing at the mental image.

"Well, yes," Roxie said. "Though it doesn't stop me from making torrential messes. Baking involves flour. Lots of flour. I haven't figured out how to contain it."

"How've the results been?" he asked, his interest genuine.

"The reviews have been fairly positive," she said, still surprised at that. "Briar's my chief tes-

ter. Though I've had Kyle stop by on several oc-
casions with Gavin, claiming to be victims of
starvation."

"Young Kyle," Richard mused. "How are
they—the girls? Their families?"

"Expanding by the minute," Roxie noted. "It's
nice, having a front-row seat to it all." She didn't
bring up the fact that for a while after the divorce,
a great chunk of her enjoyment in witnessing her
friends' lives unfold had been stolen. And she'd
resented him for that. Bitterly. She went back to
picking at her choice pork chop with lemon vinai-
grette. It was a fine meal served on a bed of baby
arugula. A shame she couldn't seem to get it to
her mouth. "This…retreat," she said, changing
the subject. "What was that about?"

He raised a brow. "I know. It doesn't sound like
me at all, does it?" There was something different
about him. Relaxed. Seeing Richard truly relax
had become a rare thing as the years stretched
from the cusp of their relationship to its scorched
ending. "I was resistant when my parents offered
to send me there over Christmas. Then I got there
and… The mountains. You wouldn't believe them.
They set me at ease in a way that nothing else has
in…" He stopped when her face fell and she went
back to cutting her meat into bite-size pieces.
Dropping his fork, he scanned the other diners
in the room, reaching for his water glass. "I'm

wondering what the pool is," he said, lowering his voice discreetly.

"On what?" she asked.

"On how long it'd take me to say exactly the wrong thing," Richard said. He took a long drink.

Roxie scanned him closely. He looked disgusted with himself. He set the water glass down evenly on the table and picked up his fork again, composed, but because she knew him, she could see the faint line etched at his brow.

Richard had always been hardest on one person: himself. Nothing had changed. Sitting back in her chair, Roxie lifted her wine and crossed one arm over her chest. "If there's a pool on you then there's probably one on me, too."

"On how long it takes you to slap me across the face?"

"More likely how long it takes me to burst into tears and weep like the wronged female I am." She shook her head. "It's a small town. People talk, often without subtlety or decent regard. If I minded, I'd have left last summer."

"Yes, but you're tougher than I am," Richard said, the faint flicker of a smile tugging at his mouth. "You've always been."

She didn't think she'd ever heard herself characterized as *tough*. She didn't feel tough and wondered if she ever had.

The waiter chose that moment to approach their table. "More wine, Mrs. Levy?"

Richard cleared his throat as Roxie stared blankly at the man. "Uh, that's fine, Wayne."

Roxie sat still as her glass was filled once more. Rubbing her lips together, she realized that her fine meal would be going to waste after all. She waved the plate away when Wayne gestured to it. "May I offer a dessert course this evening?" he asked pleasantly.

Richard looked to Roxie hopefully. His chances seemed ridiculously hinged on her appetite for sweets.

She studied the dessert card, once again uncertain. Whenever she refused dessert in the past, he knew it meant she was either sick or...well, *sick*. She didn't turn down sweets, as a rule.

Though she did feel a mite sick. Wasn't it telling, what being called by her married name could do to her?

She looked to Wayne and said, "I'll take a slice of the French silk pie to go, please."

"To go?" he said, taken aback.

"Yes," she said decidedly, taking the napkin off her lap. She set it on the table where her plate had been. "To go."

ROXIE INVITED RICHARD IN. The Victorian was dark and silent. She switched on a lamp as he roamed from the den to the kitchen, viewing her single living arrangements.

His nerves were no longer well hidden beneath his newfound ease. A pity. Over dinner, she'd nearly grown to envy it. Even now in her safe zone, she felt as strung as a sail stretched too thinly against the wind, and she didn't like it. Not here.

She invited him out to the back porch, away from the paint fumes. Away from the rooms she'd come to think of as her own. Outside it was just the wintered yard, the breeze in the high boughs of the magnolia, and Richard sitting next to her on the patio bench. She'd made tea out of habit, arranged cups and a plate of cheese straws on a tray before seeking the outdoors.

Unable to take another moment of the strained silence that had lurked, hardly broken, since dinner, Roxie asked, "What's changed, Richard?" When he glanced sideways at her, she shrugged. "I mean, besides the hair. You're more relaxed. Or you were before dinner took a turn there. You turned some sort of corner in the mountains. What was it about them that brought you back to where you need to be?" *What did you find there that you had so much trouble finding here—with me?*

That was the real question.

He set his tea in its saucer and his eyes narrowed

as he sat back in his chair. "Well, at the retreat there was this guru…" He stopped and nodded when she frowned. "Crazy, I know. I was doubtful of him at first. But it wasn't long into the retreat when he helped me see things in a new light. He helped me see me. I struggled with what happened last year. The divorce. Everything that led up to it. In the fallout, I tried to understand why I behaved that way. What kind of a newlywed strays? What kind of a man hurts the kind of woman most others dream of having?"

Roxie looked away. Maybe silence *was* better. Ignorance could be bliss.

She wasn't going to move forward, however, unless she had all the answers she needed. And she refused to stay stuck in the same conflicted place she'd been living for the past year. "What did you learn?" she asked cautiously, reaching for another cheese straw.

"That I'm a man of many faults," Richard said slowly, "and that I want to fix my mistakes."

Her mind seized on the words. Wasn't this what she'd been waiting for? "How?" she asked, measuring him and herself with care.

"You never allowed me to apologize to you before, formally."

"Richard." She shook her head. "I think enough time has passed where we can skip the formalities and get straight to the point."

He seemed to stumble a bit over her blunt delivery. "Can I ask if there's any way you can ever forgive me?"

A strong man asking for forgiveness in a sincere manner was a powerful weapon. But she'd seen him at his lowest and, try as she might, parts of her couldn't get beyond it. "I've thought about it."

As she trailed off, he turned his body toward hers and said, "What happened with Cassandra was a mistake. A terrible, terrible mistake. I hope you know that."

"Why?" Swallowing past the lump in her throat, she forced herself to ask again. "You said this guru helped you see, and I need help understanding. Why did you do it? Cassandra said you two were communicating beforehand and that you had seen each other at a conference. Did you have...feelings for her?"

"No," he said with a shake of his head. Then he stopped. Something ticked over his face, as if he were checking himself. He started again. "Well, perhaps there were some feelings, but I didn't know what they were until she and I had..."

Roxie nodded away the rest.

"So, could you ever forgive me?" he asked.

"I'm not sure," she told him. "Whatever happens between us from this day forward, I'm not going to forget it. I have to live with it."

"I know you do," he said. "I'm sorry. Seeing you standing there…your expression. I swear it felt like taking a bullet."

"Well, finding you there," Roxie said, considering, "that was like taking the whole clip." She scrubbed her hands over her face. "You were my safety net. You, our relationship, were the only truly normal things I had in my whole life. Did you know that? Did you know that I believed if there was anything in this world I could count on, it was you? Then, there you were with her." Rising, she began to pace. She was on the verge of raising her voice and yelling, and she didn't want to yell. Yelling had only ever made her uncomfortable. Or it had made *him* uncomfortable… "I gave *us* every part of myself there was to give."

His hands hung between his thighs and he lowered his head, ashamed. "I know. I know."

"So explain this to me," she went on. "Were you giving your whole self or were you just pretending? Was I too blind to see that our relationship was a one-way street?"

"No, it wasn't," he said, rising, too. "Roxie, I love you. I loved you then. I love you now."

"Then *why*?" Dear God, she was yelling. They'd been together for years, close to a decade, and she'd never yelled at him. Raising her voice, venting her frustration…it felt like a giant release valve rupturing after long neglect. By God, why hadn't she done this sooner? "Was it because we didn't fight the way other people do? Was it because the wedding got too big when you wanted it small? Was it me—did I not excite you anymore? Tell me!"

"I was afraid," he said simply, holding his arms out in a gesture of helplessness that disarmed her.

She'd never seen him helpless. "Of what?"

He took several breaths to center himself. Ever the calm one, he answered with equanimity. "Because for a while, nothing seemed like enough. I didn't feel anything for my work anymore. I couldn't bring myself to feel enough about fixing up the house. Or the wedding."

"Or us?" she prompted.

"It scared me," he said, "so badly. When you get married, it should be easy to feel excitement, but I couldn't seem to drum up the energy. I was depressed. Severely depressed. And when I should've sought help, when I should've told you, I shut you out. I shut everything out so that I could deal with the problem alone. But that only compounded the problem."

"You should have told me," she agreed. She thought of what she needed to ask next and felt sick once more. She had to force herself. "When... when Cassandra came to the house that day..." His gaze snagged on hers. There was still guilt there—and a great deal of shame. "When you held her and kissed her and...*undressed* her, what did you feel?"

Richard couldn't bring himself to answer. Roxie stood looking at him—a smaller version of him—feeling like a smaller version of herself. Cupping her hands over her nose and mouth, she walked across the cool grass in her bare feet, wishing she knew how to center herself as skillfully as he had learned to. She went up on her tiptoes, *relevé*, and picked her way through the lawn *en pointe*, concentrating on the straightness of the leg, the placement of the knee over the ankle, the hip over the knee.

The exercise was futile. The turmoil, the restlessness, continued to churn and roil and she couldn't release it as she had released the anger. Pivoting back to Richard, *en face*, she banished the years of training to the back of her mind and summoned her courage. "You know what I've realized over the past few weeks? I don't want to wait to be happy. I was happy with you. I was happy with my work. Only sometimes it felt like there was only one ball instead of two and I had to choose which court to put it in—home or work. But, damn it, I juggled because I loved both and I wasn't going to let either fail. And then, when I moved here, I realized that I couldn't remember the last time I was completely happy with everything. Can you?"

Richard frowned at her, at a loss.

"Why do you want to fight for us?" she asked. "You know it's going to be work—hard, grueling, emotional work, day in and day out until we get it right again. Is it really worth it to you?"

"I need to make things right with you," Richard told her. "I want to make things right."

"Will it make you happy, though?" she asked. "If we fall back into it, if we do right by each other, will that make you happy or are you just standing on principal?"

"I just need to make you happy again," he stated.

"This whole thing started because you forgot what it was to indulge your own happiness. Who're you doing this for now? Me or you? If it's not for both of us, then we shouldn't even be having this conversation."

"We can be happy," he asserted. "I don't know how long it will take, but I know we can both be happy again."

Her lips parted. With realization came sudden hope. "What if I want to be happy right now?"

"You can do that?"

She smiled because she didn't need three months in the mountains and a guru to tell her so.

She just needed a chance neighbor, as wise as he was Greek. She just needed the escape of this old house on Serendipity where there was room to breathe, think, and pace and to confront herself and her feelings. She just needed to yell at the man who had betrayed her, no matter how many calm, civilized years they'd spent together in their French Colonial.

The smile came fast and true, miraculous in itself. "I think I can. Not only that, I think it's what I deserve. I deserve to be happy. Right now."

Both of Richard's brows arched. Lines appeared in his brow, betraying a hint of his old skepticism. "Is that realistic?"

"If it isn't realistic, it should be," she said. "Can't it ever just be simple?"

"I don't know. I always thought if there was anything worth having, you had to work for it. Like us. But what you're telling me, I think, is that you don't want to work. You don't want to try."

"I love work," she told him. "You know that. If I wasn't a trier, I never would've left New York. I never would've given up the life my mother envisioned for me. I never would have considered for a moment that I was wrong in divorcing you. It was Cassandra, believe it or not, who made me question my motives."

"Cassandra?"

"She said something to me about her and Jefferson. They don't love each other anymore but they fear failure more than they fear unhappiness. And here you are telling me you need to make things right. Not that you want to. That you *need* to."

"Is there a difference?"

"Yes!" she shrieked, balling her hands around handfuls of her hair. "Yes, there is a huge difference, Richard! It's the difference between the brain and the soul. It's *obligation* versus *desire*. It's…it's…" She heard the words in her head and they were Byron's. "Oh, my God. It *is* apples and oranges." Clapping her hand over the lower half of her face again, she felt a wavering laugh chase through her. Could the truth really have been so simple all along?

It was Vivienne who'd been on point when she asked Byron at the wedding how he was always right.

Richard winced at the cliché. He stepped back to the bench and folded onto it.

It was then that Roxie began to see what coming here had cost him. The veneer was gone and behind it was a crestfallen man—a man she'd once loved. She found her feet moving toward him and her touch gliding across his arm in a pacifying caress. "I've spent the last two months wishing there was some way that the pieces of us that are left could amount to what we had before. But I can't make myself go back. I can only move forward."

"It's human nature, I suppose." Sliding his

glasses from his nose, he lifted the corner of his shirt.

"Let me," she whispered, taking them delicately. She used the edge of her sweater to clean the lenses, letting him collect himself. He'd come here for her. It had been honorable. Even in light of his betrayal, she could see that. Just as she could see that part of him still loved her and clung to her as she had clung to the idea of him.

But what good was an idea when you needed the tangible? What good was a half when you needed the whole, and perhaps a bit more after that? A touch of the extraordinary.

In habit, she placed the glasses back on his face and watched him lift a finger to push them against the bridge of his nose. He looked through them at her and took her hand, holding her fingers gently. "The loss is mine, and it's a big one. You're right, of course. Maybe it did start before Cassandra. Maybe I've never known how to balance passion and stability. To me, they've always seemed like two sides of a coin."

"They are," she mused. "They're opposites, but they're two halves of the same whole. Without the other, they don't amount to much. I think that's the best recipe for marriage, don't you?"

He nodded. Squeezing her hand, he asked, "Would you be okay walking me out?"

Yes, she would be okay. It was a startling

conclusion and the best closure she could have wished for.

As they left the tea and cheese straws on the patio and walked back through the house, the fatigue hit her. She had spent weeks questioning, trying to figure out what the best course of action would be concerning him. She'd thought until she couldn't think anymore, doubting herself, her own mind and heart. Now it was all over. At last. She was relieved, but drained.

As they stepped onto the front porch, he faced her. "I came here believing this would work. Your mother. She left me ten dozen messages saying… Well, you can imagine what she said."

Roxie groaned. "Marabella. Ever the complicated optimist."

He gave her a half smile. "What will you do from here?"

She glanced back at the walls of the house. "I'll live here. Through the rest of my lease, anyway. I'll work, as I always do."

"And that'll make you happy?" he questioned.

"Now that I know what I want," she said, "yes, I think it will."

"And what about Marabella? How will you handle her?"

Roxie rolled her eyes, gathering the folds of her sweater together over her middle. "Well, when I can no longer avoid her, I suppose I'll dye my hair and change my name."

He laughed quietly. "We go our separate ways from here, Roxie. And since relationships rarely end so amicably, I think it's only right to hold you."

She had gone from not wanting him to touch her ever again last March to wishing he was there to do just that in the New Year. Pressing her lips together, she decided to give herself one last test. "Okay."

He closed the space between them and wrapped her in his arms. She pressed her face into his collar as she had often done before. She closed her eyes and let her arms link around his waist.

They stood just that way for some time. She breathed him in, her brows knitting together. When finally he moved away, she blinked in surprise. The warmth of the familiar was a potent thing. But she didn't want it as she once had. There was no draw. No ache.

The hollow place inside her had sealed itself shut.

As Richard nodded to her one last time and edged toward the porch steps, Roxie saw something over his shoulder. Her breath quickened and her heart leapt wildly, tuning itself to the presence of another.

Byron. As she rubbed the space between her lungs, she felt another ache, this one sweet.

He was in casual attire—that denim shirt she'd seen him in before and Dockers. He carried flowers. White lilies cupped in lavender sprays.

His expression, however... He stood in the middle of the walkway to the house, watchful, and didn't show any further signs of approaching either the house or her as Richard made his way toward him. "Byron," he greeted with a polite nod.

"Dick," Byron said, his reply at once flat and prickly.

"Good to see you," Richard said hesitantly as he bypassed him to his car parked on the street.

"Yeah, you, too, Dick," Byron responded, not taking his eyes off Roxie. Her stomach tightened when she saw the accusation there.

She couldn't breathe, much less deny what he'd seen and assumed. As Richard drove away, Byron continued to stand there, debating, assuming, and she didn't know how to move toward him. She felt chaos for him when her chaos had just ended.

Could she afford any more chaos?

With a brusque nod of decision, he climbed the steps to the porch and all but thrust the bouquet at her. "These are from Vivi."

"Byron..."

"I just got back from dropping her and Sid off at the airport," he explained quickly, undeterred.

"They wanted to say thank you, again. And I wanted to say thank you, also. I guess I owe you one." And with that, his flight reflex kicked into high gear and he retreated. "See you."

"Byron," she said again, but he kept going. To the driveway, past the garage and down the street. Sighing, she lowered to the step. She needed to sit.

She touched her nose briefly to a sprig of lavender before setting the bouquet on the porch next to her. It was beginning to drizzle.

For a while, she sat on the porch and watched it rain.

CHAPTER ELEVEN

"THESE ARE THE numbers Grim and I have drawn up for you," Byron said, handing the paperwork over the bar of Tavern of the Graces. It was midday. The Leightons had yet to open for business and each of them held an infant dressed in a literary-themed body suit. If Byron wasn't mistaken, the quiet one with tufts of cotton hair was Poe and the bald, wiggly one was Beowulf.

Parenting level expert, he acknowledged as they pored over the spreadsheets. Olivia bounced Beowulf and her lips moved as she read. Gerald had donned his horn-rimmed spectacles and was leaning over the bar with a content young Poe gnawing on his thumb.

Byron drank the beer Olivia had poured for him off tap. Not a bad lunch either, he mused as he popped a few peanuts into his mouth. He tried not to eye the doors or think about the duchess upstairs at Belle Brides. When he drove up to the white two-story next to Hanna's Inn that housed the tavern, Flora and the boutique, he'd seen Roxie's car in the parking lot.

She'd better not be planning to come to the tavern for a midday repast, because his mission in avoiding her had gone over with surprising success so far. He used the basement equipment in the Victorian only when he was sure she was tied up with consultations or events. He felt ridiculous sometimes waiting to hear her car leave before he departed for work in the mornings. But, damn it, the bunny colony wouldn't die off until he stopped seeing her everywhere.

It had been a week. His plan was working, for the most part. It would help if Athena would stop asking him about her hips and if Priscilla would stop reminding him that he had danced with her under the stars when no one—he'd presumed—was watching. With no Roxie-related run-ins, however, he expected to flush every last cottontail from the burrow of his subconscious.

Byron ate the entire bowl of peanuts, fine-combing the details of the microbrewery the Leightons planned to open as a side venture. With Olivia's lifetime of expertise behind the bar and Gerald's cash, they had more than enough to get it off the ground. He guided them through timetables and profit margins, what they could expect from equipment, production and advertising costs.

He listened to them quibble over a name for the house beer. Despite the competitive exchange, he could feel their mutual fervor for the project.

"I'll talk to 'Cilla, too," Byron said as he filed all the information back in the packet. He handed it to Olivia. "She'd be happy to do a write-up in the paper to help spread the word once you crack the first cask. Just promise you'll let me have the first draft."

"Are you kidding? You can be one of the testers." She made a face as she sniffed, holding the baby up for inspection. "I think this newb's made himself another fine mess."

"Switch off." Gerald neatly exchanged the clean newb for the dirty one. Beowulf began to wail. "It's all right, Finnian, my lad. We'll get you a new nappy. Then you'll be a good little scallywag and catch some winks with wee Willy, eh?"

Olivia watched them exit, folding wee Willy against her. She brushed the cotton tufts with her fingertips as he nuzzled against her breast. The look on her face was a bit glazed and dreamy when she glanced at Byron again. It was startling and oddly touching to see the local firebrand so unapologetically smitten. "He's better at that than I am," she pointed out. "He generally is in any kind of a jam. He's the calm. I'm the storm."

Byron smiled. "He lives for the storm."

"He does," she said with a chuckle. "And now

he's got himself three bona fide tempests." She looked down at William and softened when he cooed at her. "Or two. Willy here's as cool as a cucumber."

"How will you manage it?" Byron asked. "The bar, the babies, the brewery…?"

"Oh, it'll be madness, I expect," she acknowledged. "But, in the words of my husband, 'it'll be smashing.'" Her brow arched finely as she measured him from tip to toe. "You'll be coming up against a whole other kind of madness when you accompany Roxie to that big Honeycutt do this Saturday. Marabella alone is a spectacle of Cirque du Soleil proportions."

"Isn't Roxie's husband escorting her to the demonstration?"

"Richard? Didn't you hear?" Olivia asked. "She sent him on down the river again."

"She…what?" Byron's frown was pronounced. He thought of Roxie and Richard's embrace last Sunday.

"I'm surprised she didn't tell you," Olivia stated. "Seeing how close the two of you have gotten." She tossed him a subtle wink.

He frowned at her for a moment more. "Excuse me," he said and turned for the door—he had to see Roxie.

When he got to her boutique, the Closed for Lunch sign on the door of Belle Brides was flipped toward the street. Byron pushed through anyway. The cheery chime of bells greeted him as did the mournful sounds of Edith Piaf. "Rox?" he called when he saw that the shop was empty. When no one answered, he wove through bedecked mannequins and dress racks to the curtained-off doorway leading into the back. "Roxie!" he called again as he ducked under the drapes.

"Byron," she said, surprised. She sat at a sewing machine while a small man in a pinstriped suit fussed with the beaded ivory train spilling over her lap onto the floor.

Byron planted his feet. "What's going on?"

She took a good look at his expression and stopped what she was doing. "Yuri, you can take your lunch break now."

"But Georgiana's dress," the man said. His words were peppered with the heavy vowels of Eastern Europe. "Your mother said she would be by later to pick it up."

"It's all right," Roxie assured him. "You can go downtown with the Grisenwalds for the sugar-flower tasting at two. I'll work through until my mother arrives."

Yuri helped her arrange the folds of pristine material before he walked around Byron, inspecting him closely. "Size 14s?" he asked, pausing to stare at the toe of Byron's brogues.

"Yeah," Byron said, a bit taken aback.

"Hmm." He glanced back at Roxie with a knowing expression before departing.

Roxie finished hanging the dress on a rack from the ceiling and pinning up the train so it didn't drag on the floor. Smoothing her hand down the beading, she tucked a long sewing needle back into the upsweep of her hair and noted that Byron's hands hadn't moved from their position at his hips. "I have a lot to do here," she warned. "Georgiana's changed dresses again." She frowned. "And you've been avoiding me. So what is it?"

"I thought you and Richard patched things up after Vivi's wedding," he tossed back at her. When she didn't argue, he asked, "Am I wrong? Because Olivia's under the impression that your waltz partner is standing right here."

"You talked your way out of the waltz."

"I don't give a damn about the waltz," he said. "However, I do give a very great damn who you're going with on Saturday."

"Nobody!" she answered, testy. Her eyes heated to larkspur flame. "Okay? Nobody! I've declined the option of a plus one."

"What about Richard?"

"What about him?" she asked in a defeated sort of way.

"Did you send him down the river like Olivia said?"

"I wouldn't put it exactly like that," she said carefully. "When I saw him, I realized that getting back together with him wasn't... It wasn't..." She faltered. When he stepped toward her, she closed her eyes and took several deep breaths. Pressing the heel of her hand against her sternum, she shook her head as a line drew between her eyes. "Would you like some chamomile tea?"

"Tea?" he asked as she skirted him.

"Yes. I need chamomile."

He was on her heels. Before she could go behind the glass counter, he brought her up short with a hand on her arm. "Hey. Look at me."

"I don't think I can do this right now." She shook her head. "Not without tea."

"Forget the tea. I'm asking you a simple question. At any point in the future do you plan on getting back together with Richard?"

"No," she said softly. "No."

He blinked as the impact hit him. "Was it you who decided this?"

"Yes, it was me," she replied, pulling out of his grasp and dodging behind the counter. She moved past the teapot and escaped by way of the waist-high hatch on the other side.

"When I saw you two—"

"You didn't ask, did you? Because if you had,

you would know that it was a goodbye that you saw." She bent down to pick up something slinky and colorful that had fallen from the lingerie rack. Her hands were trembling, he saw as she threaded the straps back through the hanger and hung it up. "I told him goodbye."

He stared at her as she moved through the clothing racks, tucking here, smoothing there. Again, anything to avoid looking at him directly. "So..." He blew out a breath. "No more Dick?"

She let out a watery laugh as she bent to the floor to pick up a stray thread. "No," she said in a voice that managed to sound both light and brittle. "It appears that I'm free of him. I'm free of him now."

When he moved toward her again, she back-pedaled and he cursed. Did he have to chase her over the entire floor to get her to see him? It was the window this time. She stepped up onto the display and straightened the embroidered bodice on the bridal mannequin before hassling with the groom's vest.

Restless, he circled the same spot over the floor, waiting for her to come down. He reached back for his neck, and he could feel how tight it was. He could feel the humming in his blood, the pulsing there around his nape. It could only mean one thing. An eruption of some kind was imminent. He tried to find some way to channel it, but she was there, in the window, point-edly ignoring him. Was this why his avoidance of her had been so successful—because she'd been avoiding him, too? "Talk to me, Rox," he said finally. "I'm going crazy here. Come down from there and talk to me."

She was on her knees, scratching something off the hem of the bride's train. A web of concentration etched itself across her brow and she pressed her lips together, shaking her head. "I lost nearly everything last year. My home. My husband. A part of my family, such as it is. Even a good part of my identity and my faith in the world as I knew it. Through it all, though…"

She stopped. Her hands stopped. Any trace of expression vanished and she looked as pale as she had when he'd seen her that spring day when her life had fallen apart. "Through it all, there was one thing I didn't lose." And, finally, she lifted her face to him. He saw emotions there, chasing each other in a turbulent flurry. "I didn't lose my friends. They got me through. They helped me move on and start over. I even gained someone new. You. When I signed the papers to lease the Victorian, I thought that in some way I might lose something of our friendship. I never thought it would be *this* that would do it."

"What?" he asked, a bit hoarse. He'd be lying if he said her emotions weren't stirring his own.

"If I had accepted Richard," she said. "If I had asked him to be with me again…would you still be my friend?"

Byron thought about it. "Yes."

Surprise trickled over her. Her lips parted.

He crossed his arms over his chest and shifted his stance. "I'm not going to lie and say it would have been easy. But yeah. At the end of the day, you could still count me in your corner. My loyalty's bigger than my pride—and that's saying something."

Relief spilled from her on a tumultuous sigh and her posture seemed to cave. "Do you know what I realized when I was standing there with him on Sunday?" At his silent question, a small smile spread across her mouth. "I realized I'd already found that thing. Not the thing that could get me from one day to the next. The one that not only could make me happy again but *had* been making me happy in brief, blinding snatches for weeks. And it all started that night you kissed me over truffles and moscato."

He began to step toward her again, lifting his hand. "Come here, duchess."

She stood, but instead of moving to him, she walked around the mannequins slowly, stepping down from the display. Touching the wall, she began to follow its curve around to the changing rooms. "I blamed it on everything else. The wine.

The aftermath with Bertie. My own loneliness. I couldn't believe I could possibly have feelings for someone again. Feelings for a friend, a confidant. After I moved into the Victorian, I realized I was thinking more about you than I was about him."

He followed her along the wall. Unable to stop himself, he skimmed his thumb across the neckline of her dress, tracing the skin above its boat shape. "Rox. *Look at me.*"

She shook her head silently and kept moving. "I've thought about it a lot, you and me. What it would be like. I haven't really been able to stop thinking about it. You've been there. Even these last few weeks when a part of you didn't want to be, you've been there for me and I've wanted things with you. I've wanted them so much I can taste them. I can taste you." Spinning, she walked backward, pointing in accusation. "That's your doing. You kissed me. Twice. It's your fault."

He nodded. "I'll take it. I'll take the blame. Just—" he cupped her jaw, tilting her eyes up to his "—look at me."

"What am I doing?" she asked, gripping him by the wrist. "I can't lose anything else. I can't lose you like I lost all those other things. You're too—" She stilled when his other hand came up to frame the other side of her jaw. "You're too essential to me. If we screw up and I lose you…? It's so easy to screw up. If I know anything—"

"You're right," he nodded. "We probably will screw up." When her gaze widened on his, he added, "Lately, with women, I'm nothing short of a complete screwup. It'd be best if we both walked away right now."

His mouth came down to hers and her grip on his wrist tightened. Her torso bowed to his as his arm hooked her around the waist, bringing her up to her toes. This time he kissed her like she was free and he was unafraid. The shock tuned her like a fork, but after a moment's pause, she kissed him back, her arms lacing around his neck, smoothing over his collar, his shoulders, his arms and coming to rest beneath his jacket against his back.

"If you don't want this," he breathed against her mouth, "you're going to have to stop me. Stop me and, I promise, I'll never touch you again."

She rose up on her toes again, fitting her front to his. "Sure about that?" She kissed him, sighing once more as they lingered, meshed, shining like a new alloy.

When she pulled back, he groaned and turned his face into her throat. She tilted her head so he could get to the perfumed pulse point he'd wanted to sip at for weeks. "No," he replied.

She turned her nose into the ridge beneath his jaw, nuzzling. "Here's a plan. We do this. We take it slow. After all, we are calm, rational adults. Aren't we?"

"Slow." She was backing up to the changing room door and he was following. The strains of "La Vie en Rose" fell through the shop. The lyrics were in French. Byron couldn't understand them, but he was pretty sure ol' Edith was telling him to do this. "Slow's good."

"Or—" Her fingers gripped his collar, tugging him nearer. "We could…" The knob turned under her bidding. The door swung open behind her. She kissed him again, hotly, arms encircling his waist, inviting him in.

He kicked the door closed behind them and shrugged his jacket free when she pushed at the lapels. The tie was next. He tugged at it. She stopped him by gripping his wrists again. She held them between their bodies, fitting her palms against his, spreading his fingers with her own. "Here," she whispered. She guided his hands to her. *Touch me*, she said with her eyes.

He maneuvered her back against the wall in unspoken affirmation. Her head tipped back against the panel, lids growing heavy as he slid his hands up over her torso in a slow sweep. When he came to her breasts, he stopped, circling. He drew wide circles on the outside then, faster, smaller, urgent. "Mmm," she moaned, closing her eyes and moving underneath the stroke when the circling turned to kneading.

Bending to her mouth, he plucked her bottom lip between his. He sampled it as his touch roamed back down her front, over her thighs, to the hem of her dress. Under. There was a noise, his, when he felt hosiery underneath, the hooks of a garter belt. His excitement hitched at the unexpected details she'd been hiding under her everyday finery.

When he lingered, tracing the lace rim of her pantyhose and the wispy edge of her thong, she opened her eyes. There was a glint there he'd never seen, deeply cast. She parted her legs a bit wider when he brushed the back of his hand against the cusp of her legs. He cupped her there, letting his thumb play over the peak of her labia, no more than a brush to taunt. In answer, she went for his belt buckle. After unlatching it, she tugged. It didn't break loose. She tugged again, then she yanked. It gave. She all but whipped it free from the belt loops.

Raising his arms to the top of the changing stall, he let her skirt fall. When she struggled with the clasp of his pants, anticipation started to gnaw. "Take it off," he ground off. "Take it all off."

"Trying." She worked the button free, unzipped him. She dragged his belt line over his hips, the briefs with them. Tipping her face up to his again, she reached around with both hands and grabbed a handful of each cheek.

He swallowed an oath, jerking in surprise and losing his balance. Planting his hands against the panel on either side of her head, he managed to stop himself from tumbling over her. The stall shook from the impact. Her nails dug in a fraction. He hissed, every inch of him going hard and taut as she nibbled the spot just below his chin. There was a smile in her voice. "Sorry. I've been wanting to do that since I stumbled in on you in the bathroom. It really is as tight as I thought it'd be. Tighter."

"I..." He fumbled. *Ah, hell.* He'd lost the ability to string sentences together. Using the only other language he had going for him, he swept her skirt over her hips again. Her touch spanned up his back and her legs spread. He stepped in.

A bead of sweat cruised down his temple as her knees rose and her legs wrapped around his, the heels of her feet flattening against his calves. He braced her up against the wall as, together, they struggled with the hooks of her garter belt. "Jesus," he said when at first neither of them was successful. "Man needs a key to get in here."

Her laugh morphed into something breathy and desperate when one clasp broke under his handling.

"Like Pandoro's box," he added absently, undoing the other with more care before freeing her.

His mouth sought hers again. His eyes were already rolling into the back of his head as her hips hitched toward his and he plunged into rapture.

She cried out and grabbed onto his hair. Shock and delight wove across her face. "Oh," she said. A wave of pleasure coursed through her, bringing a high flush to her cheeks. "Oh!"

He paused, panting. "Re-really?"

"Yes," she confirmed, laughing, crying. She nodded faintly. "Oh God, yes!" She brought his mouth back down to hers for more.

He was done. The thought entered his head, unwelcome. And another. *You own me.*

Ignoring it all, he quickened against her. She matched him stroke for stroke. Arching, sliding, they bowed and buckled, matching the strides of the other until the stall rattled, until they both felt the ecstasy of triumph, eclipsed only by the devastation that cindered beyond in its wake.

In the aftermath, she shivered and he clung. When he shivered, too, releasing an involuntary groan, his legs gave and they crumbled, as one, to the floor, replete.

ROXIE FELT SATED and resplendent sprawled with him against the wall of the changing room. Shoulder to shoulder, they both suffered various states of undress as one leaned into the other. Her updo was now more of a half do and her skin was dewy with perspiration. Dragging the back of her hand across her brow, she said, "Oh. sweet Moses. Am…am I…glowing?"

Something whistled from his throat. A chuckle? A wheeze? He said nothing, knees raised, head back, eyes closed. Another shiver coursed through him and his breath hitched. She smiled, smug and tingly.

She liked the shiver thing. She liked it a lot. "Hmm," she hummed happily, stretching her legs out, pointing her toes, arms up. As she relaxed, hugging herself, the smile turned into a wide, satisfied grin. A laugh escaped her. Then another. Another belted out on its heels. When he turned his head to her, she pressed her hand to her stomach. The laughter only grew. It rose and fell until a great chain of belly laughs rolled out of her.

He watched her, amused. "How're those endorphins workin' out for you?"

She shook her head, snorted. "Can't… I can't…" Her eyes watered. *"Pandoro!"* She snorted again and covered her face, trying to make it stop.

She heard him laughing, too. With her, at her— it didn't matter. "Yeah," he said. "Because I felt like Pandora trying to get inside your box of tempting goods over there."

She nodded, fanning her face with both hands. "I get it. I get it." As her gaze met his and she saw the laughter etched across his face, her heart swelled. She loved the sound of his laugh. It rippled across the surface, just as she remembered, floating after hers. She found her hand folded into his and wondered who had reached for whom.

"Oh, God," she muttered, winding down. Her cheeks hurt. So did the muscles of her stomach. "Thank you!"

"My pleasure. Believe me."

"Not you. I mean, yes. *You.* But God, too." When he quirked a brow at her, she enlightened him. "They lied."

"Who did?"

"I don't know. People?"

Puzzled, he asked, "About?"

"Sex, with accountants."

"Huh?"

"You know what they say." When he shook his head, she shrugged and said, "That it's boring."

"They say that?"

"It's an expression you hear. When something's really, really boring—"

"Yeah, I got that," he drawled.

"—they say it's like having sex with your accountant," she finished. "But they lied and *thank God*."

Letting go of her hand, he flicked the knot of his tie. It loosened and he undid his collar, breathing more easily. The lines of his profile drew her. She wanted to draw him, the flatness of the brow, the long ridge of the nose, the dip above the mouth. And who could forget that mouth? She'd pencil the chin and the strong blade of his jaw. She licked her lips because she could almost taste him again, the salt of his skin.

She laid her cheek against his bicep and fiddled with the buttons on his wrist. "I'll waive the cummerbund."

"Yeah?"

She grabbed his tie and fed the silk through her hands. After a few seconds' silence, he tipped his lips to her brow. She stilled as the quiet fell, the cozy kind of quiet she'd missed knowing with another. Letting her eyes close, too, she felt her breathing match his as he traced the seam between her legs. A light, tacit tease in their silent cocoon.

"Ah, Rox," he said. "What am I going to do about you?"

"What am I supposed to do about you?" She lifted a hand. "Everybody will think this is a rebound. But I don't do casual. I don't think I could if I tried."

"I tried."

"Any luck?" she asked, curious.

"When I wasn't tossing my cookies, you mean?" He pursed his lips. "No."

"Interesting." She sensed the conflict in him. In his fisted fingers. In the muscle ticking beneath his sleeve. "What do you want, Byron?"

"You." The word rushed out and she felt him tense. He hadn't meant to say that. "Damn it. I want you."

"Ditto," she admitted, going back to fussing with his tie. She settled for caressing the skin peering out from beneath his open collar. His ambergris scent stirred up all kinds of sexy reminders. It gave root to the need inside her, fanning the warm pinch in her cheeks. "I don't think I can give up the taste of you, now that I've had it."

He groaned. His hand on her thigh firmed. Tipping her head back into his hand, he warned, "Careful, duchess," and opened his mouth to hers again.

Her brows arched as the kiss, sultry, threw her back into deep water. Sliding her hand around to the hair growing over his nape, she grabbed on again, leaning into the crook of his arm. A noise in her throat betrayed her as he dove, taking her further under.

This man... If what was going on inside her was any indication, Roxie was trading the torch she'd carried for Richard for acres of wildfire. Anybody else would've said it was the rebound element. The yearlong drought that preceded it. She knew, just as she'd told him, it was something other. Two survivors skating on paper-thin ice.

Careful didn't begin to cover it.

CHAPTER TWELVE

"GOOD EVENING, SIR."

Byron was halfway out of the driver's seat of his '69 Camaro Z28. He'd spent a few weeks souping up the car in Athena's garage after both Ari and Dani had passed away and before his great-aunt made her move from the Victorian. He eyed the thin man in the penguin suit who stepped off the curb to intercept him. Straightening to his full height, he smoothed the tuxedo jacket Roxie had commissioned for him. It fit well and was even comfortable, an oddity for someone of his height. "I was invited," he said defensively.

"Very good, sir," the man said. He spoke as if he were coming off a bad head cold. Heavily congested. "I'll just take your car."

Byron's hand went to the hood of the Camaro. He'd spent an hour with her today, waxing her for tonight's outing. "You can't have her, sonny."

"Byron."

They both looked around. Much like the Camaro as it drove down the curvy highway that had led to the Honeycutt fortress, at Roxie's approach Byron's tachometer revved, the needle bowing toward the threshold of redlining. She was wearing something floor length in black satin with cap sleeves. It should've looked understated, demure. However, the skirt flared somewhere around the knee and above that it formed to her silhouette in a slight allusion to sex. Her hair was knotted to the side and she peered at him through a beaded black Venetian half mask.

Done, he thought. *And done again.*

"It's all right," she said, laying her hand on his arm. "Felix is my father's most trusted valet."

"I'm familiar with valets," Byron said, gripping his keys in his fist. "I'm also familiar with Ferris Bueller."

"Nonetheless," she said, using her perfume and wiles to extricate the keys from him. She tossed them to Felix. Leading Byron away, she murmured, "He'll take care of her."

Byron glanced back. "I'm beginning to understand how Han Solo felt when Calrissian took the *Falcon* out for a spin."

"In *Star Trek*?"

"Your tribe failed you, duchess. Seriously failed you." When she held him up from going any farther toward the white Georgian manor ahead, he asked, "What?" From the little beaded bag on her wrist, she produced a black leather half mask dotted with metallic studs. "You weren't kidding when you said masked."

"Turn around," she instructed. He did as he was told while she fit the mask into place over his eyes. She knotted it carefully at the back of his head. "How does it feel?"

Adjusting it over the bridge of his nose, he considered. "Weird. But I guess weird's not all bad."

As he turned around, she stood back, admiring the whole package. "Weird's not bad at all. Weird's kind of Roman gladiator, actually."

"A legit gladiator wouldn't be caught dead in these suspenders," he said as they began to walk again. She'd stood by her word—no cummerbund.

He whistled as they progressed to the entrance. There was no artificial lighting. The lanterns' flames danced on their wicks, giving everything they touched diaphanous shadows. As Roxie laid her hand in the crook of his arm, he felt as if he'd stepped back into a time before Camaros and Vizios, before badass visionaries like Franklin and Edison.

As the masked vigils at the door opened the deep double panels with iron scrollwork, the wood creaked. "Welcome to Versailles," Byron intoned as they passed into the black-and-white-marbled entry. Marabella had positioned herself and her wide tulle skirt in the center of the grand foyer, drawing the eye. "Crap, it's the dauphine. How low should I bow?"

"Just keep your eyes forward and avoid contact," Roxie advised, steering him wide of the family matron. She came up short, however, when a rod-backed man in a white mask and black cape somewhere out of a Gaston Leroux story stepped into their path. Her fingertips twitched on his arm and her voice lifted a fraction. "Father."

He gave her a stiff nod to go with his passing glance. "Roxanna." His attention strayed to Byron. "Mr. Strong, I presume?"

"Sir," Byron said with a nod. "We've met before."

"On the green," Leverett Honeycutt remembered. "With Hudson Browning. How is he? I haven't seen him in some time."

"Me either. I no longer work with Browning & Associates," Byron informed him. "I operate out of Fairhope with a small accounting firm."

"Do you?" Leverett asked. "Hmm."

"This is the new Richard?" a woman asked, sidling up in a metallic gold evening gown. She was nearly as tall as Leverett and as big around as a cane pole. Her dark green gaze might as well have scooped Byron up and dribbled him over ice cream. She was gorgeous, but the snide grin she aimed at Roxie made her look harsh in the low lighting. "Did you order him from a catalog?"

Byron thought he heard Roxie give an imperceptible sigh. "Byron, this is my sister Julianna. Julianna, this is my friend Byron Strong."

"A pleasure," Julianna said, laying her hand in his, inviting a kiss to her wrist.

Byron gave it a firm shake. Lowering his voice, he made sure it carried when he muttered aside to Roxie, "I thought I was more than your friend."

A small smile touched Roxie's mouth. "Shh," she said, touching a discreet finger to her lips.

The smile faded quickly when Julianna asked, "Does he do party tricks, too?" Her laughter was high-pitched and incisive.

"Julianna, don't make a fool of yourself," Leverett said, snapping the words off. He caught Marabella's signal and parted without further ado.

To Byron's surprise, Julianna's uncouth smile split apart and she seemed to deflate. Lifting a glass of pink champagne to her lips, she followed her father's progress back to her mother before zinging Roxie. "He's angry at you, not me."

"Why should he be angry at me?" Roxie asked.

"Because you got Mother in a flying tizzy over the whole Richard fiasco," Julianna told her. "You know how he hates her hysterics. He's been hissing at Georgie and me for days." She frowned at Byron. There wasn't a trace of warmth or flirtation in her now. "It doesn't help that you brought *him*."

Roxie opened her mouth to retort, but Byron

spoke out of turn. "I asked Roxie to bring me.
There's not a lot she talks about other than her
sisters. I've been with you people five...maybe
ten minutes." Raking Julianna over the coals with
his expression alone, Byron said, "It's been in-
formative."

Frown lines bracketed Julianna's mouth. She
lifted the glass again, drank deep. Someone
touched her arm from behind and she, too, left
without a word in parting.

Both of Roxie's hands tightened on Byron's
arm. He looked down at her. Her gratitude had
grown by leaps and bounds despite lurking embarrassment. "Thank you," she mouthed.

"When do the pony rides start?" he ventured.

She laughed. They began to walk again. "Before the fireworks. After the parade."

"Ha." At her knowing look, he backtracked.
"You're not joking, are you?"

"About the pony rides, yes," she said. "Everything else..."

"Roxie," Adrian said as she joined them in the
queue for the outdoors. Like all other guests, she
wore a black mask and black draping. Her dress
was a long-sleeved neck-to-toe column with little fuss. It suited her well. "Byron, excuse me. I
need to borrow the planner. The mother of the
groom just knocked back three sherries and has
announced a hostile takeover of the bridal suite."

"I'll handle it," Roxie said, nonplussed. "Tag a member of the waitstaff and ask them to send up coffee and ice water, pronto." To Byron, she said, "I'm sorry. I was going to show you to your seat."

"I'll find my way." He noted her hesitation in front of Adrian and realized it was for his sake. Lifting her hand to his mouth, he bent to skim a kiss across her knuckles then stopped just short of grazing her skin. "Wait. Am I going to meet Shrek the sheep?"

Roxie's eyes danced, laughing, under his. "Sadly, neither my mother nor sister thought Shrek's presence appropriate under the circumstances."

"Now that would have been a party." He couldn't resist a kiss to her hand, keeping his eyes locked with hers as he did so.

Adrian let him linger for a second before speaking up. "Wasn't Shrek euthanized?"

Byron gawped at her. "You serious, Bracken?" He clasped a hand to his chest. "Ah, it hurts. It hurts right here."

Roxie rubbed a circle over the base on his spine. It was the same place she'd stroked a few days ago, in the changing room at the boutique after he'd spent himself inside her. "Have Adrian show you the bar. If I don't see you before the ceremony…"

"I'll catch you later, Wonder Woman," he assured her.

Smiling, she walked away. He watched. Then he found Adrian watching him. Her mouth had curved wide and there was a perceptive glimmer there. "Did you eat a T-bone?" he queried. "I think the bone might've gotten lodged in your mouth there."

Adrian couldn't seem to contain a smug waver of glee. "Here's where usually I inform the guy that my friend—recently divorced, by the way—is far too good for the likes of him and he'd do well not to step outside the line. But you're my friend, too, and you might be just as good as she is, believe it or not. So it seems I'm at an impasse."

"Good," he said. "I know Briar serves ill-suited suitors on rye toast for breakfast at the inn, just as I know I don't have a shot in hell against your scrutiny or Olivia's shotty."

"So this is serious?"

Byron toed over the question. "I don't plan on hurting her, no."

"Well, anybody who does hurt her deserves to be euthanized a heck of lot more than Shrek." Staring him down over what he thought of as a nice button nose, Adrian added, "But that's not what I asked."

"I heard the question," he told her. "And I'll tell you as much as I know at this point, which is that we like each other, more than a little. We're attracted to each other. And, for both our sakes, we don't want to screw whatever this is up. So, for the time being, we're keeping it cautiously non-casual until we find out if we can handle the serious." Before Adrian could speak again, he said quickly, "You don't have to tell me she's coming off fresh hurt. You don't have to tell me there's risk. We're aware of it. *I'm* aware of it, and I'm still here. I'm here for her."

Her eyes had become narrow slits and she searched him with them until he might've felt sweat beading beneath the cross-strap on his back. However, her mouth slowly spread into her familiar, quiet grin and he watched her relax a fraction. "Well, I'm glad you're the one she's chosen, whether on a permanent basis or not. There's not a lot of guys I trust. You're one of them, though."

Yep, he was sweating. Swallowing, he gave her a nod. "I appreciate it, Mrs. Bracken."

She hooked her arm through his. "Come on. I'll show you to your seat."

Byron cleared his throat. "Only if you give me the lowdown on the loonies who live here."

She eyed the line of his jacket. "You got a flask hidden under the Boss? You might need it."

THERE WERE BIG weddings and then there were Honeycutt weddings. Big weddings were a tightrope walk and a juggling act. Every step had to line up; balance had to be maintained while balls stayed in the air. Roxie felt tired at the end of a big wedding, but it was the good, accomplished kind of tired.

Honeycutt weddings were a different beast altogether. Georgiana was the last Honeycutt daughter to wed, so Marabella had thrown every detail and dollar necessary into the pot to send her off in style and extravagance. There was no vacancy among the five hundred chairs during the ceremony. The reception was coordinated between dance styles and complemented by ice sculptures and a sorbet station—impressive feats with the high-priced and high-powered portable heaters running hot into the night.

Roxie never sat down at the weddings she coordinated. Yet as the reception blazed on passed midnight, she realized she hadn't had a moment to spare for Byron beyond the waltz that he generously offered to participate in. She grinned at him during the dance, knowing he gritted his teeth through it. "I told you you could disappear for the dancing. Fake a stomachache. Blame the clams."

"It's not every day Scarlett O'Hara gets married," he ruminated.

"Scarlett O'Hara was married three times," she said matter-of-factly.

"Huh. Well. *Laissez les bons temps rouler.*"

She couldn't pretend not to be impressed. "Speak French, too, do you?"

"No, baby, I speak Mardi Gras. This is ridiculous," he muttered, rolling his eyes at the Swarovski crystals strung across the canopy. "Shouldn't the wedding be simple and the marriage be…"

"Extraordinary?" she offered.

"Yeah. People get caught up in the send-off and forget the journey afterward. That's where the real energy should be spent." He tilted his head. "But then you'd be out of a job." He spun her out again, then brought her back, close. Closer than the waltz entailed. "I'm impressed with you, though, duchess. Look at you, pulling off a to-do like this without breaking a sweat. You really are Wonder Woman."

"It's not over yet," she warned. No sooner had she said it than Yuri hailed her. She apologized and regrettably left to tend to another MOG-related emergency.

A little while later the evening began to wind down, culminating with fireworks. And the newlyweds rode off into the night at the end of their parade procession in a classic white Rolls-Royce. The mother of the bride wept on her husband in dramatic fashion as the taillights disappeared. It didn't take long for Leverett to pass her off to Roxie. She saw her mother settled in her wing of the house with a sedative, then went back down to aid her team in seeing every last guest off the grounds. Her father had wanted all evidence of the party gone by daylight.

By the time Roxie had checked the grounds three times to be sure that every burnt sparkler stick and napkin had been disposed of, it was close to three in the morning. She didn't so much walk back to the white facade of her childhood home as stumble, breaking rule number one in the landscaper's book by picking her way across the St. Augustine grass.

With her shoes and mask hooked through her fingers and her skirt caught up in her other hand, she was nearly to the portico when she heard the telltale *tic-tic-tic* of the sprinklers engaging. She couldn't run if she tried so she sighed and took the icy spray-down in the face.

Yuri met her at the door. "Please tell me my father's gone to bed," she begged, weary and bedraggled.

He handed her a ready towel. "Minutes after I informed him the guests were all gone."

Thank God. If he saw her like this… If *any* of them saw her like this…

Drying the ends of her loose hair, Roxie wondered how she was going to manage the drive home, as exhausted as she was.

"I put your man in your mother's drawing room," Yuri informed her.

She stopped and stared at him. "You what?"

"Size 14 Adonis," Yuri said, leading her further into the warmth of the house. "He's just this way."

"But you said all guests were gone," she reminded him.

"He insisted you would need a ride home, so I had Jasmine fix him some coffee and show him where to go."

"To my mother's drawing room?"

"I thought it was better than your father's study."

One was as undesirable as the other. Yuri wasn't aware of that fact, though. "You were amazing tonight," she told him. "You kept the team sharp and unobtrusive and earned yourself a big fat bonus."

"This is why you are such a delightful employer. I would kiss you but Adonis might spank me." He touched his finger to his chin. "On second thought, that might not be such a bad thing."

Roxie kissed him, a *bisou* on each cheek, walked him to the door and waved him off. She closed the great oak panels and locked them. The quiet sounds echoed across the marble, as did the pads of her bare feet as she passed quietly from one room to the next. Even the servants had dragged themselves belowstairs and fallen into bed.

The door to her mother's drawing room was cracked open. Fragile light trickled out. Roxie felt her heart pick up its pace. It should have felt buoyant, the norm lately around Byron. She was robbed of that by nerves and discomfort. Filling her lungs with reinforcing air, she pushed the door open and peered inside.

The floral patterns of the room bordered on chintzy. They were on the curtains, the chairs, the sofa and the cushioned window seat overlooking Marabella's rose garden. Roxie's aversion to roses had begun early when she hid among them as a youngster from her au pair after doodling on the walls of her room. The landscaper had had to untangle her skirt from the thorns and, to her mother's horror, she'd had scratches on her arms and cheeks for days.

There was a fire in the hearth. Byron looked too manly for the room, too big for the sofa. How Marabella's hands would've fluttered if she'd seen his size 14s crossed one over the other on the table. He cupped a half-empty tumbler, arm propped on the sofa arm. With the mantel clock ticking off the seconds, he stared into the dying fire in the hearth, the only source of light.

Roxie knew it wasn't really the fire he stared at. It was the line of framed, oil-painted canvasses hanging above the hearth. Cassandra was front and center with a leather-bound ledger and their father's now deceased harlequin Great Dane,

Shep. A matching portrait hung alone in Leverett's study on the far side of the house.

Cassandra was accompanied by the rest of them: Carolina to the left, outdoors in riding clothes with her cheek pressed to that of the albino pony that had led her to several state championships; Julianna to Carolina's left, standing impossibly slim and straight in haute couture. Georgiana to Cassandra's right, sitting behind the white grand piano that had belonged to their grandmother.

Roxie couldn't bring herself to look at the final portrait on Georgiana's right. Her mother had had it commissioned six months after Roxie's debut in New York. It was as excruciating to gaze upon as looking back on that stage of her life was. "Byron." His head turned quickly and his feet lowered from the table to the floor. She lifted her shoulders, clasping her hands in front of her. "All finished."

He straightened on the sofa cushion, nodding.

When he didn't rise or speak, she licked her lips. "Would you like to go? Yuri said you wanted to take me home."

Pushing up from the sofa, he rose to his feet. "I do." He didn't approach her. His hands dipped into his pants pockets in slow motion as he searched her.

Roxie took another breath, in and out. It was

hard not to look away. Not with him regarding her with an unspoken perception that hadn't been there hours ago. Crossing her arms, she sagged against the jamb. "Go ahead," she invited.

"What?"

"Well, I assume we're not going anywhere until you get some answers." When he frowned, she added, "Byron, you're a roadmap of questions. Just ask."

His attention strayed to the portrait and there was a sad cast to his face. She'd never seen him sad. The effort it took to follow his gaze, to see what he was seeing, cost her. But look she did.

The position was first arabesque. It was the essence of perfection. Her left arm lifted high, the other level with her horizontal working leg. The pointe of her supporting leg was exquisite. The bones of her foot ached just looking at it, as if they, too, remembered all the hours she'd practiced to make it better than anyone else's. Better than her sisters. Better than old photographs of her mother as a young prima ballerina. Better than anyone else in the New York company she had been hand-selected to join before the end of private school. She was wearing a costume from *Swan Lake*, one of Marabella's own. The White Swan, a part Roxie had never danced. But her mother had had high hopes.

The painful part…the thing that had clearly left

Byron speechless, was the unnatural pallor to her skin and the distinguishable ribs poking through Odette's torso. The arms, though graceful, were bony and the legs, toothpicks.

When he still asked her nothing, Roxie went to the sideboard. There were bottles of wine hidden in the cupboard. Her mother had once been a secret night drinker before sedatives had charged in on a great, white script. Roxie poured herself a glass of pinot grigio. "I was born last. To say my mother was determined to carve a professional ballerina out of me was a dire understatement. She failed with the others. Cassandra was too ungainly and had too much trouble balancing at her height. Carolina had no inclination. She was the rebel. Georgiana gave it her best, but she didn't have the feet and Julianna certainly didn't have the heart."

She stopped and drank, her back to the fire. "Competition was bred into each of us. My sisters didn't make it as ballerinas but they all excelled in other areas. The fact that I could do something they couldn't that pleased our mother so… It fed the ambition. I didn't do it for me. I did it so that I could be the best and so that my mother's praise could make up for all the affection that never came unconditionally. Not to mention my father who never bothered with me, either. It was an ugly ambition, but it got me far. All the way to New

York, the grand stage. All the way to nosebleeds and heart palpitations and throwing up everything I ate, by choice. The first time I had my stomach pumped of diet pills, I was sixteen. The second, at nineteen, nearly killed me."

She replaced the wine bottle, cleaning the area so it looked as if she had never been there. After taking the glass around the sofa, she set it on the table. She patted the back of her dress to make sure it at least was dry before taking a seat with a whimper of gratitude on behalf of her joints. Leaning back, she waited for him to sit next to her, thigh to thigh. "I got a principal role in *Romeo and Juliet*. My mother was thrilled. She was there to see to every detail personally, from practice to rehearsal to fittings…

"Oh, God, the fittings." Combing her hair back, Roxie scowled. "She made me write down everything I ate. She'd give the list back to me the following morning with things crossed out. I was to eat less and less every day until opening night. The thing she didn't know was that I couldn't stop eating. It really is a sickness. You eat and eat and then the guilt and the shame and the self-disgust hits and you gag yourself to be rid of it. She told me I looked bloated just before my debut, before giving me a new brand of diet pills. 'These will take care of the problem,' she said. I missed the opening and was in the hospital for three weeks."

Byron shook his head. He wasn't able to look at the portrait anymore either.

"I realized if I didn't change I was going to destroy myself to the point of nonexistence," Roxie explained. "My first goal was to cut ties with my family. I didn't speak to them for over a year. The next goal was to get healthy again, which I did, little by little. And the last goal was to change my perception of myself, to change how I evaluated life and focus on what was within instead of on the outside. I realized I wanted to go back to school, to own my own business, to make other people happy. Not to compensate for my lack of happiness up to that point but because it made me happy, too, to give them the happiest day of their lives and design dresses so they could look and feel spectacular in their own skin." Rewarding herself for the retelling, she downed the rest of her pinot and settled back into the crook of his offered arm.

Byron followed suit, drinking what remained in his tumbler. "Cassandra and Julianna were here tonight. They were bridesmaids. I never saw her." He indicated his statement with a nod to Carolina's portrait.

"You probably never will," Roxie told him. "Carolina's struggle with body issues continued into her twenties. We've all had them. But Caro became more dependent on the pills than any of the rest of us. She's been in and out of rehab ever since. After her last relapse two years ago, her husband, Percy, God love him, did what I did all those years ago—he ensured that none of the rest of us contacts her again. She's okay now, I think, raising Thoroughbreds with him in Kentucky."

"Why did you come back to them?" he asked. "They don't deserve you."

Snuggling into his lapel, she allowed her eyes to close. "Because I wanted to live here and start a business on the Eastern Shore. I wanted it so badly I did it in spite of the fact that they were here. And I prided myself on being strong enough to do it with aplomb."

His arm tightened around her. "You've been through hell." He rubbed the gooseflesh still present on her arms. "And you're cold again."

"Walked through the sprinklers," she mumbled into his jacket. She was so cozy here with him. In the house she'd never felt she belonged in. With the Roxie she no longer recognized and the others staring, unsmiling, down on them. Amid the shrine to her mother's saccharine brand of perfectionism. Byron shifted away. She made a protesting noise. It was silenced when he knelt in front of her on the Persian rug. Her heart gave a lengthy tug as the light burned bright against his silhouette. He lifted her foot and began to knead.

"Ha! Careful!" she hissed as the pressure points along the arch sensitized.

He answered by focusing just there, using his thumbs to deepen the massage.

"Oh, no," she sighed. The back of her head sank into the cushion. Her eyes rolled as a jet of pure ecstasy shot through her. "Stop it. You'll spoil me."

He didn't stop. He rubbed the foot until it had warmed, until she felt sparkly and loose. Then he treated the other foot, taking his time. The logs in the fireplace split. Sparks flew. The clock chimed a quarter of an hour. His ministrations should've relaxed her. Instead, her nerve endings buzzed and her brain went into reboot, libido riding at the front of the charge. As his attentions spread up to her calves, beneath the hem of the dress, she whispered to him in the dark. "Byron. This is my parents' house."

"Is your mother planning on joining us?" he asked, kneading until the muscle beneath his hands was the consistency of tupelo honey.

"She took enough meds to knock out a small horse."

He bent over her leg to graze his lips along the inside of her knee. "What about Leverett?"

She shook her head. The bodhran drum was alive again in her chest. The buoyancy was back, too. "He never comes here."

Eyes on her, Byron addressed the buttons of his tuxedo jacket. He took it off, tossed it onto the cushion next to her. He undid his cuffs, loosening the sleeves of his dress shirt. The suspender straps went next. He shrugged them over his arms so that they fell to his waist. He undid his bowtie, popping buttons quickly down the line of his shirt before untucking the tails and pulling the shirt over his head.

Roxie stopped her jaw from dropping. She wasn't able to stop her mouth from watering. He put Perseus to shame with his well-carved shoulders, chiseled chest and washboard abs. When he gripped her under the knees and pulled her to the edge of the couch, she let him. Just as she let him lean over to kiss her navel through the satin dress. "Are we really doing this?" she asked.

He cupped her hips. Dipping his head to her breastbone, he kissed the valley between her breasts. "This museum could use a shake-up."

"Mm." He'd moved up to her neck now and was wrapping her legs around his waist.

"Make as much noise as you want," he said. "Make enough to wake up the sisters and the parentals and the creepy butler living in the basement."

"The butler lives in the tower," she jested as his hips rolled against hers and she felt his erection. Melting. She was melting into something lesser than honey and more luminous than that phyto-plankton stuff that glowed so brightly satellites could see it from space. "The basement is where they lock the naughty maids."

He chuckled, tugging at her dress. It inched down her arms and torso, revealing the bustier beneath. "Fort Knox." He skimmed the top edge. "Why is it always Fort Knox with you, Roxanna?"

"Not that again," she groaned at the sound of her full name.

He'd found the hooks along her spine and pulled her up to sitting so he could undo them one by one. "You designed this, too, didn't you?"

"Yes."

"If Lev knew what this makes me want to do to you, he'd lock me up with the naughty ones down below." He peeled the garment off, matching her stare for stare. The need there in him was naked, razor-sharp. She answered, shuddering at her own primal response.

He laid her back and stripped the dress that had fallen to her waist. They lay skin to skin when he ranged over her. She gathered him to her, beyond the point of caring whose house it was.

"Are you warm enough now, Roxanna?" he murmured.

She trembled. He made her name sound so seductive. So tender she didn't hate it anymore. "You're not going to stop calling me that, are you?"

His nose grazed against hers. He licked the seam between her lips, making her hips rise against his. "Give me one good reason why I should."

"Because it makes me ache," she whispered, realizing too late that she said it out loud.

"Here?" He bowed into her, a practiced motion that brought his rod up against her core.

Dear Lord. If he didn't get inside her already, she *would* wake the entire house. And it was her heart that ached for the sound of her name. For him, period. "Byron."

Tugging her up again, he strung her arms around his neck. "Grab hold. Like before."

She wove her fingers through his hair, her nails dragging against his scalp. They hardened as he spread his hands beneath her, boosting her so that they joined, their gazes level. She had to bear down to keep the exultant cry from tearing out of her.

Until their interlude at the boutique, she hadn't realized how empty she was. The weight of him, the intimacy, had rocked her to the brink of climax. She'd skittered over the brink without a thought for hitting the brakes and regaining control.

She came close again. He held her, tighter, as if he knew. Something greater than need took hold of her. Something hotter than passion. She felt it fill her as profoundly as he had. She felt it lighting her up, every little bit of her. Her pulse jack-rabbited at the insistency that rose like lava from the depths of her soul.

She wanted him to love her leisurely. She wanted him in slow, steady gulps. And yet she wanted to loosen his control like a well-knotted tie.

Here in this room, she wanted to make him un-steady, off balance, off the rails. She wanted to rock him like he'd rocked her.

He looked into her; he read her. It must've all been there because his expression changed. Awareness dawned. She thought she saw a sliver of alarm. He searched for several seconds before he accepted her challenge. He lifted his chin.

The table was behind him, beautiful and sturdy—rosewood with glass inlays. Roxie pushed him back until he found the edge. With a sweep of his arm, the neat stacks of picture books and magazines flipped, heaped onto the floor. She flattened her hands across his chest. The last em-bers of the fire burnished his profile so that the strong line of his brow, his prominent nose and his generous mouth looked bronzed, princely.

The glass creaked slightly when she spanned over him. His brow quirked, his lips tilting into a slight lopsided smile. It tapered off at her roving touch. Determined to make him shiver again and burn, she took her time, weaving circles over him with her palms, tracing the ridges of his abdominals, teasing the dark hair over it all, dragging the ends of her hair across his skin until goose bumps pebbled across him like orange peel and his nipples hardened to diamonds. By that point, his breath was uneven and he was having a difficult time keeping his hands to himself.

Oblique cuts. She'd researched the term for the deep V, the "sex lines," as Olivia had called them. There she indulged another fantasy she'd had of doing a thorough appraisal, as a cartographer would survey a fascinating cliff face. He tapped out as she strayed down below his pant line, her touch featherlight. "You keep going like that," he grated, hooking her under the shoulders and rearranging her over him, "and this glass isn't going to be the only thing that explodes." He didn't switch her advantage for his own, but he did pull her in, brushing the hair back from her face to kiss her. He brought her knees up, seating her over his waist.

She gripped his shoulders. Her arms straightened and she arched, receiving him. "Oh." She didn't so much utter as breathe the word. *Every time?* she thought. A random chorus of a song she'd heard in Olivia's tavern floated through her mind. Foreigner. It disappeared as his grip on her hips guided her over the first stroke and she said it again. "Oh." She rode, he steered and they climbed the intangible wall that had never felt so palpable.

He did shiver, twice, in the aftermath. She hardly noticed, however, because of the coursing tremors and electric aftershocks that had yet to subside from her. Their bodies were slick with shared perspiration. She tasted it as she kissed him openmouthed on his throat, where she'd come to lie. His arms lifted. His fingertips progressed up her backbone, down. She listened to his heartbeat. It was taking some time for both hers and his to settle into easy cadence. When he said something to her, she couldn't make sense of it. Her brain was vapor. Her limbs were gel.

He held her, caressed her, until the tremors ran their course. Subsiding, she rolled into the lovely haze of satisfaction and fatigue.

It wasn't until the clock chimed the hour that they both stirred. Byron's sigh blew against her hair. "Sun's coming up soon."

"Hmmph," she moaned, unable to move.

"Need to get you home," Byron murmured. "C'mon, duchess. We can sleep there."

We? The idea of him in her bed was all the motivation she needed. They helped each other to stand and stumbled around looking for clothing. He zipped the back of her dress and draped his jacket over her before throwing her bustier over his shoulder and taking her hand. It was in this way that they walked away from the Honeycutt mansion, attended only by the solemn blue light that brought an end to a very well-spent night indeed.

CHAPTER THIRTEEN

MARCH SIGNALED THE height of tax season. It also meant the launch of wedding season. Byron and Roxie kept busy during the day. He pulled double duty at the firm while Grim flew to Arkansas to collect his aging mother and bring her to the coast in preparation for Priscilla's due date, which was three weeks out.

Two weeks had passed from the time of Georgiana's wedding when Byron realized he'd yet to give Roxie a decent night out that didn't involve a member of his family or hers.

They planned for the coming Friday.

Byron went straight from the office to the boutique. It was close to six. She'd insisted he pick her up from the boutique when something had come up and she'd been forced to stay past closing.

Their cautiously noncasual relationship had continued without a hitch despite their work agendas. He helped her finish painting downstairs in the Victorian. She flexed her cooking muscles on nights they were both home and he acted as a willing guinea pig. After a lifetime at his father's table, scorched as it was, how bad could it be?

She fed him the spaghetti. Then Adrian's rosemary chicken. He tried various pies, spending extra time in the gym the next day. Pie was quickly becoming her specialty, and the added dose of grind at the end of every workout was more than worth his role as taster.

When she wasn't out late planning weddings, they spent nights in her bed, burning up her Egyptian-cotton sheets.

It had occurred to him that they were growing increasingly domestic. He shrugged aside whatever wariness he felt from the insight. For the first time in years, the idea of connection and intimacy with a woman wasn't making him head for open water.

It was a surprise how Roxie had a way of putting his uneasiness to bed. Well, she put *him* to bed and the rest seemed to take care of itself.

He pulled the Camaro into the shared parking lot of Flora and Belle Brides. A March wind blew, tossing treetops to and fro and sending magnolia leaves skidding across the gravel. He put on his sports coat and finger-combed his hair as he climbed the stairs to the boutique. He knocked on the glass when he found the door locked.

Roxie appeared from behind the curtain, a phone to her ear. She smiled at him and hurried to unlock the door. It swung open and she ushered him in, going up on her toes to greet his lips with hers wordlessly. Holding his arm, she lowered to her heels and said into the phone, "Yes. I'll take care of it. I'm sure it'll be splendid." At his questioned glance, she rolled her eyes. "I've got it, Mother. No, I don't need to write it down." She clasped a hand to her brow. "All right! I'm writing."

Byron grinned when she simply stood there, letting her mother prattle on. "I'm sorry," she whispered, pulling the receiver away from her mouth.

"This is what came up, I assume," he muttered.

"Yes. Pray for me." She put the phone against her chin again. "No, no. I wasn't talking to you. Yes, Mother, I was listening. It's all written down, in detail. I'm going to have to let you go." Eyeing Byron's torso, she ran her hand down the red silk of his tie. "Because I have a very important client to attend to now." She sighed, bouncing from heel to toe in an exercise he now recognized as her way of dealing with momentary stress. "Yes, you're just as important. Of course. I'm hanging up now. Mmm-hmm. Love you, too. Bye-bye." She ended the call and sagged at the knees. "Are my ears bleeding?"

He tucked her hair behind the curve of one ear. Passing the pad of his thumb over the sweet single sapphire on her lobe, he shook his head.

"Still intact. What could she possibly want from you now?"

Replacing the phone in its charger on the counter, she replied, "They're renewing their vows."

"Your parents?"

"Yes, and she's not talking a small, traditional vow-renewal ceremony. She's demanding solstice, swans and butterflies in *Bora-Bora*."

"Do it," he suggested. "It's nice there. She might decide to stay."

She blinked hopefully. "You're right! There is that."

He stepped closer until her lilac scent infused his senses. Not everyone could wear the yellow shade of her pencil dress. He rubbed the space low on her hip where he'd discovered a quatrefoil-shaped birthmark during one of their beddy-bye capers. "What do you say I get you out of here?"

"Please," she said, sending him a *kiss me* stare from underneath the dark swath of her lashes. "What's on tonight's itinerary?"

"I'm still working it out, but how's this so far? We ride around for a while, find a restaurant, fortify ourselves and have a glass of wine."

"And *then*…?" she asked.

"From there," he said, winding his arm low around her waist and bringing her up against the line of him, "we could go straight home—"

"Good so far." She grinned.

"We could listen to old music, get a little toasted and repeat exactly what we did the other night," he suggested. Because he'd wanted to before, he pressed his mouth to the tip of her ear. It was blush pink, just like her face.

"That thing with caramel syrup?"

"No, the thing where you try on another piece from your new lingerie collection. But we could tack on the caramel thing, too."

"You're right—we will need to fortify ourselves. I'll grab my coat." She rushed off in anticipation.

"Hurry, Roxanna," he told her, and wiggled his brows when she glanced over her shoulder. Her giggle echoed back to him as she disappeared behind the curtain.

The phone in his pocket vibrated. He took it out, saw Grim's name on the screen and answered instantly. "Hey, brother. Did you touch down?"

"I can't get in touch with 'Cilla," Grim said in lieu of a greeting. "I called three times in the last half hour. At work. On her cell. At home. She's not answering."

"Whoa, whoa, slow down," Byron said. "I'm sure it's fine." Alarm prickled along the base of his spine even as he leveled out his voice to combat the note of panic he heard in Grim's. "Did you try Ma and Pop's? She said she might drive over there for dinner."

"Your ma said she wasn't expecting anyone for dinner until later tonight," Grim told him. "She said 'Cilla wanted to go home first anyway from work and maybe take a nap. I'm freaking out, man."

"I'll go by there," Byron said. Roxie reappeared in her princess coat, her purse over her shoulder. There was concern on her face as she listened to his side of the conversation. She nodded quickly when he lifted a hand in question. "I'm not far away so I'll be there in a few minutes."

"I'm at the airport in Fort Smith," Grim explained. "I'll wait. There's a good signal here. And it should be easy to get a flight back if—"

"Grim, it's fine," Byron said firmly. "Ma's right. 'Cilla's probably just napping."

"Yeah." Grim sounded unconvinced. Byron knew, as Grim did, that Priscilla was notorious for two things—sleeping light and never being more than a foot away from her smartphone.

"Hang tight, buddy." Stuffing his phone in his pocket, Byron followed Roxie out the door. She locked it and they walked down the steps to the parking lot.

The drive was silent. He said nothing and, thankfully, Roxie didn't attempt to make conversation. His mind was a jumble of what-ifs.

In no instance could he justify Priscilla not answering her phone…

By the time he pulled into the subdivision, his stomach was knotted from the unwelcome possibilities. He nearly bum-rushed the door. It seemed to take forever to find the right key for the deadbolt. "'Cilla!" he called once inside. When she didn't call back to him, he tried again, louder. "'Cilla, where're you at?"

"The lights aren't on," Roxie said mutely, switching on the closest lamp on the end table next to Grim's recliner.

Dusk had fallen nearly an hour before. Byron started to reason that she simply might have gotten held up at the paper or been out late on assignment. "I'll check the garage for her car," he said, heading for the door.

"Byron," Roxie said from the kitchen. He rushed to her.

She held up Priscilla's work bag and laptop carrier.

The skin on the back of his neck drew up tight. "'Cilla!" he shouted again as he roamed from the kitchen into the home office beyond. "Answer me, damn it!"

The thud was faint. It came from above. Byron was at the stairs a few seconds after it faded. He took them two at a time. The master bedroom was all the way to the end of the hall. He bypassed the nursery and the spare bedroom and tore through the door.

She'd laid out clothes on the bed. Her shoes had been kicked off at the foot of it. The room was going dark, split only by the light from the bathroom. "'Cilla, I'm comin' in," he said and pushed through.

His feet brought him up short and his heart hit the floor. She was lying on the white terrycloth rug by the bathtub. Curled onto her left side, she'd covered herself with her towel. Her hair was wet and it spilled dark around her head. There was blood.

Byron went cold. He stood over his sister and saw someone else—someone else with reams of black hair, wearing purple jogging pants and a T-shirt she'd snagged from his dresser drawer.

She'd stayed home that day because she hadn't felt well. A bug, she told him over breakfast. *Must be coming down with something.* He'd insisted she take the day off.

He'd come home for lunch to check on her. On the way, he'd picked up lunch and a heart-shaped box of chocolate turtles as a prelude to their Valentine's Day dinner later that evening. He'd called through the house when he arrived.

He found her at the bottom of the staircase. She'd fallen. Nobody could tell him later how long she'd been there, but he'd never been able to unsee the blood.

He'd known on some level. He'd known that they would never get to meet their child. He'd known things would never be the same.

"'Cilla," he whispered, going to his knees. He started to gather her to him.

"Don't," she said, her voice teeny. "Don't move me."

He heard footsteps and looked up to see Roxie in the doorway. "Call 911!" he howled. When she nodded, reaching into her purse for her phone, he bent over Priscilla. He smoothed the hair back from her face. "Can you tell me what happened? Does anything hurt?"

"Shower." She grimaced. "I fell in the shower. Stupid," she chastised herself, closing her eyes. Tears gathered at the corners. "I took out the bath-mat to clean it. Forgot to put it back."

"You're bleeding." He snatched another towel off the rack and covered her legs, trying not to look too closely at the rivulets of blood. They had run down her legs and dried.

"I know." Her throat seemed to close and she swallowed. "By, I can't feel the baby. She's been moving all afternoon, but now…"

"'Cilla," he said, smoothing the hair back from her brow. "Look." When she peered at him, pressing her lips together until they whitened, he let out a breath. "It's gonna be okay." When a shadow of doubt crossed her, he added, "You're Lois Lane, remember? Lois Lane always comes through."

The old dialogue stopped Priscilla's chin from quivering. She sniffed. Even as the teardrops smeared across her nose and cheek, she gave him a nod and the helplessness ceased.

Strong, he thought as he gripped her hand in his. His sisters' collective strength had always been a source of awe. Seeing either of them cry was like getting hit by a bullet train.

"Ambulance is on its way," Roxie told them. She knelt at 'Cilla's back. There were other towels folded in the open cupboard. She grabbed two. "Here, let's put this one under your head. Byron, use this one to dry her hair. I'll grab a blanket. 'Cilla, we need to get you warm."

He did as he was told, rubbing the ends of Priscilla's hair. Again, he saw Dani's black waist-length tresses fanned across the carpet. His heart pounding in his ears brought him back to the present and he stifled what felt like a whimper in his throat.

Roxie returned with a blanket. As she handed it to him over Priscilla's prone form, her gaze locked with his. There was strength there, too, and assurance. "All right," she said, the words silent. "It's all right."

Byron looked away. He unfolded the blanket

and wrapped Priscilla and her swollen belly like a burrito. The assurance rolled over in his head. *It's all right. It's all right.*

He needed Priscilla to believe it. He needed himself to believe it because there was another unshakeable voice telling him it wouldn't be, and it was agonizingly familiar.

THE WAITING ROOM of the maternity ward was vacant when Roxie arrived. She was alone. Byron had ridden with Priscilla in the ambulance. Grim was trying to get a flight back. Roxie had called Vera on the drive in the Camaro to let her know what had happened.

Roxie peeked through the nursery window. A chill raced through her at the sight of empty blanket-wrapped trolleys. There were no nurses milling about.

Byron and Priscilla should've arrived before her. Roxie wondered where they were, how Priscilla and the baby were doing. Refusing to take the unoccupied nursery as a sign, she walked to the circle of chairs.

The elevator doors hummed and she turned to see Vera step onto the floor, harried. She saw Roxie and approached her at a half run. "Anything new?" she asked.

Roxie shook her head. "I haven't seen anyone."

Vera looked around the quiet space. "Somebody has to know what's going on. Come on. We'll find someone to interrogate."

As they approached the closed doors to the ward, the right one swung open and Byron stepped out. His frame was tired and he'd lost his jacket somewhere. His hair was askew where it had been perfectly combed earlier. There was a splotch of what looked like blood on the sleeve of his blue shirt. "Ma," he said in obvious relief.

She embraced him. Her hand draped, warm, over the nape of his neck as his head dropped low to her shoulder. For the space of a few seconds, she held him. Roxie could all but see the distress buzzing off him, however still he was in Vera's arms, and she fought the urge to get in on part of the familial squeeze.

"They're monitoring her now," he said. The fatigue worry had brought on was written in his hands as he scrubbed them over his face. "Her left knee's swollen, her hip's bruised, and she likely fractured something in her foot."

"The baby?" Vera asked.

"They took her in for an ultrasound. She told them she couldn't feel the baby move. They started asking her about contractions…"

"She's in labor?"

"They're not entirely sure yet. They'll need to examine her further. But the reason she can't feel the baby moving could be due to contractions, the nurse said. Her doctor's on his way."

"It could be Braxton-Hicks," Vera considered. "She's been having those for over a week now."

Byron nodded, rubbing the minute bristle of a five-o'clock shadow there. "They've got a fetal monitor hooked up. The baby's vitals look good, but they want to go ahead with the ultrasound to make sure. It's possible she might have to have a C-section."

Vera patted his arm. "Okay. It's okay."

"What about the bleeding?" Roxie asked with some hesitation.

Byron lifted his shoulders in a weary motion. "They don't know. I guess that's another reason for the ultrasound. They wouldn't tell me much since I'm not the father. Did Grim—"

"He was lucky," Vera verified. "He'll catch a return flight in a half hour or so. Let's just hope he gets here before the baby does."

"And Pop?"

"He was visiting Athena. He's on his way now."

"Athena." Byron blanched. "He didn't tell her anything, did he? It'll kill her if something goes wrong. Literally kill her."

"Byron," Vera said as he began to pace. "'Cilla will want one of us with her if labor progresses. One of us is going to have to stand beside her bed and hold her hand. If she asks for you, you need to be prepared for that. You need to be—"

"Strong," Byron said, combing his fingers through his hair. "I know."

The sight of him, anxious and unsettled, unnerved Roxie. She reached out to him when he passed by her. "Maybe you should sit."

"No," he said with a shake of his head. "I don't need to sit. I need…"

When he trailed off, at a loss, Vera said, "Take a walk. It'll help you untangle what's going on in your head."

"But what if—"

"We'll text you immediately," his mother told him. "Go. We'll be here."

Byron looked from her to Roxie. For a moment, she thought he would come to her. Then he looked back at Vera and gave a short nod. "My phone's on me. As soon as you know…"

"You'll know," Vera told him. "Trust me."

As he turned to go, Roxie saw that the back of Byron's neck was flaming red. Her lips parted. The pain emanating off him was profound. "Maybe one of us should go with him," she muttered. *Maybe I should go with him.*

Vera waited until Byron had walked beyond the elevator doors. For the first time since confronting him, worry crossed her face. "He's in a race against his own demons right now. As much as I hate him being alone when he's hurting, he'll want to be left on his own until he sorts out what he's feeling, at least somewhat." Vera linked her arm through Roxie's and led her back to the chairs. They took two of the hard seats by the window. "It was the same before, with Dani. The way he found her. In the days that followed, even after she lost the baby, he never thought she wouldn't pull through. He closed everything out and put all his thought and energy into getting her from one step to the next. To say he was heartbroken when she didn't... Well, that was just the start of it. It took him some time—before he was ready to let the rest of us back in again."

"He told me a little bit about it," Roxie admitted. "About her. Still, I can hardly imagine what he went through."

"He talked to you about Dani?" Vera said curiously. "That's encouraging. To my knowledge, he doesn't talk to anyone at all about it. Even we, as his family, try not to bring it up. He survived it, but the wound's still there and it's a big one."

Roxie frowned. The last few weeks had been incredible. They'd been heavenly. But little things had struck her here and there. She'd ignored them mostly, reminding herself of their decision to keep things "cautiously noncasual," since neither of them had had a relationship to speak of since their respective spouses.

She remembered now, though, waking up alone most mornings. Almost every night he'd gone to sleep in her bed yet he was always up before her the next day, sometimes already over at his place dressed and ready for work.

She was an early riser, so she knew how soon he had to get up to beat her out of the sheets. Up to this point, she'd convinced herself it was the constraints of their workday schedules. Weekends, however, proved the same. She wondered if he had made a conscious effort to avoid waking up with her.

The odd time Byron did sleep in her bed, Roxie had noticed that he always wound up lying with his back to her. She'd blamed this on the his-her-side-of-the-bed complex. But now she couldn't help but reconsider.

Vera was right. Despite the fact that he'd opened up once or twice about Dani—his marriage to her, even her death—it had only been in small spurts. And she'd yet to witness an occasion when the subject didn't put him ill at ease.

This wasn't the time to think about that, Roxie knew. He was torn up over Priscilla and the complications that might arise from her fall. What would it do to him if something happened to Priscilla or her baby?

Much as it had before, it would unravel him, bit by bit, until there was little left. He'd rebuilt himself once. To do so again would be inconceivable. "This is different," Roxie told Vera, certain even if none of the rest of them were. "It's going to be different this time. I know it."

"You're sweet to say so," Vera murmured, smile wavering. "This family has been through its fair share of hurdles. But in this case, I hope you're right, dear. For everyone's sake."

BY TWO O'CLOCK the following morning, Byron had paced the entire maternity ward a dozen times or more. He'd drunk bad coffee, enough to exceed his high tolerance. It'd made him jittery and tetchy. Nobody approached him as he paced. Not Roxie. Not his mother. Not his father, once he arrived. Grim raced off the elevator shortly before midnight, still wearing the clothes he'd said goodbye in the morning before, looking as worse for wear as Byron felt.

When news came that they would go ahead with the C-section, Byron had taken off his tie and unpinned his collar. "It won't be long now," Vera murmured to him as she and Constantine settled into chairs, side by side. Their hands locked.

Constantine had been strangely reticent. Byron had never thought of him as old, but he looked it now with anxiety apparent in his fast-tapping heel and the lines of his visage.

Through adolescence, Byron had come to rely

on his parents' combined strength. It had forged itself through Vivienne's accident and subsequent recovery. It had proved itself again and practically saved Byron's life when Dani lost her own. He'd never seen either of them flag once.

The fact that his father looked like he was teetering on the edge of a breakdown made the knots of Byron's stomach slimy. It made them multiply. It was one of the reasons he hadn't been able to join them and Roxie in sitting. To look too closely, to see all the terrible possibilities on his father's face that Byron had experienced and they had all witnessed years earlier… It was effort enough to keep himself from flying apart at the seams.

He wasn't completely convinced that he hadn't done so already. He kept it tethered. He kept it silent, the same storm he'd felt six years ago. The one he'd come out of as a lesser version of himself. It had cost so much, too much, to become somebody new.

Leaning against the window of the nursery, he frowned deeply. Where were the babies? Sure, it was a small town and March might not be the biggest season for births, but he'd been here long enough to see the sun go down and nearly long enough to see the next one rise, and there were still none.

It's not a metaphor. He repeated it to himself to make sure he understood it. But like the assurance that things were going to be "all right," it didn't help much. He wanted to stop looking, to stop staring at the nurses who looked as if they needed something to do, but he couldn't look away from the empty heaters and trolleys where babies should've been.

First there was Vivienne, who'd learned at the age of thirteen she would never be able to carry her own children. Then him losing Dani before she could carry their baby to full term. Now Priscilla?

Had his family not been through enough?

The bitterness, the anger felt so much safer than helplessness. If not comforting, it was at least comfortable. He'd lived there with anger for so long; he'd left a nice little cave should he ever want to come back and visit. Breathing carefully, he felt his neck burn and the heaviness in his chest, making even the involuntary rise of his lungs and ribs feel arduous. It would be unwise to hermit inside his anger, but he could see no alternative that didn't involve losing another large piece of himself should Priscilla or her child not come through the delivery.

He felt a touch on his arm and jerked.

Roxie held up her hand. "Sorry," she said quietly. "I didn't mean to sneak up on you."

"What are you still doing here?" he asked, pressing his brow into his hand. The window's glass was cool under his palm but he wasn't absorbing that cool like he needed to.

"Waiting for news," she said simply. She held out a thermos. "Here."

He shook his head. "I can't take another caffeine hit."

"It's not coffee," she said, her voice unchanged. It was level, smooth.

He resented her calm. He shrugged, trying to throw off the automatic irritation. It wasn't her that bothered him. It was the situation. Repeating that to himself, he took the thermos and sniffed the opening inside the lid. "What is it?"

"Just drink it," she told him. "It might help."

It didn't smell like liquor. Byron took a sip. His brows arched as he lowered it in surprise, swallowing the tea with ease. "Where did you get this?"

He shrugged. "It's Briar's blend. I keep a few bags in my purse."

It was Athena's tea. He took another sip. It hit the spot, somewhat. The heat, however, didn't help the high-pressure situation around his collar.

As he continued to drink, she reached out again, rubbing up and down his arm. "Are you okay?"

He sniffed. It was a loaded question, one he couldn't think about answering at the current moment. So he said, "You should've gone home hours ago. It's after midnight. You've got an event at noon."

"I'm staying," she told him. By her tone, she wasn't negotiating that fact.

"Why?" he demanded.

She regarded him closely, searching him. When he only looked at her in challenge, she closed the space between them. "Why did you wait for me? After Georgiana's wedding."

He sipped the tea, hoping it would soothe the conflict he felt between the past and the present, the old Byron—the one who had bitch-slapped him as soon as he'd seen Priscilla on the bathroom floor—versus the new Byron.

He might have been lost in his own neuroses, but he'd seen her. He'd seen Roxie watching his parents, the unity between them. It hadn't quite been envy on her face, though not far from it.

Roxie longed for that natural understanding with someone. She craved the timeless intimacy that was his parents' relationship, even as they were going through hell.

He could see that she wanted that, the type of partnership that wasn't weakened by the hard times but fortified by them.

She'd told Byron she didn't do casual and what they had together thus far wasn't. But he realized that some part of her sought more than what they did have, much more.

He wondered if that was what she'd come to want with him. It struck an arrow of fear in him he hadn't seen coming. Suddenly, he was left wondering how he'd ever thought he could be more than what he was—a widower with deep-rooted issues involving commitment with women who weren't and never would be his wife.

The hand on his arm didn't drop as his silence reigned between them. Instead it squeezed. "Nobody's eaten yet. There's a cafeteria. Why don't I go grab something for everyone and we can all have a bite?"

He felt sick just thinking about eating, so he shook his head, tight-lipped.

"Okay," she said in understanding. Again, she looked at him. She had a way—she'd always had a way—of looking into him. Deep, deep into him. "You're exhausted. Come back and sit down with your parents. At least until we find out—"

"No, Roxie," he answered, firm. "I can't eat. I can't sit. I can't talk. I just need to stand, right here. I just need—"

"You just need them to be okay," she murmured and nodded. "They will be, Byron. I know they will."

"How do you know that?" he asked. "Do you know what could go wrong in there? Do you have any idea?"

"It's easy to dwell on the negative," she acknowledged. "I understand that. But I can't stand to see you torturing yourself. I can't stand to see you alone."

He didn't know how else to deal with it. In her own way, she was asking him to lean on her, to open up to her. She was offering to take the brunt of whatever was eating him up from the inside out.

If she knew how much there was to this storm, how dark and ugly it was, she wouldn't be here. She wouldn't want to take it on. She couldn't possibly. And he cared, damn it. He cared too much about her to let her fall victim to it.

If he showed her, she'd run for the hills—and who could blame her?

Movement beyond the window snagged his attention. Roxie gasped as a trio of nurses in surgical scrubs ushered in a trolley. Grim was on their heels, dressed head to toe in his OR garb. The mask was still over his mouth. When he saw them through the window, Byron saw his eyes curve in a familiar smile. He pointed to the trolley.

A nurse moved just enough for Byron to see what was in it. Like a kid in a candy-store window, he pressed his face to the glass to get a better look.

"It's a girl," Roxie breathed. She gripped Byron's arm, dancing up and down on her toes.

"Byron, it's a girl! You have a niece. Vera! Constantine! Come see her! She's here!"

Byron shook his head, unable to take it all in. He looked again to Grimsby. Closer now, he saw that his friend's eyes were watery. He removed his mask and nodded. "They made it!" he said mutely.

"Oh." Roxie pressed her hand to the glass as they wheeled the trolley over to the heaters. "Look at her. She's gorgeous." Glancing sideways, she tilted her head. "Byron? Are you all right?"

He shook his head, swallowing for the third or fourth time against the lump in his throat. He backed away a step. Another.

A long arm hooked him around his shoulders. His father stood with him. There were tears coursing down his long face. He tightened his bolstering grip. "Look at that," he said, and laughed weakly. "That there's a miracle. You need to see it as much as we do, son."

"I…" The squalling newborn calmed as she felt the warmth above her. Her eyes were closed tight and her cheeks were squished. Still, she sought the heat and the light with her upturned face, fingers wriggling, legs unfurling. Byron closed his mouth quickly. The emotions were there, looking for release and dangerously close to overspill.

Vera was on his other side, taking his hand. "You're an uncle," she said. The statement sounded wondrous. She took the flask Constantine pulled from his pocket. *"Opa,"* she cheered once before lifting it to her mouth.

Constantine chuckled. "You're damn right *opa*." He took a hit then tapped the flask against Byron's front.

Byron wrapped his fingers around it. He raised the flask in salute to Priscilla and Grim's daughter and the next generation before tipping back the ouzo.

CHAPTER FOURTEEN

ROXIE KNOCKED ON the door to the Strongs' house, carrying two new pie tins as well as two gifts. Priscilla and the baby, Evangeline, had spent a week in the hospital due to the high-risk nature of the delivery. Vera had invited Roxie to dinner for a welcome-home party. It would be the first Strong gathering, only Vivienne and Sidney absent, since the newest member of the family entered the world.

As thrilled as she was by the invite, Roxie had toyed with the idea of not attending. It seemed so special, this first dinner together to celebrate Evangeline's birth. She wasn't family and, to her knowledge, she'd be the only non-family member present. Also, the invitation had come straight from Vera herself and not her son.

Roxie juggled the boxes she held as she took off her sunglasses and slipped them into her bag. Everything had turned out okay with Priscilla and Evangeline. Priscilla's foot was healing, though she'd been instructed to stay off it for a while— nearly impossible for a new mother. But both

Priscilla's and Grim's mothers were helping out in that regard. Byron was also lending a hand when he could.

More than that, Byron had been going over to the Grimsbys' house for dinner most nights. So Roxie had stopped setting the dining room table for dinner. She'd also stopped lighting candles and playing music to await his arrival with a bottle of wine, because those same nights were the ones he stayed out late and went up to the garage loft to crash in his own bed.

The few nights he did spend with her weren't as easy as they had been. Conversation was stagnated over dinner. He went to bed with her after but it was quietly. And always, afterward, she found herself sleeping with her front to his back, his face to the wall.

Somewhere around finding Priscilla on the floor and the baby's delivery, a part of him—a large part—had closed itself off from her. But whatever he had gone through personally—how scared he'd been—it couldn't possibly be his excuse anymore with everything turning up roses for the Strong family. Which led her to wonder precisely *why* was he turning away from her.

The door opened and Vera greeted her. "So glad you're here," she said, welcoming her inside the house for the first time. It was very open, one room flowing into the next with few walls to separate the inhabitants from one another. There was a sign near the door with a Lewis Carroll quote: "We're all mad here." "Fair warning," Vera muttered when she caught Roxie staring at it. She took some of the boxes. "We're outside. It's a beautiful day."

"Yes," Roxie agreed. "Spring's coming." *Finally*. She handed over the pie tins. "My best so far. Pecan on the bottom, lemon meringue on the top. They smell so good that I had a little brainstorm in the car on the way over here. What do you think of me combining the two fillings? It could be something like pecan-lemon-meringue surprise."

"I think that you're starting to think like a master baker," Vera commended. "These will be perfect for dinner."

"Don't you mean dessert?" Roxie asked as she followed her into the kitchen.

"Well, Con's grilling, you see," Vera explained. "He insisted on cooking for his granddaughter for the first time. I told him his granddaughter wouldn't actually be eating his fare. He refused to listen. So in a half hour, we'll be throwing away what was once a perfectly fine steak platter and serving your pie for dinner instead."

Roxie looked out the window onto the deck. "Um. Vera?" She pointed at the grill and the man standing in front of it with a water hose.

Vera cursed an impressive streak when she saw the fire blazing high above the grate. Quickly, she ducked under the sink and fumbled for the fire extinguisher. "Who sold that man a bottle of lighter fluid?"

Roxie dodged Vera's path as she tore through the door. She barreled her husband out of the way and opened fire with white foam to keep the flames from reaching the walls of the porch. With black smoke hanging in the air, Vera turned on her husband. He spread his hands in explanation. She retaliated and an impressive argument commenced.

Despite several minutes of scolding, Constantine used tender fingers to brush the ash from Vera's hair. He brought her close, his charred chef's hat bending, a top-heavy mushroom, as he leaned to her level. Roxie heard his voice drop to match his suggestive grin. Vera's tone lost its edge. She began to laugh, brushing foam from his apron appropriately labeled NSFW. He laughed, too, until they were laughing at each other. They kissed in front of the flame-roasted steaks as bits of ash and foam floated away with the wind.

Roxie felt the tenderness collide with her chest. She rubbed absently at her breastbone, feeling her smile fade by a margin.

"What happened?"

She pivoted to find Byron a few feet behind

her. He carried a brown paper bag and a gift of
his own. Caught, she cleared her throat. "Uh, your
father. I believe he burned dinner."

"Huh." And he shrugged like a near miss with a
house fire was an everyday event. His gaze settled
over her. He didn't smile, but she saw his quick
perusal. She'd worn a breezy floral sundress and
brown wedge heels with straps that ribboned up
her calves, both a taste of summer. It didn't hurt
that she knew the shoes brought attention to her
legs, the gams he liked so much.

It was a petty play, perhaps. Schoolgirl-worthy
tactics. But she had to give it a shot. She needed
him to decide. She couldn't bear to wake up one
more morning in sheets gone cold after another
night with him. She wasn't built for casual dating.
Apparently, she wasn't built for this new version
of "cautiously noncasual" either.

"You look nice," he told her.

"Thank you." She thought she saw a flash
of longing there, but he turned away to set the
paper bag on the counter. She fought the urge
to smooth her hands down the line of his back.
What's wrong? she'd wanted to ask him for days
now. *Why are you doing this?* Her pulse rocked
hard under the hurt she'd been downplaying, with
the hope that things would change soon and he'd
go back to being her Byron. "What's in the bag?"
she asked, keeping her voice light.

"I stopped by the BBQ place," he explained, re-trieving a platter from the cupboard and dumping the scrumptious-smelling honey-BBQ chicken on it. "Figured we'd need a backup plan."

"This happens a lot around here," she guessed. When he only hummed in answer, she went on, "It's a surprise Vera doesn't have a contingency plan of her own."

"She loves him," Byron said, snagging a Stella Artois from the fridge. He cracked the cap with his fist. "Want one?"

"No," she declined. After setting the gifts on the table behind her, she clasped her hands to-gether at her waist. "Byron. Can we talk?"

"The others will be getting here soon," he re-minded her.

Just end it. The errant thought entered her head with another pained twang. *Why drag it out? Why put me through this? Why sleep with me then turn cold again by morning?* The questions screamed in her head.

This was his parents' house. More, it was a party for Priscilla and Evangeline. *Later.*

He was right. It wasn't long before the Grims-bys arrived along with Tobias's mother, a thin woman in her late sixties who smiled warmly and spoke softly. Outside on the chaise longue where they'd found a spot of sunshine, she spoke kindly to Roxie. "When Tobias told me Byron had found himself another girl, I didn't know whether to thank the heavens or pass out cold."

Roxie tried to conjure a genuine grin. "Which did you do?"

"I wound up thanking the good Lord after my youngest son, Michael, picked me up off the floor," Mrs. Grimsby admitted with a great laugh.

Roxie, too, giggled. She laughed more as she sat down with the rest of the party around the picnic table on the lawn overlooking a stretch of blue bay. Shadows were long in the afternoon. Baby Evangeline took a turn in each person's arms. When she started to fuss in Byron's, he got up instantly and walked off to find another sunny spot closer to the water. He turned out of the cool breeze, hunching his shoulders so they shielded the baby girl from the chill and bouncing her gently in his arms.

This hurt, too, watching him. Even the simple pleasure of being with his family was beginning to pain her. They made her feel like a part of it, and pretending that things hadn't gone puzzlingly stilted between her and Byron hurt. The BBQ was great, but as anxious as she'd been to try it, she declined a slice of pie as everyone else made quick work of the pecan and lemon meringue.

They passed gifts to the new parents. Oohs and aahs winged around the table at the various springy baby outfits. In addition, Evangeline received a silver spoon from the Strongs complete with the Greek key motif. From Mrs. Grimsby, she received a crocheted blanket so beautiful Roxie marveled over the handiwork. Tobias's mother chuckled over her offer of a job. From Byron, Evangeline received a pair of infant-sized shoes and a book of children's poetry. Roxie gleaned that there was a significance to the gift that she couldn't quantify.

"Does she not know the story?" Vera asked, pinpointing her son.

Byron lifted his beer. "I try to avoid the story of my conception around women I'm dating," he said, and drank.

"You have to hear it," Priscilla told Roxie. "Dad and Ma met at college. She was this sweet, innocent freshman and he was this long-haired hippie."

"Wait a minute," Constantine said, cutting in quickly. "That sweet, innocent freshman was wearing a Van Halen T-shirt."

"And the long-haired hippie was completely nude," Byron added.

"Nude?" Roxie asked, shocked.

"Well, he was wearing a sandwich board," Vera said, unable to contain a reminiscent grin. "And sneakers. He was the center of a one-man peace rally. The board had *Peace on Earth* painted on it in big letters. He was handing out flowers to passersby, reciting British and Epicurean poetry in lyrical fashion."

"I get the sandwich board," Roxie mused. "But the sneakers?"

Constantine winced. "I couldn't outrun campus police in bare feet."

"It was my first day on campus," Vera remembered. "I went wandering, trying to get my bearings, and there he was. I'd never seen anything like him. He was tall, dark, handsome…"

"She'd never seen a naked man who wasn't nailed to a crucifix," Priscilla explained.

Vera nodded. "There was that. He had dark unruly hair, just like Jesus's. Though he had something Jesus definitely did not—his own brand of raw sexual magnetism." Groans sounded from her children but Vera ignored them, carrying on. "He handed me a red rose and asked me if I'd like to join him in song. I told him it was my first day. He said he was a second-year senior, which was his segue into telling me his name, Constantine Strong, and that if ever I needed help of any kind he was willing to drop everything, sandwich board and all, and come running. He wound up writing his number on my palm while holding the flower between his teeth."

"Smooth," Grim commended.

Constantine's smile was downright jaunty. "Thank you, sir."

"I couldn't look away from him," Vera recalled. "I knew I was staring and that I shouldn't, but it was like Psyche gazing upon Cupid for the first time."

"Really, Ma?" Byron intervened. "Pop looked like Jesus *and* Cupid?"

"Were you there?" Vera asked him pointedly.

"I wasn't far behind," Byron retorted.

"Please don't stop." Roxie egged Vera on, thoroughly entertained.

"He smiled at me one last time, put the flower in my hand again and kissed my wrist. I suppose I knew then."

Priscilla cupped her chin in her hand. "My father, ladies and gentlemen. Corrupting good little Catholic girls since 1981."

Roxie shook her head. "I still don't get what that has to do with poetry, though."

"Because of the poem," Priscilla informed her. "He recited Lord Byron to her after kissing her wrist."

"Byron," Roxie said in surprise.

"Yes," Vera confirmed, dipping her head in a nod to her son.

Constantine reached for his wife, tugging on her sleeve. "She had me from the first."

As the others commemorated the retelling, Roxie sat next to Byron's tense form. The parallels were there. His first meeting with Dani had happened around the first day of college. It had clearly been that elusive, fairy-tale love at first sight followed by a lifetime of devotion, however brief.

"Roxie's present is next," Vera announced, handing it across the tabletop to Priscilla and Grim.

"You shouldn't have," Priscilla said as she tugged at the bow. "This wrapping's better than Grandmother Delacroix's."

"Let's not mention that old biddy's name at my table," Constantine warned, earning an elbow in the ribs from his wife.

"Wow," Priscilla exclaimed. From the gift box, she withdrew an Irish lace gown. It was hand-stitched and befitted a baptism or christening. "Roxie! This is unbelievable!"

"I heard you and Grim talking at the hospital about taking Evangeline to the Gulf once the weather warms for an unofficial baptism," Roxie said. "I didn't know if she had anything to wear. This is probably a bit more formal than you'd like for her—"

"You can't have it back," Priscilla told her. She held it to her, smoothing the fabric. Then she nearly knocked Roxie off her seat by rising from her side of the bench with a hand from her husband and limping on her medical walking boot around the table so that she could give

Roxie a hug. "Thank you," she said, squeezing her. "Thank you so much."

"You're welcome," Roxie replied. Tears pinched the back of her eyes. She loved these people. She loved everything about them, from their quirky individualism to their open affectionate ways, the support they offered in unconstrained, unconditional quantities. She loved—

"There's another box here," Grim pointed out. "Roxie, this is your wrapping."

"Oh," she said, straightening from Priscilla's embrace. "I forgot. That one's actually for Byron."

Catcalls went up among the group. Byron waved them off. "All right, all right," he said good-naturedly as he took the small present from Grim. "You sure you want me to open this in front of the rabble?"

"It's not embarrassing, I promise," she said.

He unwrapped the bow and loosened the lid. He peered inside and blinked at the contents.

"What is it?" Vera asked, intrigued by her son's reaction.

Byron slowly unraveled the item from the box. It was a scarf. The pattern was Greek key, black and blue. As he held it between his hands, Roxie explained to his family, "Because of me, he lost his scarf on Valentine's Day and I promised to replace it. I'm sorry it took me so long to make," she added to Byron. "I blame all the sewing for Georgiana's wedding."

"It's nice," he said. "Thank you."

"You're welcome," she replied. His eyes had lifted to her and they were holding. She refused to look away first. Again, she saw the flash, the tenderness behind it. Her heart rolled and fluttered until she felt breathy and mystified.

"Well," Vera said, watching them just as the others were. "Good story time, kids. Now, Izzy." She turned to Mrs. Grimsby. "Tell us how you met Tobias's father."

Affirmative chants went up among Priscilla and Constantine as Grim protested, "No, no, no!" and Mrs. Grimsby's great laugh abounded. All the while, Byron looked at Roxie and she looked at him, wanting to touch him, wanting him to touch her in a way that wasn't polite or withdrawn.

As everyone helped clear off the table, Grim offered Roxie a turn with Evangeline. Roxie walked her farther into the garden and settled on a bench swing with a faded cushion and creaky chains. She wrapped the baby girl snugly inside the blanket Mrs. Grimsby had made for her and rocked her. She hummed a tune. "Tennessee Waltz," she realized after a few bars. She smiled over the young face as the shadows merged and the sun broke like a golden egg over Mobile's horizon, its bedazzling contents leaking across the rippled bay.

It wasn't until Priscilla came out to the garden to collect Evangeline for her next feeding that Roxie saw Byron watching from the deck rail. She gripped the edge of the swing, letting it come to a standstill, and Priscilla took Evangeline into the house. How long had he been standing there?

She couldn't read him anymore. With her, he'd always been so clear about what was right and what he wanted. But lately he'd closed off and left her knocking on the foxhole door. She couldn't stand it another moment.

Bracing herself, she walked to him. "I'd like to speak with you now."

"We should go in," he said by way of an answer.

"What do you want, Byron?" When his lips parted at the question, she lifted her shoulders. "It's a simple question, one you seemed to know the answer to when you came to the boutique that day. You said you wanted me, remember? And you meant it. I know you meant it. So what's changed?"

"Who says anything's changed?"

"You have," she said, planting her feet. She wasn't backing down. There was too much on her chest and she had to relieve it. "You've said it plenty over the last week, whether it was by avoiding my gaze or turning away from me. Not talking."

"My family's here, Roxie. They're inside. Let's not do this."

"You've avoided it at home. You haven't slept with me in three nights."

"When did we determine we had to sleep in the same bed?"

"Never," she said. "But before this week, you were there every night with me. And, sure, you turned away from me plenty then, too, once we'd exhausted each other. But I didn't feel completely shut out."

"I haven't shut you out."

"And now you're lying," she said, stricken. "You're lying to me. Richard may have taken off my sister's clothes and climbed between her legs. But he never once lied to me."

Byron scrubbed the back of his neck, releasing a sigh. "What do you want to hear?"

"Tell me you don't want me." Her voice rose on the charge. She couldn't help it. She'd held it in too long. She'd held it in with Richard, Cassandra, her mother and her father. She'd wanted desperately for Byron to be different.

And, damn it, he'd seduced her on the sofa in her mother's off-limits sitting room. So she sure as hell could yell at him on his parents' deck for breaking her heart. "I'll apologize to Vera and Priscilla," she said. "I can't go another day with them treating me like one of the family if you've stopped having feelings for me. Have you, Byron? It stopped for Richard and he never told me."

She saw his teeth as his lips peeled from them. "I can't believe you're comparing me to *him*."

"He shut me out, just as you're doing. He strung me along, whether he had good intentions or not. He didn't open up to me about his demons either. That was why he and I failed."

"He cheated on you."

"He severed communication," Roxie said. "So much so that he was compelled to turn to *her* for answers."

"That's different," Byron said. "I'd never betray you like he did. I'd never be unfaithful. And besides, we're not married, Roxie. We don't even love each other."

The statement, so finite, set her back a step. She felt much as she thought he might have when she'd struck him with a closed fist a year ago. Her mouth opened, closed. Pressing her lips together, she worked it all back underneath the surface. The shock, the hurt. She pushed it all into its black box and sealed it and herself closed, just as he had. "You're right," she said with a tight nod. "You're absolutely right."

Byron looked at her with dawning apprehension. She looked away because she didn't want to see the tsunami in his eyes. "Don't do that, Roxie," he said, quiet. "Don't love me."

She swallowed again, fighting for composure, fighting for dignity and strength. "You're the only one who said anything about love."

"You can't love me," he pointed out. "I told you I'd screw things up. I told you I couldn't make relationships work…"

When he trailed off, she added, "You told me you didn't believe in taking risks unless it was extraordinary? You told me that you're a one-and-only kind of guy? Yes, you did," she realized. She blinked quickly to erase the mist gathering at the corners of her eyes. "Excuse me."

Before she could bypass him, he asked her, "Why are you here, duchess? Still? Why do you stick around when people hurt you?"

The question struck her off guard. "I guess…" She sighed, tremulous. "I guess it's just waiting… Waiting for someone to care deeply enough that they're willing to wade through their emotional bog, their own personal shit, to share themselves enough, to fight for me. Fight for us." She felt as if she'd been leached of blood. "No more," she promised.

He watched her go to the door. "Where're you going?"

"You've been pushing me away for days, Byron," she reminded him. She pulled the sliding door open. "This is me taking the hint." She gave a half laugh. "You'd think after thirty years of being pushed away by Leverett Honeycutt, four sisters and a cheating husband, I'd know. I'd have learned by now. I guess I should thank you. You've finally made it sink in."

She veered into the kitchen, then stopped when she found Constantine, Vera and Grim at the sink. The men were pretending not to listen. Vera looked as stricken as Roxie felt.

Quickly, Roxie grabbed her purse off the nook table. She wrestled her coat on and braced herself once more as she faced Byron's mother. "Thank you," Roxie said, working the brittle crack out of her voice. "Thank you for a lovely evening."

"You're welcome anytime," Vera replied, sincere.

Roxie felt too choked up to reply. She all but raced for the door, unable to bring herself to say goodbye to the rest.

At her car, she threw her bag into the backseat. As she slammed the door closed, she heard running behind her. "Wait a minute," Byron called when she opened the driver's door.

She thought about ignoring him. She thought about driving away, perhaps even running over his toes. Whirling on him, she shouted, "What if I did love you?" It brought him to a halt. "So what? So what, Byron? Loving someone, being loved—it's not the end of the world!"

His jaw hung loose. It took a few seconds for

him to close it. Bracing his hands on his hips, he frowned in answer. *Yes, it is*, he answered silently.

His gaze was so blue and so sad, she had trouble inhaling. "It doesn't have to be," she told him. She lifted her hands. "If this was a magical, extraordinary, once-in-a-lifetime connection, you wouldn't give a thought to the risk. But it isn't. I just wish you hadn't made me believe that you were in. All of you *in*."

Frustrated with the emotions spilling freely down her cheeks, she swiped the back of her hand under her eyes. "I won't wait around for things to change. I'm sick of waiting. I'm sick of being hurt. And, for once, I don't want to fight." He'd taken the fight out of her.

That might've been scarier than loving someone she knew she shouldn't have loved so soon after she'd loved another who hadn't cared enough about her.

She opened the driver's door to get into the car, but he grabbed on. He held her by the elbow, his grip tight as he struggled with what to say. "I do care," he said at last, the words gravelly.

She weighed the conflict on his face, the turmoil over watching her go. All of which he could have prevented. "Just not enough?"

"You asked me what I wanted back there," he interjected. "You asked me."

She paused, searching him. "And?"

Some of the softness blazed behind his hard features and he shook his head. "I should've done it the right way. I should've cut you loose when I realized I was going to screw it up. But I couldn't give you up. Not completely. I couldn't let you go." He cursed. "I don't want you to go now."

"Oh, God." She covered her mouth. "Why? Why do you have to make this so hard?"

Why did I have to love you?

He moved in. She shook her head, but his arm circled her, tugging her toward him. "Please," he said when she planted her feet once more. "Please let me hold you."

She breathed unsteadily. Her knees nearly buckled. "Tell me what hurts. Just tell me. Tell me why you've closed off." Balling her hands in his shirt, she stopped herself from diving into him without any of what she needed. "Tell me the risk with me is worth letting it all go."

"I…" The battle in him bled through the exterior. He looked at her through eyes that both wanted and resisted. His arm tightened around her waist. "I don't…" He exhaled raggedly. "I don't know how. I'm sorry. I'm so sorry."

She ground her teeth to keep the emotions locked back where they belonged. His chest rose and fell under her fists. She wanted nothing more than to rest her head there. Her temples pounded and the ache in her had gone brambled and edged. It was like having a porcupine lodged there. "Okay," she whispered. She'd asked too much of him. "It's okay." Giving in, she laid her brow against his sternum.

For some time, they stood in just that way, neither completely together nor completely apart. She recalled how Richard had held her in the end. How despite the comfort of the familiar she'd felt little. It had made closing that chapter of her life with him in it easier, knowing there were no crumbs left behind.

There weren't just crumbs between her and Byron. There were great, splintered fragments of an emotional Pangaea. The pain spilled into the gulfs between, oceans far too wide for crossing.

She pulled away. Pushing her hair back from her shoulders, she felt the struggle vibrating off him in miserable strains. No, none of this was easy. "You'll tell your family I said goodbye?"

He pressed his lips together and looked beyond her. A muscle along his jaw rapidly ticked away the seconds.

"I'll give it a day or two," she decided, "before I call Vera. By Monday, you'll have your house back."

His gaze seized on her again, his brows coming together. As she opened the driver's door wider and lowered to the seat, he stepped forward. "Roxie..." he protested.

She shut the door and cranked the car. After putting it in Reverse, she placed her hand on the back of the passenger seat and backed out of the driveway. As she pulled out onto the highway and accelerated, she tried not to look in her rearview.

CHAPTER FIFTEEN

THE HOUSE ON Fairgrove Avenue had been run-down a good bit by the time Constantine and Vera decided to roll up their proverbial sleeves and scoop it off the auction block for a second chance.

It was Byron, however, who volunteered for the task of *literally* rolling up the sleeves of his hardy plaid button-up shirt and single-mindedly attacking the overgrown yard with a Weed Eater. When that didn't work, he searched his father's toolbox full of odds and ends and found a decently edged seven-and-a-quarter-inch circular saw blade.

After modifying the Weed Eater with the new blade and applying a pair of clear safety glasses, he was able to get the weeds down to a manageable height. He put Ari's old push mower through hell, chopping the growth down to a ragged carpet.

Despite March's last cold snap, he'd worked up a fine sweat beneath the plaid. Still, he needed to keep going. He scanned the interior, noticed his mother's penciled instructions on the walls of the house for what needed to go. After rooting around the shed for a while, he found a promising item among the rusted inventory that the negligent previous owners had left behind.

When Constantine arrived at the house close to sundown, he found his son amid a massacre of Sheetrock, swinging a sledgehammer with all his might at a third wall. The sound of Papa Roach's "Last Resort" pounded against what was left of the downstairs floor. Constantine shouted Byron's name three times before crossing the space to turn down the portable speaker.

Byron stopped in midswing, frowning when he saw the man watching him, hands on hips, eyebrows quirked in a quizzical manner. It was only then that Byron realized how hard he was breathing, that his throat was dry and that the muscles in his arms were damn near shaking from the unbroken exertion of the last hour. He pushed the safety glasses to the top of his head and swiped a hand over his slick face, cursing inwardly. "Pop."

Constantine pressed his lips together as he took in the scene. "So," he said. "Whatcha been doin'?"

Byron glanced around. It was the first time he'd stopped to look since he started. He shrugged at the destruction, still trying to get a grip on himself. "Uh, you know," he uttered. "Stuff."

Constantine nodded as his gaze roved back to Byron's face. "You wanna sit down?"

"Sure," Byron answered without argument as his father kicked an overturned painter's bucket across the floor. He crumbled to it, passing the sleeve of his shirt across his brow. Lifting his chin in thanks, Byron took the flask his father handed him and imbibed a generous nip.

Avoiding Constantine's steady gaze as the man positioned his ridiculously long frame on a matching bucket, he took his time screwing the cap back on the flask.

Constantine took the flask back and had a drink himself. As he lowered it, he said thoughtfully, "By the way…that wall you're doing a number on there…that one stays."

Byron stared at him, blank. When humor didn't cross Constantine's expression, he realized his father was serious.

Ah, hell.

Passing a hand from the top of his head to his brow, he swept grains of plaster from his hair and felt the fine coating of dust he'd have a tough time shampooing out later. There was definitely a tremor in his muscles and it wasn't going away. Feeling the weakness behind it, he steeled himself.

Constantine licked his lips after taking another drink of ouzo. His eyes were lowered now, too. "Son…"

The word and the sentiment behind it brought

something up Byron's neck—heat riding on the coattails of embarrassment and desperation he hadn't quite worked out. Not even with frickin' saw blades and sledgehammers. He dropped his head and let it hang low, closing his eyes and wishing the ouzo had killed the sick taste in his mouth.

Constantine shifted on the bucket and sniffed. "The last time I caught you listening to Papa Roach, it was 2001. Vivi was in recovery from the accident. You and Dani had had a fight of some sort. I don't recall what for—"

"I do," Byron heard himself saying. He didn't lift his head as he explained. "I'd made her father mad."

"Ah. Soft-tempered Javier." Constantine chuckled, knowing. "However did you manage that?"

"I opened my mouth."

Constantine laughed a little harder before settling back into solemn reminiscence. "I think it might even have been a day or two after you found out—"

"About 'Cilla and Grim. Yeah." Byron nodded. "Yeah, it was."

"You remember what you were doing at that point?" Constantine asked.

Byron hitched up the legs of his jeans and placed his elbows on his knees. He tapped the heel of one foot on the floor, pursed his lips. "Throwing a few darts?"

"You don't throw darts with a crossbow."

The ghost of a smile tapped the corner of Byron's mouth. "Maybe not in your day, grandpa."

"You had a black eye," Constantine went on. "A busted nose. You never did get around to telling me where those came from."

"Grim," Byron blurted for the record's sake. He spread his fingers, studied the lines. "He didn't take too kindly to me trying to kick his ass for going behind my back with 'Cilla."

"That's only half the story as I heard it," Constantine said wisely.

The smile grew, upside down and close-lipped as the red tinge in Byron's neck spread.

Constantine confirmed his findings. "It was you who taught both your sisters how to throw a mean punch. And 'Cilla's the only person in this family who can get just as riled over something as you."

Byron's foot scraped across the floor as he toed away a crinkled, abandoned cigarette butt. "It was *you* who taught us all that 'make love not war' business. Or failed to teach us."

"She did what she did out of love, same as you."

"She nearly broke my nose," Byron pointed out.

"Noses like ours tend not to get out of the way of much."

It nearly made Byron bust up with laughter—just as his father had intended. But the flash of mirth was quickly dragged back by the lingering touches of desperation and the sick taste on the back of his tongue. His smile faded. "What's your point, Pop?"

"I'm getting to it," Constantine promised. "I love you. You know that."

"It's that bad, huh?" Byron muttered, bouncing his foot a bit harder.

"I'm responsible, you see," Constantine went on all the same. "All your life I've told you one truth above all others."

"This isn't about Roe v Wade again, is it?" Byron quipped, trying to slow down what was coming. Whatever it was, it was going to smash into his splintered resolve with the same Mack truck he'd seen Roxie go head-to-head with last year.

"Strongs are like what?"

"Penguins, *pappou*." Byron heaved a sigh. He was starting to think as much of penguins as he did about fast-breeding bunnies. "Penguins."

"We mate *once*," Constantine continued, slowing the words down, "for life. And those mates are equal to us in every way. Always."

"Yep." Byron bobbed his head. "That's the truth as I know it."

"And because I told you this all your life…because I pounded it into your head and gave you these expectations of yourself, you walked away from something recently. Something wonderful. And it's all my fault."

Byron looked up at his father, finally. The man's eyes were damp and red-tinged and they regarded Byron with guilt and grief.

Constantine Strong was known as a sentimental man. He'd cried at many corners of Byron's life, and not just at the bad times. He cried religiously at weddings. He'd wept at the birth of each of his children. Graduations turned into monsoons. Tears had sprung forth the first time any of them had said the words *I love you*. In English. In Greek.

When Byron was younger, he'd turned away from these patriarchal displays of emotion. He'd teased his father for them. Then maturity stepped in—adulthood—and Byron began to understand in a surprisingly subtle way that despite all his bravado and that stiff upper lip he'd worked so hard to convince everyone that he had, he wasn't *unlike* Constantine at all. He was, in fact, an apple who'd fallen close to the tree and, over time, had rolled back into the embrace of its roots to rest against the trunk.

Now he stared, blinking fast, into his father's heart and felt his lower lip start to tremble. *Oil! Oil!* "Don't, Pop," he said.

Constantine would not be undermined. "It is a truth," he asserted, "proven well in our family, over time. We've embraced it, all of us. And… forgive me for saying it…but I think you might be hiding behind it."

"I'm not *hiding* behind anything," Byron bit off then stopped. Reassessed. He sheathed the automatic response and shoved it out of reach. He was exhausted. From the frenzy of manual labor as well as the effort to hold everything in place that wasn't there anymore.

Roxie. God, he missed Roxie.

Byron shook his head quickly. "Whatever this looks like to you—to anyone—this is *not* duck and cover. Give me some credit."

"It came between you," Constantine noted. "The family truth came between you and the person you love."

"The person I…" Byron lowered his head once more and grabbed the back of his neck with both hands to keep the tremors from reaching the surface.

"Don't kid yourself. You're over the moon for her," Constantine said. "You know how I know? Because of all those combustive reasons why you do love her—the untamped smile, the warmth that I'm sure you feel down in your bones, her gentleness and unbridled compassion—even the fact that she is who she is in spite of who her family would like her to be—they're the same things that made me fall hard for your mother."

"*Don't* bring you and Ma into this. It's not fair."

"But you made her walk away because you've been led to believe that your truth lies elsewhere. With someone else. And you've never contemplated any other life but that."

Byron's voice was muffled when he interjected. "When did you start sounding like Mr. Miyagi? I must've missed the invitation to the dojo."

"All right," Constantine said, rubbing his hands together in contemplation. "I guess I'll try putting this in words you can understand." He narrowed his eyes on Byron's face, dropped his voice low and rasped, "'In Okinawa, belt means no need rope to hold up pants.'"

"Oh, Jesus," Byron said, but Constantine went on with the performance.

He reached out and tapped Byron's heart. "'Karate here.'" He pointed to his belt line. "'Karate never here. Understand?'"

Byron had pressed his lips together. Beyond the emotional exchange, beyond the sick feeling and the fatigue, his father could still lighten the mood like nobody else. "If it's not there, sensei," he said, eyeing his father's belt, "then why are the rest of us always catching you and Ma pawing at each other?"

"'Wax on, wax off,'" Constantine said with a shrug.

Byron laughed despite himself. It was short. It came forward against his bidding. But he laughed. He pressed a hand over his eyes. "Why did I ask? Why did I even—"

"Understand, Byron-san?"

Lowering the hand, Byron eyed his father in a weary but fond manner. "'Wouldn't a flyswatter be easier?'"

"Bonsai!"

"Okay." Byron took the flask from Constantine's jacket pocket. "I'm going to go ahead and cut off the ouzo. I'm not sure it's helping either of us."

"Yeah," Constantine agreed as he leaned forward and wound an arm around Byron's shoulders. "If your mother asks whether we talked, let's neither of us speak of this." He patted Byron on the back and touched his brow to the crown of Byron's head. "You okay, *moro mou*?"

Byron swallowed. "Maybe." Then admitted, "This might've gotten me closer. Maybe."

"Don't sound so surprised."

"By the way," Byron added. "It's not your fault that I am the way I am. And, in case I don't say it enough… I love you, too."

Constantine sniffed, his hold tightening.

Byron breathed carefully. It nearly hurt to do

so. Something heavy and wide had been lodged inside his chest for a couple of days. *Now I know I've got a heart 'cause it's breaking.* "Can we man it up a little around here again?" he nearly begged.

Constantine nodded at the half-finished demo job. "Let's finish what you started here. We'll take a joint skelping from the boss lady over that third wall, though." Reaching for the portable speaker, he unplugged Byron's iPhone and replaced it with his own, queuing up a less angry playlist.

Byron stood and palmed the sledgehammer, ready. He stopped abruptly when music poured into the room again. "You couldn't have come up with something a little more butch?" he said, lifting his arms in question at the sound of REO Speedwagon.

"It's either REO or Carly Simon," Constantine explained, picking up a hammer and fitting safety goggles into place. "Your call."

Byron pursed his lips. "REO's good," he decided and went back to the demolition.

"You're sure we can't change your mind?"

Roxie smoothed the folds from the contract on the tabletop in front of her, trying to comb through the legal jargon. Pinching the skin between her eyes, she read the first few paragraphs as classic rock clashed from one tavern wall to the next. Olivia's regulars weren't a quiet bunch.

Picking up the pen, she angled the form so that she could sign.

Vera hadn't touched the chilled white zinfandel she'd requested. They sat at a table in the corner, away from the bar and pool tables. As Roxie finished looping her signature over the line, Vera watched in solemn meditation.

Roxie placed the pen cap back on, set it on the paperwork and scooted it to Vera's fingertips. Tilting her glass of water to her lips, she sipped as Vera stacked the papers and placed them in her folder. "You'll have the check for the remainder of the lease by midweek," Roxie promised.

"Con and I are willing to waive that."

"I insist," Roxie said. "I'll put it in the mail first thing tomorrow. As for the furniture, Cole and James have offered to lend a hand. They'll have it out by tomorrow evening."

Vera sighed. "If you'll allow me, I'd like to speak plainly for a moment. It's about what happened at the house the other afternoon."

"I'm sorry, Vera," Roxie said instantly. "I'm sorry I made such a mess of things at Evangeline's welcome-home party."

"You weren't the only one who made a mess of things." Vera picked up her wine. "My son's made quite a mess of things with you, it seems. Con blames himself. And, in retrospect, I blame myself a little bit, as well."

"What for?" Roxie asked with a frown.

"When Dani passed away, I didn't know how to talk to Byron," Vera mused. "I was there for him in every way I did know how, but there were too many times I let him retreat into the quiet. I told myself to be patient, to let him find his way. That's always been Byron's mode of operation, since he was a child. But I didn't know that by not cracking him open, by not making him address what he was feeling, that he would continue to avoid it so determinedly. It never occurred to me that it might ruin any woman's chances of reaching him ever again."

Roxie shook her head. "There's no reason to blame yourself. What happened between Byron and me…it was foolish of us. We were friends, now we're not. We both lost something in the mix. Something really special."

"He lost a *great deal* by letting you go," Vera said. "Friendship's only the start of it. You make him very happy, Roxie—happier than I've seen him in years. It did me well to see that. I think he wants to be with you. He's just been closed off for so long, he isn't certain how to proceed without hurting either of you more than he already has."

"It's safer not to feel. I can understand that, and I'm not so much angry as I am sad."

"He's the same," Vera ventured. "Low. And…

maybe I'm overstepping my bounds, even as his mother, but I'll say this—it's safer, the road he's chosen. It won't make him happier, though. He won't be truly happy again until he realizes that. I just hope… I hope by that point it's not too late for him to have all the things he still could've if he'd tried now. Part of the problem is he doesn't believe he can have everything he had before. He doesn't believe he can commit his whole self to another marriage and he certainly doesn't believe he has another shot at a family."

Roxie blinked at the sting behind her eyes, surprised by it. Raising her hand, she pretended to check her eyeliner. When she was sure that her eyes were dry again, she cleared her throat and lowered her hand back to her lap. "I hope he does, too. Even if it's not me. It doesn't have to be me. Everyone deserves to be happy. Someone like Byron especially."

Vera grasped Roxie's hand. "I'm selfish. I want it to be you."

Roxie tried to laugh but failed. She held on to her choked emotions for a moment. "You have a beautiful family. You've all been so kind and generous. You made me feel like I belonged. It has meant more than you could possibly know."

"Oh, for God's sake, come here." Vera hugged her around the neck in a gesture that was just as touching as Priscilla's days before. Maybe even more so.

Roxie held on tight. The maternal embrace should've sweetened the hurt. It only made her feel the loss of Byron and his family that much more.

"You let me know how that pecan-lemon-meringue surprise turns out," Vera said.

Roxie hiccupped. She settled for a nod.

It wasn't until after Vera departed with the paperwork that a third drink clunked onto the tabletop in front of Roxie. She recognized the amazing Lewis Painkiller.

Olivia topped it off with a cherry before banding her arm around Roxie's waist in commiserating support. "Is it time for me to go into the men-are-stupid invective?"

Roxie did manage a smile. "I don't think so."

"How 'bout the you're-better-off-without-him rant?" An idea crept across Olivia's face and she perked up. *"Or..."*

"I'm scared," Roxie claimed.

Olivia held up a finger. "Hold that thought. Gerald!" she called to her husband behind the bar. "Get me an amp!"

"What are you doing?" Roxie asked.

A mic passed hand-to-hand from the bar to Roxie's table. Olivia cursed at it when it wouldn't switch on. She tapped it and half the crowd ducked at the deafening sound from the speakers. "Is this bitch on now?" Olivia asked, putting it to her mouth. "'Bout damn time." She lifted her hand to the crowd, simpered. "Hi, everybody. It's your favorite kickass bartender, back from maternity leave."

Wolf whistles and rebel yells cascaded through the crowd. Gerald hit the old-fashioned order-up bell behind the bar and grinned at his wife.

Olivia held up a hand. "Thank you, thank you," she said. "I know you've missed me. And since it's my first official night back behind the bar, I think we should have a little fun." She glanced sideways at Roxie. "Y'all know Roxie, right?"

Roxie's eyes widened in awareness as attention and more whistling greeted her. She offered those assembled a stilted smile before narrowing her eyes on Olivia.

Olivia chuckled. "You all know how great she is. So I'm going to give you the chance of a lifetime. We're going to have ourselves a little—" she wiggled her brows "—auction."

Cheers went up through the crowd and Roxie nearly shrank into her seat. Diving for the mic, she groaned when Olivia danced out of her reach.

"One night only!" Olivia continued, merciless. "We know that our girl is far outside the league of any man here..." General agreement went up among the men in question. "So whoever wins her will be required to treat her like the lady she is. Buy her a few drinks. Make her smile. Proceeds will go to the charity of her choice, which is…" She held the mic up to Roxie's chin.

"I'm going to kill you," Roxie said into it.

"Yes! Murderesses for Hire. My favorite." Olivia pumped her fist into the air. "Is everybody ready?"

"Me! I'm not ready!" Roxie hissed as she watched bidders fumble for cash.

"Oh, come on," Olivia said, lowering the mic. "I can't stand to see you this sad all over again. And this way we all have fun." She put the mic to her mouth once more. "The bidding starts at twenty-five dollars. Do I have any takers?"

"Thirty dollars!"

"Oh, mother help me," Roxie said, dropping her face into her hands. As the bidding continued, she groped blindly for the Painkiller in the glass on the table. She'd gulped half of it by the time the bidding escalated to a hundred dollars. If this went on, she'd have to ante up on her liquor intake and order a Face-Eraser. For the knock-out.

"Do I have a hundred and twenty-five dollars?" Olivia called out. "Come *on*, gentlemen. This is Roxie Honeycutt we're talking about here! That's like having Grace Kelly in the house!"

Roxie groaned again as the bidding rose, using the straw from her water glass to suck the Painkiller down faster.

"Five hundred dollars!"

Everyone pivoted toward the bar. Roxie looked around and her heart bounded in relief when she saw Gerald standing on top of it holding five crisp one-hundred-dollar bills overhead. Hoots of laughter rose through the room. "Oh," Roxie breathed as he jumped down and made his way through the throng to stop the proceedings. "Oh, thank you!" she cheered, leaping up from the chair and throwing her arms around his neck. "Thank you, Gerald! *Thank you!*"

"Take the money, Mrs. Leighton," Gerald said when Olivia propped a hand on her round hip. He held out the Benjamins and lowered his brow when she stared good and hard. "You've had your fun. Take the money and give our good friend Roxie a break."

Olivia took the hush money, trying to hide a smile while she counted it. As she lifted herself onto her toes to brush her mouth across his, she murmured as an aside to Roxie, "Just so you know, he doesn't put out until he's had tequila. Lots and lots of tequila."

Gerald chuckled, patted his wife on the bottom, then, as she backed off announcing an end to the contest, he dipped his head in a polite bow to Roxie. "Shall we order another round?"

"Absolutely," Roxie agreed heartily as she took a seat again and thanked every star for the friends she had left.

"IT'S NOT A good day today," the attendant told Byron a little while after he entered the nursing home.

Byron held up the caramels. He'd also brought flowers today. White hyacinths from the garden of the Victorian. They had bloomed early this year. He'd mixed a few clustered shoots with small branches from the Japanese magnolia and wrapped the bouquet in a layer of newspaper to protect against the weather. With spring only a few days out, the rain had decided to challenge the wind for sway over the coastal lowlands. "What do you mean?" he asked, dropping the hood back on his raincoat. "Is everything all right?"

As caretakers were trained to do, the nurse hid much behind a placid gaze. "It's nothing serious. There's been more pollen in the air so her coughing is worse. She's resting now."

"I won't agitate her," Byron pledged. "I'd just like to hold her hand for a few minutes."

The nurse's mouth slowly bowed. "Are you the nephew?"

"The better one, yes," Byron confirmed.

She nodded. "She told me if you visited to let you back or there'd be hell to pay." Motioning him forward, she said, "This way."

Byron tailed her to the door of Athena's suite. The nurse knocked and called out, letting Athena know she had a visitor.

The room beyond was dim. With the curtains pulled, the light from the television was the only thing left to penetrate the darkness. There was an old movie playing on low volume. The needle-point chairs were empty and, as the nurse strolled into the room, Byron saw that Athena was tucked into bed. He lingered on the threshold until the nurse propped Athena higher in the comfortable pillows stacked at the head and rearranged the sheet and comforter. Athena sought the door and smiled when she saw him.

He held up the bouquet. "May I come in?"

"Yes, of course," she said on a quiet laugh. The nurse took his raincoat and left him with instructions to call the front desk if necessary.

Byron showed the flowers to Athena. "Hyacinths," she observed, pleased. "Blooming already?"

"Yes, ma'am," he said, changing out the drooping bouquet from the vase on the table between the chairs for the new one. In the bathroom, he freshened the water before putting the vase back where he'd found it. "The lady said you weren't up to your old tricks today." Scooting a chair closer to the bedside, he took a moment before sitting to place his hand over the ones she'd clasped on top of the covers and plant a kiss on her nose. "Everything okay?"

"They can't keep a good girl down," Athena informed him. "Not even here." She took a caramel when he handed it to her, tutting happily.

Byron lowered to the seat and eyed the black-and-white film stars onscreen. "All right! Bogie. Pass the popcorn."

Athena sighed as Humphrey Bogart's stoic visage filled the screen. "You remember, don't you, how you and Ari stayed up summer nights to watch Bogie film noirs?"

"*The Maltese Falcon* was his favorite." Byron nodded as he unwrapped a caramel for himself.

"Which was yours?"

"*Key Largo,*" he said readily. "Though if 'Cilla stayed up with us, we were forced to watch *Casablanca*. All she had to do was bat her eyes at Ari."

Athena began to chuckle. It deepened into a cough. As it rattled into her chest, Byron snatched a tissue from the box at her bedside and tucked it against her hand. She pressed it to her lips and waved him off when he hovered. "Don't fuss over me," she said, shooing him back into his chair.

"I shouldn't have brought the flowers."

She shook her head, wiping her nose and mouth. She sniffed. "What is this place without flowers? A box with no soul?"

He gripped her hand when it came to rest at her side. "I've been thinking."

"Deep thoughts, I see," she discerned. "Tell me about them."

He leaned toward her. "I think you should move back home to the Victorian."

Her frown was pronounced. Before she could protest, he said, "Before you say no, hear me out. I think you and Vivi were right. It is too much house for one man. We can turn the sitting room into a bedroom. We could hire a home nurse. Ma and Pop could lend a hand when necessary..."

"Nephew."

"I'd take care of you," he assured her. "You'd be home."

"Oh, *paidi mou*." She cupped her hand warmly around his cheek. "No auntie's ever had so fine a nephew as you."

"I mean it."

"Yes. But this is where I am. This is where I'll stay."

When Byron shook his head automatically, Athena grasped his ear in a habit from his boyhood that instantly brought him to attention. "You listen to me, Byron Atticus. However long I lived there, it wasn't the Victorian that was ever my home. My home is wherever my Ari was. I have no illusions about that. The house belongs to you." Shrewdness bled into her exotic eyes. "Especially since your father tells me that Roxie has given up her lease for *you*."

Byron's jaw tensed. "He told you that, huh?" Shifting on the chair, he gripped his knees. "What else did he tell you?"

"That you're both hurt," she said, "and you don't seem to know where to place your next step."

"She's gone," Byron said, dipping his chin to avoid that wise stare. "There is no next step."

"He was talking about you, the man you've made yourself out to be." When Byron's brows came together, Athena inhaled. A wheeze rose with her chest but she went on. "It takes more strength than we're certain we are capable of to move on after the one we love moves on to the next life. Your strength has always been your greatest gift. These past six years, it has shined in ways that you cannot see. It's shined so brightly, I've admired it. Envied it, perhaps."

"I took notes from the best," Byron admitted.

Athena pet the hair on the back of his head. "There is such a thing as too much strength. We rebuild. We make an inner fortress, if you will, with stones so thick piled high enough that no one can conquer them. No one but ourselves. No matter how the light may shine without, no matter how the chambers may want that light to shine within, we stay behind the stone. We may wish to, but we do not tear down those walls we worked so hard to build. I know a bit about this," she said, dabbing the center of his chin with a light fingertip. "I have known loss and I speak to you as someone who has retreated. But it is not me who has the luxury of time. We are lucky in life to find the love that we have had—me with Ari Papadakis. You with your Daniella. It is a rare thing to find someone else we can love as much as we once did. It is even rarer to open ourselves to it, to leave what was behind and embrace the new. And there are those, Byron, like you, who have enough time left to enjoy it. To learn about one another as loved ones do. To make babies together as you ought. To lie down and rest beside each other night after night and know life again in its purest form."

Byron had raised his clasped hands. He rested his chin on them, pressing his knuckles to his mouth. The voices of Bogart and Hepburn bantered back and forth in the interlude as he culled up enough will to broach what he'd been holding back since Evangeline's birth. "What the hell's the matter with me, Athena?" he whispered. "Why can't I wake up?"

"You've woken up every day for the past six years," she informed him. "You've gotten up and dressed and gone on with it. You survived. But survival is just the beginning, a small step up from simple existence."

She scrubbed his temples, head low again. "That's...blunt. Thank you, Auntie."

"You've already taken the first step beyond that anyway," she informed him.

He raised his eyes to hers. "I have?"

"Yes. You admit the house is too much for one man. Why?"

Rubbing his palms together, he thought about the Victorian and the things that weren't there anymore. "It's quiet," he muttered. "It's quiet there without her."

"Uh-huh. What else?"

He exhaled, releasing the air trapped inside him. "I wanted the house. Growing up, visiting you and Ari in the Victorian was my great escape. Everything seemed simpler there. Time even seemed to stretch. Over the last few years, the idea of moving there was just an ideal. It wasn't that I couldn't imagine myself growing old in those rooms alone. I don't think I ever thought about the reality of having it to myself. It wasn't until Roxie..."

She smiled softly at him. "It wasn't until she moved in that you realized you could never live there alone."

"She filled it," he said and he felt his lip twitch at the corner. "With her paint and music, messes and fabric. Somehow she made it hers as much as mine. I started to want us, as much as the house. I started to see us both there."

"What's so bad about that?"

"Nothing," he said with a shake of his head. "But then 'Cilla had her fall. And the whole baby thing… It messed me up. I realized how far Roxie and I had come in a few weeks, how much it meant. The inertia got to me. I remembered how fast it could change, how quickly it could all fall apart. Disappear."

"You let your fear lead you."

"Yes," he said, nodded. "Hell, yes."

"And so you pushed her away."

"Worse. I pushed her to the point of leaving." He scowled. "I hurt her. I didn't have to hurt her."

"Why would you do a thing like that, Byron Atticus?"

"Because I'm a jackass."

Athena's eyes widened. "Yes, good." She began to laugh and cough again.

He got up to get her a glass of tepid water. As she drank, noise from the television drew his attention for the first time since the discussion had begun. Audrey was singing.

He turned toward the voice. It sang without music. It sang a familiar song he didn't know the words to. A French song. "La Vie en Rose." He listened and watched, as transfixed as Bogie himself.

"Byron?"

Byron pried his gaze from the TV. "Sorry. What did you say?"

Athena lowered her chin at him and amusement danced across her features, making them young again even if only for an instant. "I said, 'go get the girl.' And don't take no for an answer."

The grin that crept across his mouth was wide. He bent to kiss the back of her hand. Placing his palm over the blue-veined expanse, he told her, "There's a wily gentleman two doors down who's wheeled his chair passed your door three times since I've been here."

She rolled her eyes skyward, muttering a Greek entreaty for mercy. "You leave the matchmaking to bored old ladies. Now get out of here before I use that spray bottle on the windowsill for something other than flower misting."

CHAPTER SIXTEEN

THE RAIN DIDN'T stop the prep for Roxie's latest event. With banishing thoughts from all parties involved in the affair, clouds broke and gave the Farmers and the Housings the rooftop nuptials they'd planned for with an added display of heat lightning over the Gulf to the south to spice up the untamed vista.

The reception was rocking belowstairs in the ballroom of the spacious condominium that was located not far off Fort Morgan and well removed from the popular white-sand beaches of Gulf Shores and Orange Beach. The rain continued to hold off for Roxie and her team as they broke down chairs and disassembled the arrangements for the altar, but a light salty mist dampened things enough to make negotiating the rooftop slippery. She took off her shoes before climbing the ladder to begin unwinding the branches of the arbor, handing each piece carefully to Yuri so he could pack them in a box.

They were losing the light. The sun had crept below the earth's ledge a while ago and only a sliver of daylight hung around. They'd be lucky to finish before dark, and Roxie didn't look forward to navigating the rooftop by night. Handing another branch down to Yuri, she waited for him to take it. "Yuri?" she said, shaking it to gain his attention.

"Did I miss something?" he asked, "or was Adonis on the guest list tonight?"

"What?" Roxie glanced over his head. She froze. "Oh, God. What is he doing here?"

"Looking for you, it seems," Yuri determined. He took the branch from her as well as her hand. "Before you fall..."

Roxie followed his urging down the ladder. As Yuri climbed up to finish what she had started, she couldn't bring herself to move.

Byron came to her, walking down what had been an aisle moments before. He walked over fallen petals. The breeze tossed his hair across his brow. Was it just her or did he look more handsome than usual? How was that even remotely possible? The gray suit was one she hadn't seen before and he'd left his collar open with no tie, an oddity for him unless he was stressed in some way. Yet he looked unflappable. The slippery roof didn't even mess up his stride.

As he slowly drew to a halt, she tried not to stare too lovingly at him. Even after it all, even with the razor's edge of hurt he'd caused still alive inside her, she couldn't help but turn her face up to his like a UV-starved sunflower that had survived the storm.

Yuri cleared his throat behind her, snapping her out of the haze. She blinked, not offering one word in greeting; she just stood and stared at him like a lovesick moron.

"How was the wedding?" he asked.

"Hello," she said back. She frowned. *Oh*. That wasn't right.

He smiled at her anyway, slowly, until it dug into his cheeks, and he nodded. "Hi. How was the wedding?" he asked again.

She spread her fingers, searching herself. How *had* the wedding been? It was difficult to think when he was looking at her in that unbroken manner. "It was…sweet. Very sweet. How did you find me?"

"Adrian. She told me you had a wedding today."

"And you were just passing by?" she guessed, knowing Fairhope was almost an hour away.

"No. I drove like a bat out of hell to catch you before it was all over."

Why? "Is everything all right? Priscilla and the baby? They're still…?"

"Wonderful," he finished with a fond smile. "Yeah."

She nodded. "Good. That's good."

Yuri groaned from somewhere behind them.

"Do you know the banana slug is the world's slowest mollusk?"

As Roxie glanced back at him, confused, Byron asked, "Oh, yeah? What do those bad boys top out at? Point zero zero something, I'm sure."

"Slower," Yuri drawled, pointedly narrowing his eyes on Roxie. "Glacial. Like coral."

"Coral doesn't move," she informed him.

"No. It does not."

Roxie frowned at him and looked back to Byron. "Perhaps we should talk—in private," she said so that Yuri could hear.

"The honeymoon suite is currently available," Yuri noted handily.

Byron chuckled as Roxie sighed. "Come on," she said, bending to retrieve her shoes. He beat her to it. "Thank you," she said, taking them by the center straps. To Yuri, she asked, "Downstairs, can you and Jasmine manage things without—"

"Go," Yuri said as he broke down the last of the arbor.

Byron offered her his hand at the stairs. She was flustered by the gesture. She held it as she put her shoes on and they climbed down to wait for the elevator with other members of her team. By the time they reached the garage level, neither had said much. She gave the others some instruction about what to put where. Byron waited near his Camaro next to the half wall that looked out onto the beach. He'd retrieved a knapsack from the car. "What's that for?" she asked, joining him.

"I'll show you," he said, offering her his hand again.

He led her to the beach, stopping only at the end of the empty boardwalk to remove his shoes. She kicked hers off again and followed him down to the sand. Sea oats bowed under a steady northeast wind. The waves pounded the shore. The sea foam was thick. Wishing she'd thought to grab her jacket, she crossed her arms over her chest as he picked a spot along the last tidal line. "Here's good, huh?" he asked, looking out over the water.

"For what?" she asked, putting her back to the wind.

He glanced at her and saw that she was cold. Unzipping the knapsack, he pulled out a plush blanket and laid it on the sand. Tugging her hand, he said, "Have a seat, duchess."

Duchess. It had been a while since anyone had referred to her by the fond nickname. It put her at ease because it had arisen from her friendship with him.

She folded her legs beneath her as she lowered to the blanket. He knelt beside her and unraveled another blanket from the sack. Draping it around her shoulders, he pulled the ends closed over her front. "Better?" he asked.

She squinted as next he revealed two drinking glasses from the bag's contents as well as a bottle-shaped package in brown wrapping. Champagne, she saw as he removed the paper. "Byron, what is this?"

"Hold these for me?" he asked, putting a glass in each of her hands. He unraveled the foil from around the cork and worked it until it popped free into his cupped palm. After pouring champagne into the glasses, he took one for himself, then plunked the bottle down into the sand. Stretching his long legs out, he extended the glass to hers. "Cheers."

"What are we toasting to?" she asked with a bewildered laugh.

He stopped just short of taking a sip, then shrugged. "Another great wedding on the books?"

He'd driven a chilled bottle of champagne all the way out to Fort Morgan to wish her a job well done? As she tipped the fizzy substance to her mouth, her heartbeat lightened. She licked her lips, tasting Dom and trying not to remember the taste of him. Was this her friend Byron, the one she'd thought she'd lost?

The longing was great for both Byrons she'd known—the friend and the lover.

"I'm glad you're still wearing your cocktail dress," he pointed out, eyeing the blanket over her shoulders.

"Why?" she asked.

"Don't you always dress up for champagne?"

She smiled, recalling the conversation they'd once had over a bathtub and Billie Holiday. Unable to help it, she ran the back of her fingers over the outer seam of his jacket sleeve. "So...that's the reason for all this?" she assumed, encompassing the blankets and bubbly with an upturned hand.

"Mmm." He drank and turned his gaze out to sea, a hint of a smile dwelling around the corners of his eyes. The wild air blew the hair back from his brow. Roxie shivered, bringing his attention back to her. He set down the glass and adjusted the blanket so that it fell over her legs, too. "Still cold?"

She shook her head. "I'm fine," she said. "Byron, you need to tell me what's going on here. The last time I saw you...it convinced me we'd never be here in this place again." She sighed when he only looked at her. "It made me think we'd never be friends again."

"I told you, duchess," he said, the words as soft as his gaze, "I'd always be your friend." When she swallowed, he edged closer. "Hey." He canted his head against hers and murmured, "You never lost me. I'm right here."

Her hold on his sleeve tightened. His scent teased her and she squeezed her eyes closed as she turned her nose into him the slightest bit.

"I'm sorry," he whispered. "I'm so sorry, Rox."

She nodded, too overwhelmed to speak.

"I hate that I made you think you'd lost me. And I hate that I acted like a chicken when you did something incredibly brave."

"I did?" she asked.

"Yeah. I saw you get hurt last year, the kind of hurt that most people don't come back from. But most people aren't you." His smile was tender. "You opened yourself up, enough to maybe love someone whose issues know no bounds."

When she said nothing, his arm linked around her waist. "You know what I love about you most, Rox?"

Her eyes opened. The bodhran was back again. It pounded into the quiet between them.

"I love that you knew I could move on even when I was convinced that I couldn't. I love that your belief in me was stronger than my fears."

"Was it?" she asked, tilting her face up to question his.

He held her tighter. "Yeah, it was," he said, back to a whisper.

She took a deep breath. "Can I ask you a question?"

"Anything."

"Do you think there's one great love for everyone?" she asked as she had once before. "Only one?"

His eyes caressed her features and he said, "I believe there's love and there's the extraordinary. I know that that's not something many people find once. Once is a miracle. Twice is a phenomenon that I know now not to take for granted."

She couldn't breathe.

"It was foolish and cruel of me to claim that we don't love each other when it's me who loved you first." He exhaled raggedly when her hand came up to cup her mouth. "I think I fell in love with you the first time you smiled at me. The day we met. Do you remember when that was? You were getting married. You were getting married to somebody else and I thought, 'It's okay. It's okay if I love this one because she'll always belong to somebody else and I'm safe.' And then you didn't."

"And you weren't," she realized. "You love me."

"Yes," he said, pressing his cheek to hers. "Yes, Roxanna Honeycutt. I love you very much."

"Is…" She slid her hand up his collar. "Is it okay if I cry now?"

He laughed. "Yeah. Yeah, go ahead."

He held her as she wept silently into his shoulder, absorbing the quiet hitches that rose from her chest and shook her. He held her for a while in the peace that bloomed on the cries' heels.

Words spilled into the blissful void. His. "You know…" His voice was the slightest bit husky and it danced along her skin. "I've always liked beach weddings best, I think. There's something about 'em. Waves. Flip-flops. Tradition dictates sunset, but I'm starting to think dawn is more symbolic."

"Hmm." She thought about it, aware again of the endless whoosh of water and wave. "People would have to get up early to attend. Really early. Who would show?"

"The ones who matter," he said simply.

She beamed at the thought. "Oh. I like that. I like that very much."

He nodded as her gaze climbed back to his. "Think about it. Champagne and shrimp cocktails for breakfast. Everybody could bring swimsuits and call it a beach day. Everybody loves a beach day, right?" When she only smiled at him, he continued, "Then they all leave and the happy couple retires to the honeymoon suite—early. And check out late the next morning."

"Have you been thinking about this for a while?"

"Yeah, I have. And I think it could work. But you're the wedding planner. What're your thoughts?"

"It sounds wonderful," she said wistfully. "But somebody wise once told me that it's not the wedding that counts. It's the marriage."

"You're right. That person was wise." The amusement fled his face though the fondness remained as his gaze drank from hers. "I haven't just been thinking about it. I want it."

Her lips parted in surprise. The glass she'd been lifting to her mouth lowered as the words seized her.

"I want it all," he continued, "and it's you who's made me want it again—the wedding, the marriage, everything and anything that comes with it. *All of it.* I want you and me in Athena and Ari's old Victorian, day in and day out, doing them proud."

She shook her head, dizzy with the beautiful pictures he painted. "I…"

"You make me believe that it can be extraordinary," he told her. "*You* are extraordinary. You make me *feel* extraordinary." He took her glass and set it in the sand with his own. Shifting, he took something out of his pants pocket. A small box. He set it in the cradle of her palm.

"I…" she said again, blinking at the box. She wasn't imagining it. It was there.

"Open it," he invited.

She lifted her other hand to the lid and pried it back. "Oh," she sighed, reaching up to touch it. She stopped herself just in time.

It was gorgeous. The ring was vintage. A halo diamond in rose gold. The band was etched with a significant pattern: Greek key. She knew just by looking at it that it was a family heirloom of some kind, which made it mean that much more…

"And so," Byron said, cupping his hand underneath the one cradling the box. "I promise you this, duchess. I promise that I will be that man at the altar waiting for you as you walk down the aisle in your white dress. I promise that it will be me giving you those vows and honoring them all the days of my life, without exception. I promise that, no matter what color you paint the walls of the Victorian—and I'm sure there will be many—those walls will see us love and fight and make up, unremittingly. I promise I won't give up—on me or you, on us, whatever comes…family…"

"Byron," she breathed, swelling with emotion as she saw the possibilities in him. All the possibilities he spoke of and more. "Oh, Byron."

"It's not a question of if," he continued. "It's *when*. Until then, what do you say? When dawn breaks on this beach that day will you take me… and my parents—and a handful of siblings and one kooky great-aunt?"

She could do nothing but stare at him. Just stare and wish and dream.

"Do you know what the key pattern represents?" he asked, talking fast as he took the box from her. He wedged the ring from the cushion and took her hand. "As far back as ancient Greece, it meant love and devotion. It means unity. Infinity. But most of all, it represents the bonds of friendship, because even those old pagan fuddy-duddies knew that a marriage should begin with nothing less."

Her pulse washed against her ears. There were no words to match his—she was out. Yet she wasn't the least bit empty. In truth, she'd never felt so full.

"It's Athena's ring," he explained. "Ari gave it to her. Not when they were first married. They barely knew each other then. He gave it to her after they admitted finally that they loved each other as a husband and wife should."

"It's so beautiful," she said. And its history made it more so.

"She gave it to me to give to you," he told her. "Just as she gave me the house so I wouldn't go on thinking that I have to grow old alone. After you came along, I stopped wishing for that."

Roxie looked beyond the ring. She looked beyond the words. She looked at Byron, all that he was and would be. He'd loved the old Roxie and the new one. He'd seen her at her best and her worst, and still he loved her. He knew what forever meant. And after everything he'd been through, he offered her his forever.

Grabbing his face in both hands, she kissed him. She kissed him long and deep, buffered against the wind by his strength and buoyed against the tide by his love. "Say it again," she murmured against him. "Say it. Once more."

"I love you, *matia mou*."

Roxie nodded, blind. "Yes. Yes, I will take

you…just so long as you promise not to make me wait too long—"

"No. No, duchess. I couldn't."

"—because it all sounds so wonderful." She wiped her eyes on the back of her hand. "So wonderful, I could just…dance and dance and dance." She finished laughing, her eyes full. And she was sure they danced with stars—beaded, crystalline, and fiercely luminescent— because the stars were dancing inside her. Her laugh turned watery as she asked, "How's that for a rebound?"

"Let those who talk call it a rebound," he challenged. "Because we followed it up, didn't we? A three-point shot from the top of the key to clinch it."

"Just like in polo. Right?"

He shook with silent laughter and kissed her. "I still have a bone to pick with that tribe of yours," he murmured, smiling against her lips.

They lingered that way for some time. Lips grazing. Her cheeks growing wetter, his smile broader as he used the pads of his thumbs to wipe her tears.

After a while, he reached under his coat into the lining of his jacket. Music floated, muted and slow, into the night. At her questioning glance, he raised a brow. "You said you could just dance. So…" Rising, he offered her a hand. "Will you dance with me, duchess?"

She let him bring her to her feet. Wordlessly, she led him beyond the blankets, down to the line in the sand where the water had risen and the surface was packed and stable. There she pulled him close as waves kissed their feet.

Before they linked together, he placed the ring on her hand and kissed it. She draped her arms over his shoulders in answer, pressing her cheek against his chest.

The moon rose as they swayed to Ella and Louis, as his chin came to rest above her brow. They danced until the tide and the sea changed. Lightning webbed across distant clouds, but they didn't stray from the beach, *their beach*. They stayed long enough to greet sleep from their blankets on the shore. Long enough to greet the first light of the new day that came after.

* * * * *

LARGER-PRINT BOOKS!
GET 2 FREE LARGER-PRINT NOVELS PLUS
2 FREE GIFTS!

♥ HARLEQUIN®

Romance

From the Heart, For the Heart

YES! Please send me 2 FREE LARGER-PRINT Harlequin® Romance novels and my 2 FREE gifts (gifts are worth about $10). After receiving them, if I don't wish to receive any more books, I can return the shipping statement marked "cancel." If I don't cancel, I will receive 4 brand-new novels every month and be billed just $5.09 per book in the U.S. or $5.49 per book in Canada. That's a savings of at least 15% off the cover price! It's quite a bargain! Shipping and handling is just 50¢ per book in the U.S. and 75¢ per book in Canada.* I understand that accepting the 2 free books and gifts places me under no obligation to buy anything. I can always return a shipment and cancel at any time. Even if I never buy another book, the two free books and gifts are mine to keep forever.

119/319 HDN GHWC

Name _____ (PLEASE PRINT)

Address _____ Apt. #

City _____ State/Prov. _____ Zip/Postal Code

Signature (if under 18, a parent or guardian must sign)

Mail to the **Reader Service:**
IN U.S.A.: P.O. Box 1867, Buffalo, NY 14240-1867
IN CANADA: P.O. Box 609, Fort Erie, Ontario L2A 5X3

Want to try two free books from another line?
Call 1-800-873-8635 or visit www.ReaderService.com.

* Terms and prices subject to change without notice. Prices do not include applicable taxes. Sales tax applicable in N.Y. Canadian residents will be charged applicable taxes. Offer not valid in Quebec. This offer is limited to one order per household. Not valid for current subscribers to Harlequin Romance Larger-Print books. All orders subject to credit approval. Credit or debit balances in a customer's account(s) may be offset by any other outstanding balance owed by or to the customer. Please allow 4 to 6 weeks for delivery. Offer available while quantities last.

Your Privacy—The Reader Service is committed to protecting your privacy. Our Privacy Policy is available online at www.ReaderService.com or upon request from the Reader Service.

We make a portion of our mailing list available to reputable third parties that offer products we believe may interest you. If you prefer that we not exchange your name with third parties, or if you wish to clarify or modify your communication preferences, please visit us at www.ReaderService.com/consumerchoice or write to us at Reader Service Preference Service, P.O. Box 9062, Buffalo, NY 14240-9062. Include your complete name and address.

HRLP15

REQUEST YOUR FREE BOOKS!
2 FREE WHOLESOME ROMANCE NOVELS IN LARGER PRINT
PLUS 2 FREE MYSTERY GIFTS

✶✶✶✶✶✶✶✶✶✶✶✶✶✶✶✶✶✶✶✶✶

HEARTWARMING™

Wholesome, tender romances

LARGER-PRINT BOOKS!
GET 2 FREE LARGER-PRINT NOVELS PLUS
2 FREE GIFTS!

HARLEQUIN®

INTRIGUE
BREATHTAKING ROMANTIC SUSPENSE